Planet Fall

Kestrel Class Saga
Book 6

By
Toby Neighbors

Planet Fall - Kestrel Class Saga Book 6
© 2020, Toby Neighbors

Published by Mythic Adventure Publishing, LLC
Idaho, USA

Books By Toby Neighbors

Toby Neighbors Online

www.TobyNeighbors.com

GOODREADS
www.GoodReads.com/TobyNeighbors

FACEBOOK
www.Facebook.com/TobyNeighborsAuthor

INSTAGRAM
Instagram @TobyTheWriter

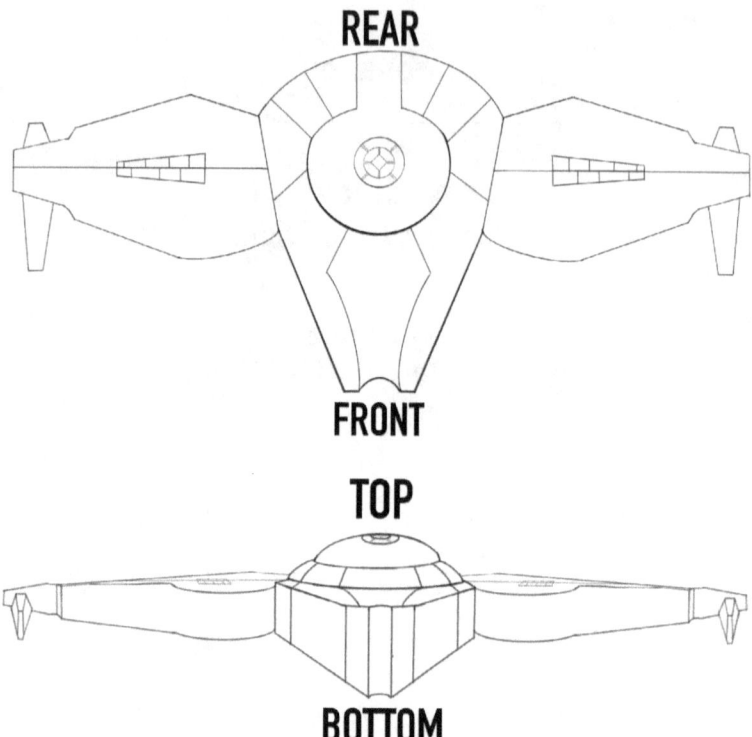
REAR

FRONT

TOP

BOTTOM

MID LEVEL

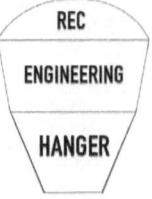

CREW LOUNGE | SICK BAY

CREW
CREW

BRIDGE

CREW
CREW

OPEN TO HANGER

UPPER LEVEL

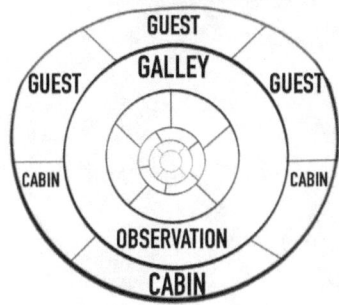

GUEST

GUEST | GALLEY | GUEST

CABIN | CABIN

OBSERVATION

CABIN

LOWER LEVEL

REC

ENGINEERING

HANGER

THE MODULUS
ECHO

Chapter 1

Ben watched as the *Modulus Echo* flew toward Royal City. The only human settlement on Gershwin was aptly named. It was the home world of the royal family, their private planet and posh playground. The city consisted of a half dozen buildings lining one edge of a lake. There was a royal palace in the center of the town. It was a massive building created to display the wealth and grandeur of the royal family. A hotel tower housed any guests invited to experience life in the private world. Everything else in the city was there to facilitate whatever whim might strike the guests.

The city was stunning. From the bridge of the ship, Ben could see the dazzling lake fed by a waterfall from the mountains surrounding the far edge. A spaceport was located beyond the mountains, out of sight from the city's pampered guests. Ben couldn't help but wonder why the aliens hadn't taken the city right from the start. Yet the small landing force had chosen to make planet fall on another continent and seemed content to build their own settlement in the uninhabited world.

"Wow," Kim said from the pilot's seat in the center of the bridge. "Would you look at that?"

"Where is everyone?" Magnum asked.

"Hiding, I suppose," Ben replied.

The posh royal city seemed deserted. There were no people moving about on the cobblestone streets, and no lights inside the buildings, which were made of polished steel and glass.

"I'm taking us down," Kim said.

The *Echo* hovered gracefully before descending to the ground in a large open space directly in front of the royal palace. There was still no sign of the people who had been left in the city, not even contact from the city's flight control.

"I'll see what I can find with Captain Lawrence and his officers," Ben said. "You can start back as soon as we're off the ship."

"How'd I get stuck shuttling soldiers while you explore the city?" Kim asked.

"Luck, I guess," Ben said.

"You want me to come with you?" Magnum asked. The big man still had his Lancet assault rifle slung across his back.

"No," Ben said. "You stay here and make sure the Confederates don't get into our supplies."

Magnum nodded.

"I'll be running a systems check and monitoring communications," Nance said. "Keep in mind, your com-link won't reach us once we leave the area."

"Yeah, we better find some better equipment," Kim said. "I don't like being out of touch."

"I'll see what I can do," Ben said. "They have to have something in the city. I would think it would be state of the art to ensure the royals never miss a call."

"Watch your back," Kim said as Ben headed for the stairs.

Down in the cargo bay, twenty officers were waiting by the rear hatch. Their leader, Captain Oliver Lawrence, was a tall, thin man with a wide jaw and dark eyes. The officers were all dressed in black uniforms, and each carried a pistol in a holster with a flap that covered the weapon's handle. Ben went straight to the controls and pulled the lever to lower the hatch.

"We're here," Ben said. "But we haven't heard from anyone, not even flight control."

"That figures," Lawrence said. "With the royal family gone, the locals have probably moved out of this area."

"It's a perfect target," a lieutenant said. The name badge on his chest was hard to read, but Ben made out Gabianelli, E.

"Odds are good that they're near the landing site," Lawrence continued. "They'll be waiting there for rescue."

"Which isn't coming," Ben said as the hatch settled onto the red cobblestones. "For now, let's see what we can find while the ship goes back to shuttle the troops for you."

Ben led the way out of the ship. It felt as if he had stepped back in time. The buildings around him were nothing like the prefab structures he was accustomed to, or even the industrial style of space stations. They were more like jewels on display. Wide steps made of polished marble led to the royal palace.

"Might as well start in there," Lieutenant Gabianelli said.

"No," Lawrence replied. "Let's leave the palace to the crew of the *Plato*. They got us here in once piece. And they might not be happy about a bunch of rebels camping out in the royal residence."

"I'd rather not be in any of the buildings, Captain," said another officer, a woman with her hair pulled into a tight bun hidden under her hat. Her name badge read Dallas, G. "They won't offer any protection in a fight."

"But they might have resources," Lawrence said.

Ben tapped the button on his collar, activating his com-link. "We're clear, Kim."

"Alright, see you in an hour," Kim replied, her voice small and chirpy on the tiny com-link.

The *Modulus Echo* lifted straight up into the air. The group of officers, with Ben in tow, hurried to a glass building that had wide double doors to avoid the ship's downwash as it rose upward and took flight. The doors opened automatically as the group approached, swinging silently on well-maintained hinges. Ben had never seen doors that didn't slide apart, but the glass doors opened like flower petals to soak in the sunlight.

The rebels acted nonplussed, but Ben knew they were just as impressed with the city as he was. It was opulence on a scale none had ever witnessed before. Ben knew that just one week's stay on Gershwin cost more than most people made in a year. And the waiting list was years long if a person could even get the clearance to make the trip. There were never more than a couple of hundred guests on the planet at one time, and only four hundred service industry professionals could call the planet home. The workers served in rotating shifts, never more than five years at a time, except for the palace staff who never left.

Inside the glass building, which was part shopping complex and part recreational space, the soldiers spread out. Ben could see all the way through to the waterfront on the far side of the building. There were restaurants on the far side, with balconies full of tables that stretched out over the water of the lake. The group stopped at a holographic display that showed what was on the upper floors. There were cosmetic surgeons, hair and nail salons, and a variety of spa facilities from mud baths to massage parlors.

"Doesn't look like anything that would help us," Captain Lawrence said. "Let's try one of the other buildings."

"There has to be a comms station in the tower," Ben said.

"Good idea, and we might find shelter for the brigade," Lawrence said. "Dallas, you take command of this building. There has to be food in the restaurants. We'll need it once the troops arrive."

"Roger that, Captain," the female officer said.

The rest of the group, including Ben, left the building and went toward the tower. It was a tall, round building, essentially a cylinder with glass all around. The rooms inside had panoramic views through the glass walls. Ben thought it strange that such fragile, antiquated materials were used to construct the buildings in such an important place. Transparent steel was only slightly less opaque than glass, and far stronger. Yet the pampered guests in the royal world expected nothing but the highest quality. From a distance, the glass reflected the bright sunshine so that the buildings looked like shining gems. Yet when they got close, Ben could see through the glass. The tower had a large lobby with thickly cushioned chairs and sofas, smartly arranged on exotic rugs. Beyond the seating area was a large desk with a cascading water feature behind it. Ben was not a military tactician, but the thick wood and granite countertop looked sturdy enough to take cover behind in a firefight.

"This has promise," Lieutenant Gabianelli said.

"There are interior rooms," Captain Lawrence said. "Perhaps enough for the brigade to take cover in a fight. Let's get someone up on the roof."

"Roger that, Captain," Gabianelli said.

The lieutenant jogged away toward a bank of elevators. The captain activated the hotel's computer systems and pointed behind him.

"Comms systems are that way," Lawrence said to Ben.

Ben nodded and hurried past the reception area and into the employee section of the hotel. There were offices and a storage room with everything from towels to toothbrushes. One room was marked Security, and another was listed as Communications. Ben went inside and found a sophisticated array of computers and communications gear. One was labeled Near Space and another was marked Deep Space Transmissions. Ben quickly tapped a few keys and brought the holographic displays up. It took a few minutes of searching, but he found the local frequency radio and began testing channels.

"*Modulus Echo, Modulus Echo,* this is Ben. Can you hear me?"

When there was no answer, he changed the radio frequency and tried again. Eventually, he found the right channel.

"We read you, Ben," Nance said. Her voice was crystal clear. "We're back at the landing site. Are you okay?"

"Yes," Ben replied as he marked down the *Echo*'s communication frequency on a note board with a blue marker. "But the city is deserted. I've got to find the channel for the landing port."

"Ben, you may not be able to reach them," Kim said. "Those mountains will block your signal, and I doubt that there are any satellites left in orbit to bounce a signal off of."

"She's right," Nance said. "We'll have to fly over and see what's happening at the spaceport once we get the soldiers ferried to the city."

"Alright," Ben said. "At least we have communication with you. Pass on the frequency to the *Plato*. There's not much we can do if they come under attack, but at least we'll know."

"Do you think that's a possibility?" Nance asked.

"At this stage of the game, I'm not taking anything for granted," Ben said. "Stay alert."

"Will do," Kim replied. "See you soon."

"I'm counting on it," Ben said.

Chapter 2

The *Everest* was in hyperspace again. She had made a short intermediary jump just to get out of danger in the Celeste system. The big battle cruiser had waited for the Krah ships she knew would come after them. With their lasers and missiles on standby, they fired as soon as the ships dropped out of hyperspace. Four Krah ships did their best to evade the *Everest*'s barrage and even counterattacked with their own kinetic weapons, but it was a useless exercise. Without overwhelming force, or surprise, they were no match against a proper warship. General Pershing wondered how they had been able to conquer their own galaxy.

Once the Krah ships had been defeated, Pershing ordered the ship to set a course for the Mersa system. After they made the jump, she left the bridge and went to find out what had happened to the *Modulus Echo*. The bridge was the command center of the ship, but there were other sections where crew members saw to the various systems that kept the big capital ship running. One of these was the ship's flight control center. Their responsibility was to keep track of the smaller vessels coming from and going to the *Everest*. Someone had given the *Modulus Echo* permission to leave the ship, and their best hope for closing the wormhole and defeating the Krah was either dead in the Celeste system, or worse, captured. Pershing knew the crew of the small Kestrel class ship was very capable of looking after themselves. They had successfully evaded the Royal Imperium Fleet, but she didn't want them running either. They had agreed to work with her, but she doubted their intentions. Odds were high that if they ran from the Celeste system and weren't pursued, they would simply disappear. The galaxy was a big place, and General Pershing didn't have the time or resources to track them down.

"Officer on deck!" a sergeant shouted as General Pershing stepped into the flight control center.

"As you were," Pershing said.

The crew members manning the half dozen stations all turned and looked at her. They were enlisted personnel, and she could see the fear in their eyes.

"The *Modulus Echo*," Pershing said coldly. "Where did it go? Why did it leave?"

There was a moment of silence as the tension rose to an uncomfortable degree in the small control room. Finally, a young man with a round face cleared his throat. He spoke without ever looking up from Pershing's shoes.

"They said… They said they needed to go off-ship to make repairs," he stammered.

"Off-ship?" Pershing said. "What repairs require a vessel to leave the hangar to make repairs?"

"I'm sorry, General," the round-faced man said. "I didn't know what to think. It was your personal ship."

"That ship could be the only hope for the galaxy," Pershing said. "And now we've lost her."

"I don't understand," the enlisted man said, still not looking up.

"No, you wouldn't," Pershing said.

She was too angry to stay. The crew of the *Everest* wasn't actually hers to command. She had taken control during the fighting, but Admiral General Dietz was the ranking officer. He had frozen when the Krah attacked, so Pershing had taken command, but she wouldn't push the limits of her authority by cracking down on the foolish air controller who had let the *Modulus Echo* leave the hangar. She had to choose her battles wisely, and the fight for control of the Royal Imperium forces that would be brought to bear against the Krah was the most important thing. She couldn't waste what little advantage she had over the newly appointed commander in chief.

Walking back to the admiral's salon, Pershing considered her options. She would need to get eyes back on the Celeste system. But she also needed to find out if the *Modulus Echo* or any of the other Royal Imperium ships had made it out of the system. The Krah were desperate to control the space around Gershwin and the wormhole, which made sense from a strategic perspective, but Pershing feared there might be more to it. Chances were high that the Krah had more vessels coming into the system. Or maybe they just needed to warn their compatriots of the dangers they faced in the human galaxy. Pershing wanted the wormhole closed, or at the very least for the space around it to be filled with warships that could capture or destroy any vessel passing through from the alien galaxy. But the Krah had adapted. Simply by spreading their forces out, they had become exponentially more formidable. She needed time for further interrogation of the prisoner who called himself Grubat. He claimed to be a chieftain in the alien culture, yet he answered all her questions. Perhaps he feared more aggressive interrogation techniques, but Pershing didn't think so. It was more likely that he was playing her somehow, working to gain an advantage that she hadn't seen yet.

At the doorway to the salon, she was forced to press a buzzer and wait to be allowed in. The small insults and petty politics of the Royal Imperium military seemed ridiculous to her. Yet she was forced to endure them, even though three Royal Imperium battle cruisers had just been run out of the Celeste system with their tails between their legs. She could only hope the other battleships survived the surprise attack.

The door slid open, and Duke Simeon looked at her. She could see shame in his gaze but didn't say anything about it. He had quickly run when the attack came. He might view himself as a military man, but he didn't have the experience or the discipline. Of course, fighting on a ship where a person had no real control over the battle outside their tiny fraction of responsibility was difficult to endure. The best a person could do was to stay at their station, see to their duties, and hope the ship didn't vaporize around them.

"General," Duke Simeon said in a husky tone.

"Your Grace," Pershing said with a slight bow. "I trust all is well?"

The duke stepped back and allowed Pershing to step into the room. The normally spartan office space had been filled with luxury furnishings. The queen sat poised on a sofa, her back straight, her eyes fixed on the display screen that showed the swirl of hyperspace outside the ship. Admiral General Arnold Dietz looked visibly shaken. His skin was pale, and Pershing saw his hand tremble as he raised a glass of liquor from the small bar in the corner.

"We are well enough as can be expected," Queen Ultane snapped. "What is the condition of the ship?"

"The *Everest* took no damage in the fighting," Pershing said, "and acquitted ourselves well after the initial hyperspace jump. I'm confident that we are no longer being pursued."

"Confident?" Dietz said. "How can anyone be confident of anything anymore?"

"The ships following us were destroyed," Pershing said. "We're on our way back to the Mersa system. May I speak freely, sir?"

Dietz nodded.

"We need more ships. Every moment we wait to retake the Celeste system, the greater the odds of the Krah increasing their numbers."

"What if there are no more ships?" Queen Ultane asked. "What if we simply give them Celeste and defend the surrounding systems?"

"Do you know something I don't?" Pershing asked.

"No," the queen snapped. "But word of this defeat will not inspire confidence in your leadership, General. I doubt more ships will come to join your fight."

"Then we perform a defensive withdrawal from this quadrant, but we'll only be postponing the inevitable."

"Don't be so certain," Dietz said. "We fought well, you said so yourself. This one ship destroyed four of theirs. They could dash themselves against our defenses until they have no strength left."

"Perhaps if the wormhole was closed," Pershing said. "For all we know, they could have a virtually limitless number of ships to reinforce their fleet. Plus, they have the advantage in numbers. You saw how quickly they adapted to our tactics. They are skilled engineers. With each system they conquer, their strength will grow. They can turn the wreckage of our ships into new vessels or more weapons to use against us."

"So attacking them is the only answer?" Queen Ultane said.

"In my opinion, yes," Pershing said.

She knew that no matter what the royal family did, she would find a way to fight the aliens. The rebels had proven that even common citizens would rally around a worthy cause. If she had to recruit from the riffraff and arm them with sticks and stones, she would do it.

"What do you need us to do?" Duke Simeon said.

"Get me more ships," Pershing said. "In the meantime, I intend to find out as much as possible from the prisoner."

"Fine," Dietz said. "We'll get more ships."

"You can't promise that," Queen Ultane said.

"I can promise to try," Dietz said. "That's what a good leader does—empower those around him. If the general needs more resources, we'll get them."

Pershing bowed to the queen and saluted Admiral General Dietz. It was more a matter of habit than respect, but she didn't really have a choice. They were going to support her war against the Krah, and the least she could do was behave as they expected. She turned without another word and left them staring after her.

Chapter 3

All around him, the Krah were celebrating their victory, but Trooper Le Croix, formerly Major Le Croix of the Royal Imperium Special Forces, felt no joy. Despite Yarl Cherbak's insistence that Le Croix had helped him escape from the humans who attacked their party in the mountains, most of the Krah distrusted the enhanced human. The Krah were never talkative, but many refused to acknowledge him at all, and he could feel the isolation building like humidity before a tropical storm. A sense of loneliness had settled in on Le Croix. Chieftain Grubat had been his friend, and Le Croix felt guilty that he hadn't been able to save the Krah leader who had accepted him so completely. During the attack, Grubat had been taken prisoner, and there was no doubt that General Alicia Pershing would do whatever it took to get the information she needed from her captive.

To make his situation even worse, the itching and burning around his enhancements had gotten worse. It was so bad at times he couldn't stop himself from scratching the inflamed flesh around his enhanced legs. He tried not to let the other Krah warriors see him, but the itching would not stop. And keeping busy was becoming harder and harder, with no one willing to let him help with the small projects around the camp. Alpha Vistol had called a halt to all expansion, and the focus of the camp had shifted to defense. Le Croix was officially a trooper, having been promoted by High Priest Alwain, and was allowed to stand watch with the other warriors. The only way Le Croix could hope to win back their confidence was to show his prowess in battle, but that seemed less and less likely with the return of the Krah fleet into orbit. Reports indicated that the Krah had driven the humans away, and Alpha Vistol had ordered a strong defensive arrangement of the Krah ships in the system to ensure they weren't defeated again.

While the camp celebrated the victory in space, Le Croix volunteered to stand watch. He was alone on the wall, staring out into the darkness. He knew the Spec Ops team had night vision and that he was probably an easy target for a sniper in the forest. They could take him out, along with anyone else who was visible above the wooden palisade that surrounded the camp. But Le Croix didn't fear death. Not that he wanted to die, but he wasn't sure he wanted to live either. He was a traitor, a man without allegiance, enhanced by the Krah in ways that he still couldn't understand but with a growing suspicion that his body was rejecting the artificial legs they had given him. The skin around his headdress was beginning to chafe as well, and it was only a matter of time before someone noticed. If he couldn't utilize the enhancements, he would be rejected as Krah. And more than anything, Le Croix feared living as a cripple. He could get by on prosthetic legs, but the Krah had taken his eyes too. Humanity didn't have the technology to replace eyes, and that would mean Le Croix would be blind. Perhaps, he reasoned, it would be better to die than to live without the enhancements the Krah had given him.

"I thought I would find you here," Cherbak said as he approached along the fighting platforms that lined the wall. "You should be celebrating."

"Someone has to stand watch," Le Croix said.

"Perhaps," Cherbak said. "Although without the support of their fleet, it's more likely that the humans have fled."

"They'll be back," Le Croix said.

"And when they return, we will crush them," Yarl Cherbak said. "You cannot blame yourself for Chieftain Grubat's loss."

"Why not?" Le Croix replied. "Everyone else does."

"Not me," Cherbak said. "Not Alpha Vistol. Who else matters?"

Le Croix turned back to see the large bonfires roaring in the camp. It was not unlike a human settlement. The class structures were more rigid, and the Krah were less interested in romance, but in many ways, they were the same. Most of the warriors and workers were drunk already. The defenses were down to a bare minimum, which made it the perfect time for a sneak attack. The young Krah were loud. In fact, there was so much noise in the camp that Le Croix feared they would be attacked and no one would even hear it.

"You have word from the ships?" Le Croix said.

"Indeed," Yarl Cherbak said. "The *En'Galla* survived the human invasion. I'll be returning to her as soon as the debris around the planet is cleared."

"Congratulations," Le Croix said.

He had fought Yarl Cherbak in a battle of honor and won. When the Spec Ops team ambushed them in the mountains, Le Croix had saved Cherbak's life. Since then, the two had become friends, and Le Croix knew that Yarl Cherbak's only hope to restore his honor and reputation was on the *En'Galla*. With a ship to command, Yarl Cherbak could enter the service of another chieftain and, in time, rise in rank.

"Brooding isn't the way of a true warrior," Cherbak said. "Come with me to the *En'Galla*. We will prove our worth together."

"That's a kind offer," Le Croix said. "But Alpha Vistol made it clear he wants me to stay here. I'm not sure why."

"You are the only link to the humans and the way they think," Le Croix said. "The other prisoner has lost his faculties."

Le Croix remembered Prince Godfred for the first time since his enhancement. He felt guilty that he had failed to protect the ranking member of the royal family, but he knew there was nothing that could have been done to save the craven prince. The Krah detested fear, and cowards were outcasts in their society. Le Croix and the crown prince were both prisoners of the Krah at first, but he could have done more for Godfred once he was accepted by the aliens. He made a mental note to find where the prince was being kept and do whatever he could for him.

"I have my place, and you have yours," Le Croix told Yarl Cherbak. "I appreciate your support. You have mine. Once the system is secure, perhaps things will change. If they do, I will look for you."

Cherbak nodded, then left the platform without saying another word. Le Croix wasn't sure if the Yarl actually trusted him. They had grown closer after the ambush in the mountains, but perhaps it was simply a debt that needed to be paid. Affection and friendship weren't traits valued by the Krah.

The burning itch around Le Croix's hips returned suddenly. It was a maddening sensation. He glanced both directions along the wall's fighting platform before discreetly rubbing his free hand across the inflamed area. It was a reminder of his failures, a physical torment that was only a fraction of the torture he endured mentally. He was a traitor, a turncoat who had betrayed his own people and joined the enemy. And soon, the Krah would discover his secret. When that happened, they would reject him. Le Croix would be a man with no people, no hope, and no way to escape the hell his life would become.

Death was better, there was no doubt. And it was out there in the darkness, Le Croix knew it. The commando team was watching the settlement. They were probably watching him at that very moment. The only thing Le Croix didn't understand was what they could possibly be waiting for.

Chapter 4

"Reinforcements have all been delivered," Kim said. "Including the crew from the *Plato*."

"That's good," Ben said, his voice clear over the *Echo*'s bridge speakers.

"You coming back on board?" Kim asked as she stood up and stretched.

"Soon," Ben said. "I'm trying to help Captain Lawrence switch over to a long-range frequency on the hotel's comms system."

"Okay, but you know that won't do them much good, right?" Kim said. "I mean, it's not like anyone else is monitoring those channels."

"Analog signals can bounce off the atmosphere and hold up for long distances," Nance said.

"Do we even have the equipment to pick up analog signals?" Kim asked.

"It's a safety measure," Ben said. "All communications gear is supposed to have an emergency analog setting."

"Fine, so get it done and let's get off this rock," Kim said. "We've done our part and then some."

"I hear you," Ben said. "Give me half an hour. Then we can hop over the mountains and check on the spaceport."

Kim turned and looked at Nance and Magnum. "He knows the soldiers can do that, right? I mean, the longer we hang around on Gershwin, the greater the odds that General Pershing returns, and I'd rather not be around for that."

Magnum chuckled, and Nance typed some commands into her computer without looking up. Kim decided she needed to stretch her legs. She would have been happy to leave the planet right away and fly as far from the Celeste system as possible, but she wouldn't leave without Ben. And getting off-world wouldn't be as simple as she was making it out to be. They had disrupted the debris cloud getting down to the planet. It would take time for Gershwin's gravity to pull the wreckage back into a steady orbit. Then there was the alien fleet. She didn't like thinking about them. The *Echo*'s flux shield might fend them off long enough to make the jump to hyperspace, but the aliens knew how to track them. There was no telling how many of the strange-looking vessels might follow them through space no matter where they went.

"I'm getting something to eat," Kim said. "Be back in a few minutes."

"Okay," Nance said without looking up.

Kim wondered briefly how Magnum handled the way Nance seemed emotionally absent. Kim liked Nance. She was like a little sister to her, but Nance had trouble relating to people. She preferred her computers and the strict rules of a good operating system. Since leaving Torrent Four, and probably for a long time before that, Nance hadn't left the ship without protest. And while she wasn't cold or uncaring, Nance had a difficult time expressing her emotions. Kim knew she had affection for Ben and Magnum, even for Kim herself, but Nance rarely even looked her in the eye.

As she climbed the stairs to the upper deck, she shifted her thinking from people to food. There was one good thing that came from working with the Royal Imperium—they had more than enough food for the first time in their lives. Kim knew that, on dozens of planets, people would fight and kill for a fraction of the food General Pershing had delivered to the *Echo*, most of which was still stored in their cargo bay. And it wasn't simply protein bricks and seasoning packets. It was actual food—fresh and frozen fruits, vegetables, and meat of all kinds. There were sacks of rice, flour, beans, and sugar. There were vacuum-sealed packages of preserved foods too. And spices, not just artificial seasoning packets, but actual containers of dried herbs and spices. They even had large containers full of salt.

In addition to the food, there was a wide variety of drinks, from fruit juice to alcohol, coffee, and tea. They had enough food to live on for over a year, maybe more. It was the first time in her life that she hadn't worried about how much she was eating or what she would do when the food ran out. In the galley, she prepared herself a sandwich with real meat, real cheese, fresh lettuce, onions, and pickles. She even slathered the thick slabs of bread with a liberal amount of spicy brown mustard. The sandwich, when she finished, was too big. She knew she couldn't eat it all, so she cut it in half and put each on small plates. Then she carried a sandwich across the observation gallery to Professor Jones's quarters and knocked lightly on the door. It swished open almost immediately.

The old man looked harried. His hair was sticking out from his head, and his clothes were wrinkled. There was a musky, unpleasant smell from the room too. Not that Kim doubted that the Professor's obsession had him too busy to bother with basic hygiene.

"I come bearing gifts," she said.

"Oh, how thoughtful of you," he said. "Would you like to come inside?"

"No," Kim said quickly. The room was covered with the professor's work. Every surface had a digital slate or data pad carefully arranged. Some had academic texts on them, others were filled with complicated mathematic formulas. "I just brought you something to eat."

"That's exceedingly kind. I'm hungry," Professor Jones declared as if he had just realized his need to eat.

Kim didn't bother asking the older man how long it had been since he stopped working to rest or eat. She had seen Ben in similar conditions. It was like once an idea or project took hold, they couldn't think of anything else until it was completed. He took the plate and smiled.

"I'm close," he said. "The answer is there, and soon I'll find it."

"The answer?" Kim asked.

"To the wormhole problem. I know we can close it, but it's a delicate matter."

Kim nodded. "Is there anything we can do to help?"

"No, no, no," he said, his mouth already stuffed with food. "Just a little more time, I think."

Kim smiled then headed back to get her own sandwich. Food seemed less appealing somehow. She couldn't get the professor's words out of her head. Why was it their responsibility to fix the galaxy's problems? Perhaps it was their fault the wormhole was opened, but if they hadn't fired the rocket, she knew the galaxy wouldn't be better off. And she, along with Ben, Nance, and Magnum, would all be dead, or worse, in a Royal Imperium torture chamber. Yet, even though all they had wanted to do was live their lives, they had been forced to break the Royal Imperium's oppressive laws and run for their lives at every turn. They weren't warriors and the *Modulus Echo* wasn't a battleship, yet somehow they had managed to almost single-handedly sway the fight between the Imperium and the Confederacy. And if that wasn't enough, they had been roped into dealing with the alien problem too.

She took a bite of her sandwich and couldn't help but marvel at the taste. But even delicious food couldn't distract her from the fear that nagged at her. They seemed to be in a safe place, far from any obvious threat, but the reality was that they were in an occupied world. The aliens may have set up shop in another continent, but they had traveled through space to reach Gershwin, and Kim had no doubt they could mount an attack on Royal City if they wanted to.

Leaving the planet was the obvious answer, getting to orbit and making the jump to hyperspace wouldn't be easy, but it was possible. Yet she also knew that if the professor could find a way to close the wormhole, they would have to stay and see it through. Kim was tired of the responsibility. She wanted to live. What they needed was distance and time from the Royal Imperium. She couldn't stop worrying that something was going to happen, and the people she cared about would be robbed of the opportunities they so richly deserved. She couldn't let that happen, but she feared it was beyond her control.

"Kim," Nance said via their com-link. Her voice sounded small and distant through the tiny speaker pinned to Kim's jumpsuit collar. "Ben's on his way back. We can leave when you're ready."

"Great," Kim said, looking at the remnants of her sandwich. "I'll be right down."

She wanted to see Ben. It made her nervous when he was off the ship without her. But she had a feeling that his return would only lead to more responsibilities, more danger. And she didn't want any part of that.

Chapter 5

Ben made his way out of the tower that had been taken over by the Confederate soldiers. They numbered just over two hundred, but they filled the lobby of the hotel with so much organized chaos that Ben was glad when he stepped outside. The air of Gershwin was cool and sweet. But despite the feeling of wonder Ben felt about the pristine royal world, he felt like an outsider. The unblemished planet was a stark contrast to Torrent Four where Ben and the rest of the crew of the *Modulus Echo* had spent most of their lives. Torrent Four was a trash world, filled with the debris of a global war that had left the environment ravaged and the landscape littered with the wreckage of millions of ships.

Gershwin, on the other hand, was beautiful. Royal City was small, just a short strip of cobblestone, with beautiful buildings lining the lake. On the other side of the street was a huge green space, immaculately maintained by a host of automated landscaping drones. Water was being projected by tiny sprinkler heads that popped up from the deep grass. Flowers were pruned, and carefully manicured hedges lined the edges of the park. There were paths that meandered through the green space, and Ben wanted to take Kim on a walk. He wanted to breathe clean air and feel the cool kiss of twilight with the woman he loved beside him. Instead, he passed a trio of soldiers setting up a large automated high-caliber rifle on his way to his ship.

The *Modulus Echo* looked like an antique compared to the glistening buildings on the other side of the street, including the royal palace. The metal was tainted with a dark patina, and the heat shield tiles, which covered most of the ship's hull, were streaked with black scorch marks. It would be dark soon, and Ben was tired. He wanted to go to his cabin and sleep, but the gaping hole in the hull of the port wing still needed repairs. And if Ben could convince the others to stay long enough, he wanted to load the ship's missile racks before they left the planet.

The rear hatch was closed, and Ben was forced to go in through the air lock on the side of the ship. He cycled the air lock and stepped through the portal into the cargo bay. It was filled with pallets of supplies, mostly food but also medical supplies and weapons. He passed through and climbed wearily up the stairs to the ship's main deck, just as Kim was coming down from the galley on the third level of the ship.

"Hi, stranger," she said.

"Hi, Kim," Ben replied as she jumped into his arms. He held her close. "Did you miss me?"

"Terribly," she whispered back. "Can we leave now?"

Ben pulled back and looked at her. He didn't say anything, but the look on his face must have given him away, and Kim looked disappointed.

"Let's get everyone together and talk," Ben said.

They moved over to the bridge, where Nance was still at her computer station. Magnum stood up and gave Ben a high five. There was no doubt that the crew felt as if they had succeeded by escaping from General Pershing's command. Ben had nothing but respect for the general, but their goals were completely different. The general wanted to use the *Echo* to wage war, while Ben wanted to ensure his friends and the ship avoided it as much as possible.

"Any problems?" Ben asked Nance.

"No, all systems are good," Nance said. "Even the port wing engine is functional."

"At least the new conduit kept the wiring from melting on entry through the atmosphere," Ben said. "I'd feel better if we made a full repair."

"Are you kidding me?" Kim said. "We should get off this planet and out of the system as soon as possible."

"We could make repairs in space," Magnum suggested.

"True, but getting out of here isn't going to be easy," Ben said.

"Why don't we just lie low?" Nance asked. "Gershwin is a big world. There are plenty of places to hide. And we have plenty of supplies."

"But we have no idea what the aliens are doing," Ben said.

"Live and let live, I say," Kim replied.

"Here's what I'm proposing," Ben said. "We rest here tonight. Make a few repairs, perhaps even get a little help from the Confederates reloading the missiles. In the morning, we hop over the mountains, check in on the spaceport, then we head up and take a look at what the aliens are up to."

"So we can leave the system?" Kim asked.

"That's one possibility," Ben said.

"You really want to stay?" Nance asked.

"No," Ben said. "But I've been thinking about the commandos. They're cut off. Completely on their own."

"The commandos?" Kim said, her voice louder than it needed to be. "Ben, we don't owe them anything. You know that, right?"

"What I know is that without help, they're most likely going to get hunted down and killed out there."

"That's the risk they took when they joined the Royal Imperium military," Kim said.

"We might be able to help," Magnum admitted.

"And let's say you're right," Kim continued to vent her frustrations. "We manage to pick them up without getting ourselves killed in the process. Then what? We'll have to go to another Royal Imperium installation to drop them off, and guess who'll be waiting for us? That's right, our friend, the general. And I don't think she'll buy the repair story either."

"We don't have to take them off-world," Ben said. "We can bring them right back here."

"It's a waste of time and fuel," Kim said. "But whatever."

"What are the Confederates planning?" Nance asked.

"They're going to hold this position," Ben said. "Look for places to dig in and fight if the aliens come around."

"All the more reason we should make ourselves scarce," Kim said.

"One more day, that's all I'm asking," Ben said. "Where's the professor?"

"He's still in his quarters," Nance said.

"Has he had any luck?" Ben asked.

Kim looked down. She was an amazing pilot, and a passionate person in general, but she had no poker face. Ben knew if he pushed her, she would lash out. Instead, he waited.

She looked up, started to say something, then looked down again.

"He says he's close," Kim finally replied.

"Close?" Ben asked. "Do you know what that means?"

"Do I look like a science nerd?" Kim snapped. "I made the man a sandwich. He said he was close to solving the problem. I didn't stick around for a lesson, Ben. But yeah, I think he's got some ideas."

Ben felt responsible for the wormhole that their flux rocket had opened in the Celeste system. They hadn't expected the gravity event they started to suck in most of the Royal Imperium Fleet and their massive space station, yet it had. The enormous mass powered the flux rocket's gravity event to create the wormhole. The aliens who had come through that portal were a different matter, but Ben felt responsible for closing the wormhole, or at the very least, sharing the procedure Professor Jones came up with. The Royal Imperium could close the wormhole whenever and however they wanted, as long as they had the means. If Ben could hand that information over to them, he would feel no qualms about leaving the system.

"Maybe he'll have a plan by the time we collect the commando team," Ben said.

"We don't even know they want to be *collected*," Kim said, emphasizing the last word and turning her statement into an attack. "But hey, what do I know? I'm just the pilot, right?"

"Kim, we're leaving the system," Ben said. "I promise."

"Yeah? Well, just don't wait too long. I'd rather not have to fight my way through a swarm of alien ships, you know?"

Ben nodded and looked over at Nance.

"I'll run a systems check," she said. "It might not hurt to swap the Zexum tanks. Getting out of orbit burns more fuel than jumping through hyperspace."

"Good idea," Ben said. "I'll repair the port wing. Magnum, could you see if the Confederates can spare a few people? We'll mount the missiles and head over the mountains at first light."

Magnum nodded. Nance began typing away at her computer. Kim just stood looking at Ben.

"You want to give me a hand?" Ben asked her.

"No, thank you," she said. "I'd rather not get my hands dirty."

"So what are you going to do?" Ben asked.

"Maybe I'll go for a walk."

"I'd feel better if you stayed close to the ship."

"And I would feel better if you didn't treat me like a child. I can handle myself around a bunch of soldiers."

"I'm not worried about them," Ben said. "You said it yourself—the aliens could attack at any time. If that happens, I want us in the air."

"Oh, so now you're worried," she said.

"I just don't want to lose you," he said, taking her hand and leading her away from the bridge.

She didn't resist, not even when he led her down the stairs and into the engineering bay, where he finally turned to face her. Encouraged by her lack of resistance, he pulled her close.

"I'm sorry," he said quietly.

"You and your stupid conscience," she said. "If you get me killed, I'll never speak to you again."

Ben laughed but Kim didn't. And he could see the concern in her eyes.

"One day," Ben said. "That's all we need."

"You don't know that," Kim said. "Ten thousand ships could come through the wormhole in a day, for all we know."

Her voice was full of concern, but her body leaned into him. She wasn't trembling, and she wasn't angry at him. She felt relaxed as he slid his hands around to the small of her back.

"Just let me get the ship in order," Ben said. "And maybe catch a few hours of sleep. We could all use some rest."

"I know," Kim said. "But I would rest a lot better if we were in another system."

"Soon," Ben said.

He kissed her softly, and she responded to him. Her hands were on his shoulders, and even though he wasn't big like Magnum or overly muscled like the commandos that had spent so much time aboard the *Echo*, her touch made him feel taller and stronger. It was a strange thing to his mind, one that didn't make rational sense. But whenever he was close to Kim, he felt an irresistible urge to protect her and make her happy.

"Are we okay?" he asked as he pulled back from her kiss.

"Always," Kim said.

She pulled him close and hugged him tightly. A dozen chores needed his attention, but he didn't care. He felt like he could stay in her embrace forever.

Chapter 6

The forest was thick around a rocky knoll where the commando team had set up camp. There were no tents, no equipment caches, just the eight members of the team and whatever equipment they carried. Their beds were nothing more than boughs cut from the evergreen trees around them, with no cover. They slept in shifts and kept careful watch for movement from the aliens. From the knoll, they could see the alien settlement. Days, sometimes even weeks, in enemy territory with little or no word from the command was not unusual, but it was clear to Staff Sergeant Visher that something had happened. Despite their ambush on the aliens, they seemed more at ease than ever before.

Corporal Dial woke up when his wrist link buzzed silently. It sent a small but strong current into his arm that woke him instantly. He rolled over, checked his weapon to make sure the safety was still on, and then moved over beside Staff Sergeant Visher.

"Anything happen in the night?"

"Negative," Visher replied. "And no movement this morning either."

"You think they're lying low?"

"Maybe, but it's more like they aren't worried about us or anything else."

"What do you think that means?"

Visher shrugged his shoulders. "Probably nothing. Who the hell knows what these creatures think?"

At that moment, an alien with mechanical legs came crawling over the top of the wooden wall they had built to surround their camp.

"I don't know about you, but that's some creepy shit right there," Corporal Dial said.

"Yeah," Visher said, looking at the alien's spidery legs through his rifle's telescopic scope. "We ain't dealing with rebels anymore, are we?"

"No, Staff Sergeant," Dial replied. "What is that thing doing?"

"Making repairs," Visher said. "Or improvements. I can't tell for sure. But that's a worker. I don't ever see the big ones with head tentacles doing the menial labor."

"It's too bad we don't have drones to give us eyes inside the palisade. I'd like to know what Major Le Croix is doing."

"He was on watch last night. It was the perfect opportunity to send us a signal, but he didn't. And he has to know we're out here watching."

"So he's not a prisoner. He's gone over," Dial said sadly.

"Looks that way," Visher said.

"Well, I'll take over for now. Get some rest. I'll wake you if anything changes."

"Roger that," Visher said.

The older man's joints popped as he got up. The commandos were trained to surveil their targets, sometimes for days at a time, and while they could sit or lie for hours without moving to avoid detection, they were used to a more active lifestyle. Spying on their enemies was tedious business, but important. Sooner or later, they knew the general would return, hopefully with reinforcements. The more they knew about their enemy, the better prepared they would be in planning a successful mission.

Not that Corporal Dial expected the attack to be difficult. The wooden wall probably gave the aliens a sense of protection, but a single grenade would knock a hole in it big enough for the humans to get through. And if they had air strike capability, they could bomb the entire camp without risking a single soldier's life. The aliens seemed unfamiliar with modern weapons, which gave Corporal Dial and most of the commando team a sense of superiority. They felt they could wipe out most of the aliens on their own, just with the weapons they carried.

Dial glanced down and saw the digital ammo count on his rifle. It fired both lasers and projectile rounds. He had it loaded with .45-caliber reaper rounds, which were made from depleted uranium. The weapon held sixty bullets and could fire in a variety of modes from single shot to full auto. At the moment, he had the barrel extender in place and his adjustable telescopic scope set to sniper mode. From his spot on the knoll, he could easily pick off the sentries posted on the alien settlement's wooden walls, but that wasn't their mission. They were a recon force. The intelligence they gathered as they waited for word from General Pershing was more important than killing the individual aliens.

The rest of the second unit, which Corporal Dial was in charge of, got up and spread out without a word, relieving the first unit that Staff Sergeant Visher led. If the commandos engaged in conversation, they did it so quietly that Dial didn't hear them. He waited several minutes into their watch before calling for a comms check.

"Second unit," he said quietly, utilizing the throat mic that was standard issue for Special Forces commandos. "Report."

"All clear to the south," Corporal Amadi said.

"Clear to the west," Private Felix reported.

"I've got a herd of elk moving through the forest," Private Rhoades said. "That's some real good eating. I could get us one with a laser shot from here."

"Negative," Dial said. "This isn't a camping trip, Private."

"You ever had fresh elk tenderloin cooked over a fire?" Rhoades argued. "It's the best thing you'll ever eat, I guarantee it."

"Man, he just doesn't get it," Amadi said.

"Rhoades," Dial said calmly. "We are here to observe and report. We can't do that if we're harvesting animals in the forest and building fires."

"Roger that," Rhoades said. "But it seems like overkill. One person could sit up here and watch the camp. They haven't done anything outside the walls after our ambush."

"They haven't done anything yet," Dial said. "Our job is to watch and see if they do."

"And what happens if they come out, Corporal?" Private Felix asked.

"That depends on what they do," Dial said.

A few seconds later, the door that was built into the wall surrounding the camp swung open. Dial tensed as he raised his rifle to look through the scope. He adjusted the digital zoom so that he could see the entire door area. He expected some of the warriors to come charging out. If they moved fast from the settlement and into the trees, it would give them cover and make the commando team's weapons less effective. But it wasn't warriors moving out of the camp, but the workers with their long, folding mechanical legs. Several began working on the door, while others spread out on either side and inspected the wall.

Dial zoomed in his scope so that he could see through the opening and into the camp itself. There were strange-looking spacecraft spread out on the far side, next to the mountains. Dial could only see one, but it seemed obvious that the aliens were using the ships as their main housing. He could see aliens moving about the camp, but what drew his eye was a wooden cage. It was big, perhaps two square meters. A sturdy cube for keeping prisoners. Dial reached up and touched the scope's record sensor. He zoomed in as far as the scope would go and propped the gun on a rock to hold it steady. The scope worked to focus for several seconds. Corporal Dial could see a figure in the cage, but he couldn't make out who it was. He expected to see Major Le Croix locked inside the pen, but when the image finally came into focus, he saw a bedraggled Prince Godfred instead.

"Holy…" Dial said.

"You got something?" Corporal Amadi asked.

"Wake the staff sergeant," Dial said. "This changes everything."

Chapter 7

"Why do things always take longer than you expect?" Kim asked.

"I don't know," Ben replied.

Outside the ship, a group of Confederates was helping Magnum load the missiles onto the wings of the *Modulus Echo*. Ben liked the firepower but preferred the look of the ship without the weapons. He felt better after a full night's sleep, and he rested better after he had checked for damage on the port wing, repaired the hull, and replaced the missing heat tiles.

"All systems are in the green," Nance said from the computer station where she was a fixture. "Auxiliary battery banks are both at one hundred percent."

"Good," Kim said. "I'm itching to get off the ground."

"Me too," Ben said. "There's not been any answer from the spaceport."

"That's probably because they aren't monitoring the old frequencies," Kim said. "We don't even know if they have a qualified radio operator over there."

"Once the weapons are installed, it should only take fifteen minutes to cross the mountains," Nance said.

"Should, but we know how that goes," Kim replied. "Things rarely go as planned around here. How much d'you want to bet we don't leave the planet today?"

"No, I'm not taking that bet," Ben said. "Don't be so negative."

"I'm just being realistic," Kim said.

"Looks like they're loading the last missile," Nance said.

"I'll radio Captain Lawrence," Ben said. "We'll lift off as soon as the Confederates are clear."

Kim flexed her arms and popped the knuckles on both hands. "I'll start the preflight checklist."

Ten minutes later, the old but fully functional Kestrel class engines roared to life. Ben was surprised by how loud they sounded in atmosphere when they were silent in space. Magnum was back on board and settling into his seat at the weapons console. They still hadn't found a suitable seat for him, and the big man looked almost comical in the small chair at his station.

"All hatches are closed and secured," Nance said.

"We're cleared for takeoff," Ben said.

"Alright, let's go," Kim said.

The ship was old, an outdated hybrid model that could fly in atmosphere and hard vacuum equally well. She had been a luxury vessel back in her day, and while Ben hadn't restored her completely, the engines and ship systems were in perfect working order. The *Echo* rose straight up into the air and hovered over the city like her namesake. Kestrels were predators known for hovering, and the *Echo* had no trouble holding her position above Royal City.

"Look at that view," Ben said.

The large bridge display screen showed the high-resolution video feed from external cameras mounted on the bow of the ship. They could see across the city, over the green space and surrounding forest. There were green meadows and a tree-lined river in the distance. The beauty of Gershwin was unrivaled. Ben thought it a shame that so many people lived in worlds that were little more than garbage heaps, while so few would ever step foot on the royal home world.

"Beautiful," Nance said.

"I prefer space," Kim said. "Don't get me wrong, this is nice, but it feels a little claustrophobic to me."

"Let's get moving, then," Ben said. "You won't have to wait too long."

The ship turned gracefully, pivoting in the air and then gliding toward the mountains.

"I'll have to gain some altitude," Kim said.

"I have the passage through the mountains plotted already," Nance said. "It should be on your screen."

"I've got it," Kim said. "Thank you."

They flew through the mountains, rather than above them. The view was spectacular. The peaks were covered with snow that was brilliant white, and crystal-clear streams flowed to the edge of towering cliffs before falling hundreds of feet to pristine pools that were lined with huge moss-covered boulders. Tall, pointed evergreen trees were growing in the valleys and along the steep sides of the mountains.

Winds buffeted the *Echo* as she made her way through the pass. Kim tried flying higher, then lower, but the erratic winds seemed to come out of nowhere, always pushing them closer to the mountains. Kim used her experience piloting kites through the canyons on Torrent Four and kept them safe, even though the *Echo* seemed too large at times. More than once, the ship's wingtips flew dangerously close to the unforgiving cliff faces or mountain ledges, but they took no damage. And just as

Nance had predicted, fifteen minutes later, they came through the pass and onto a wide, flat plain.

The spaceport looked like a star. At the center were the flight control station, refueling equipment, and a hanger with two luxury air transports. Branching out from the center were six long tracks with enclosed people movers, and at the end of each was a landing pad that was also a launchpad. They were all empty, and from a distance, the port seemed abandoned.

"Looks like a ghost town," Kim said as she guided the Kestrel class ship toward the port.

"If the locals are hiding, it makes sense that we wouldn't see them," Ben said.

"There are only two buildings down there," Kim said. "How can they be hiding there?"

"Perhaps there are underground facilities," Nance suggested.

"Take us down and we'll check it out," Ben said.

"Shouldn't they be manning their comms?" Kim asked. "Even if they're hiding?"

Ben felt foolish. "Of course," he said. "I forgot."

He tapped a few keys on his console and brought up the ship's communications program. He set the system to an all-frequency broadcast, then spoke into the mic built into his console. "Gershwin Landing Station, this is the *Modulus Echo*. Does anyone read me? Over."

He waited, but there was no response. Kim was busy landing the ship, but Magnum and Nance looked at Ben with surprise. He keyed the mic and tried again.

"Gershwin Landing Station, this is the *Modulus Echo*. We were part of the Royal Imperium force working to retake the system. If there is anyone there, please respond. Over."

Nothing came back to the ship, not even static. It was as if the system was powered down. Ben nodded at Magnum, who headed immediately downstairs.

"That's strange," Kim said.

"Magnum and I are going to check this out," Ben said. "As soon as we're off the ship, I want you to take off."

"And go where?" Nance asked.

"Just circle above us until we signal you," Ben said. "Something's wrong."

"What did I tell you?" Kim said.

"Your com-links may not reach us once we take off again," Nance said.

"I know, but once we're in the station, we'll use their gear," Ben said.

"Unless it's offline," Kim said.

"Then we'll signal you visually," Ben said. "We aren't looking for trouble, but we need to find out what's happening here."

"My money is on the aliens," Kim said. "They probably took out the locals first thing."

"Maybe, but if they did, we need to know it," Ben said.

"Just be careful," Kim added. "If the aliens did attack, there may be more in the station."

Ben felt a lump in his throat. He had to swallow several times before he could speak.

"We will," he managed to say before leaving the bridge.

He went downstairs and was met by Magnum, who was coming out of the engineering bay. He had two rifles and held one out to Ben, who took it and began checking to make sure it had power packs. The Lancet ARs were laser weapons, meaning they used batteries instead of bullets. Magnum had a belt with several more battery packs slung over his shoulder. Ben hoped they wouldn't need them, but he checked his pistol. It was also fully charged and had an extra battery in a slot of his holster.

"You have your com-link on?" Ben asked.

Magnum nodded.

"Let's use the air lock," Ben said. "It takes less time to cycle and the girls can get in the air sooner."

They walked over to the air lock and opened the inner door. It closed with a heavy thump behind them, and Ben's heart rate increased as Magnum pulled the lever to cycle the air lock. Ben tapped his com-link to activate it.

"We're heading out the air lock," Ben said.

"I see you," Nance said. "We'll keep eyes on the station. I've got radar going, and we're scanning comm frequencies."

"Good," Ben said as the outer door opened.

The spaceport was automated. The weight of the *Echo* on the landing pad activated the people mover, which was zooming toward them on the long, narrow track. Ben was thankful the entire top was transparent and he could see that the transport was empty.

"Give us a second and we'll be clear," he told Kim and Nance.

"Roger that," Kim said.

Ben and Magnum went over and waited at the gate until the people mover came to a complete stop. The gate lifted automatically, and a woman's voice said, *Welcome to Gershwin, birthplace of kings.*

The door to the transport slid open, and Ben stepped inside. The transport was large enough for a dozen people. It was a simple people mover, essentially two bench seats along either side of the transport. He and Magnum sat facing each other and with views across the plains and toward the mountains. The dome of the conveyance was so clean and clear it was almost invisible. They saw the *Echo* take off and circle upward.

"Can you still read me?" Ben said into his com-link.

"Barely," Nance said.

The people mover started, gliding easily along the track. Ben turned his attention to the two buildings at the center of the port. One was a tall, elegant building with large windows. The other was a hangar with a massive door that rotated up and in. The door to the hangar was open, and Ben could see that the transports were not inside.

"No transports," Ben said.

"We didn't see them in the mountain pass," Magnum said.

"And they weren't in the city. The Confederates searched all the buildings. There's no place to store them."

The people mover slowed down as it approached the central hub, changed tracks, and then moved around to the front of the taller building.

Welcome to Gershwin Landing Station, the automated voice said as the doors of the people mover opened. *Have a wonderful stay.*

Ben and Magnum stepped off the people mover and went straight to the door of the tall building. A sign over the doorway said Welcome Center, and both doors swished open as they approached. Inside was a large lobby that reminded Ben of the hotel tower. Only, the furniture was askew.

"Bodies," Magnum said.

Ben's blood ran cold. He could see several people lying face down on the broad marble tiles that lined the floor. A sickly-sweet smell wafted out of the welcome center. Ben tapped his com-link.

"This is Ben," he said. "Can you read me?"

"We can," Kim said, her voice crackling with static. "What's the word?"

"You may have been right," Ben replied. "We have dead bodies in the welcome center. Not sure who or what killed them, but from the odor, I'm sure they're dead. Magnum and I are going in."

Chapter 8

General Pershing was with Grubat in the interrogation room when the *Everest* came out of hyperspace. She felt the familiar stretch of time that always occurred whenever they jumped into or out of hyperspace. The hours had flown by. Pershing hadn't eaten or slept in so long she couldn't even remember the last time she had taken time to look after herself. But the information she gleaned was incredible.

Grubat was sitting in a chair with his legs shackled together. A table separated the alien from Pershing. Grubat's wrists were enclosed in metal cuffs that were attached to the tabletop. He didn't move much, but the thick tendrils of his headdress were in constant motion. They waved gracefully, almost as if they were underwater or perhaps immune to gravity. Pershing had learned that they were extrasensory devices that not only received and deciphered information from the air around the alien, but were also a sign of rank and prowess in battle.

She wanted to stay and continue the interrogation, but time was precious and she was needed on the bridge. And while she found the alien fascinating, she also knew that she couldn't accept Grubat at his word. For all she knew, he could be lying about everything. He was a captive, an enemy with no incentive to tell the truth. He was talking, but that might merely be a ploy to stay alive. Worse still, he could be doing something she was completely unaware of. Only time would tell, and she felt that it was going too fast.

"Have the prisoner put in a cell," Pershing told the guard behind her. "And double the watch. No one speaks to the prisoner without my permission."

"Yes, General," the guard said.

She turned and left without a word to Grubat. Her nature wanted to thank him for his openness, but he was a prisoner with no right. He would have to talk or be made to talk, and while she felt he was being cooperative, he wasn't her ally. There was no reason to be cordial with the alien, and unless there was a reason for it, she refused to do it.

General Pershing hurried from the detention center on the lowest level of the ship. If the *Everest* was fired on, the least important sections of the vessel would be the most vulnerable, including the detention center where any prisoners were kept. She took a lift up to the main deck which ran the length of the battle cruiser, almost exactly in the center of the vast ship. Only officers and personnel that needed to be on the main deck were allowed access. She stepped off the lift and hurried toward the bridge. She had a small concern that Admiral General Dietz might have found his courage and decided to take command from her again, but he was not on the bridge.

"Report!" Pershing said as she came into the command center of the ship.

"Commander on the bridge!" said the security officer.

The ship's ranking officer was a captain with experience running the ship. Most of the appointed officers had career military veterans who carried out their orders and actually oversaw the duties of the commander on the ship. The *Everest* had Captain Pointer, a short, bulky man with a shiny, bald head. He had dark skin and thick eyebrows. Pershing saw a thick patch of whiskers showing on both of his round cheeks.

"General, we have entered the Mersa system," Captain Pointer said. "Four hours to reach the orbit of Mersa Prime. I was just about to radio system control."

"What other vessels are in the system?" Pershing asked, after noting the various bleeps on the holographic plot.

"There are two trade vessels, the weather drone operating ship *Nova,* and twelve small craft that show new transponder codes not in the Nav Net or our data banks."

"New ships?" Pershing asked.

"Correct, General. Flight control has scrambled a squad of fast-attack ships to investigate."

"I have an idea who they might be," Pershing said. "Open a comm channel to those ships."

The communications officer spoke, "Channel is open, General."

"Confederate vessels, this is General Pershing on the R-I-F *Everest.* Is Holt still with you?"

There was a slight pause, then a man replied, "Yes, I'm here, General. Against my better judgment, I might add."

"Very good," Pershing said before turning to Captain Pointer. "Have those fast-attack ships stand down and return to Mersa Station. Those are our ships."

There were murmurs on the bridge, but no one spoke loud enough to be overheard by Pershing. She wasn't surprised by their shock. Working with the rebels was a difficult pill to swallow even for her, and it had been her idea to begin with.

"Holt," she continued. "Have your squadron form behind the *Everest*. We aren't expecting trouble, but let's stay alert for the possibility."

"Roger that, General," the Confederate grumbled.

"Make orbit, Captain, then await my orders," Pershing ordered.

She left the bridge and went to the communications center, which was a small room farther down the main corridor of the ship. It was manned by three technicians at all times who monitored all incoming communications signals. She stepped into their domain, and after an awkward moment of standing and saluting, they settled back down.

"I need the video of this interrogation sent out," Pershing said, handing over a tiny data chip. She had recorded her lengthy questioning of the prisoner, Chieftain Grubat, on a tiny personal video recorder she kept on her person at all times. It was a handy device when dealing with politicians who had no qualms about lying. She had never been forced to use the evidence it recorded before, but she had activated it when questioning the prisoner and hoped it would get the rest of the fleet to see that the rumors of the invasion were true.

"Send it to whom, General?" one of the technicians asked.

"Everyone," Pershing said. "Send it everywhere. It's the only information we have about the Krah. If something happens to us, the intelligence we have gleaned can't be lost."

"So a general broadcast?"

"Yes, go wide, as wide as possible."

"We could post it to the networks too," another of the technicians said. "It'll probably go viral on its own."

"Do it," Pershing ordered. "And continue to broadcast the call for all ships to report here to the Mersa system."

Confident that the communications techs would do as she ordered them, Pershing headed back to Admiral General Dietz's salon. She needed to give him an update, and hopefully convince him to leave the *Everest*. If he was going to be the commander in chief, he couldn't be fighting on the front lines, and Pershing needed every ship she could get. Perhaps he could settle on Mersa Station and take charge of the fleet as it arrived in the system. Pershing was confident the other ships would come once they saw her video interrogation of the alien her commandos had captured. In the meantime, she needed to get back to the Celeste system and find out what the aliens were doing. Her initial victory had been short lived, and she needed a more sustainable way to retake the system and push the aliens back to their own galaxy. She silently cursed herself for losing Professor Jones and the *Modulus Echo*, but she would find them again soon. As long as they were still alive, she would find them. And make them pay for their betrayal.

Chapter 9

It wasn't the first dead body Ben had ever seen. Death was common on Torrent Four, and bodies were often left in the salvage fields where they died. Ben had even killed on occasion when there was no other option. Yet the dead bodies in the luxury setting of the welcome center on Gershwin seemed terrifyingly out of place.

"Blunt force," Magnum said.

The big man was bent over one of the bodies. Ben could see more scattered around the large lobby. The dead were all dressed in fine clothes. There was no sign of the workers who had lived or been stationed on the planet.

"What's that mark on her neck?" Ben asked.

The corpse in question was a slender woman wearing a long, silky gown. The outfit itself seemed strange, considering she must have been with the guests who were fleeing the planet.

"It looks like a welt," Magnum said. "Like maybe someone pulled off a necklace."

Ben walked over to a heavyset man whose dead body was sprawled on the polished tiles. Blood had pooled under him and turned into a sticky sludge. Ben leaned down and checked his pockets. There was no wallet, no money clip, not even a wrist link, even though a light strip showed on his otherwise tan arms where some sort of watch used to be.

"Have they all been robbed?" Ben asked.

"That would be my guess," Magnum said. "In the panic and pressure of the situation, the workers turned on the guests."

"And then stole the transports to escape in," Ben said. "But where would they go? There isn't another spaceport on this planet."

"It's a big place," Magnum said. "I doubt smugglers would have much trouble getting on and off-world without being noticed."

"Right under the nose of the Royal Imperium?" Ben asked. "That's crazy."

"Or maybe the royals were so confident that they were safe that they didn't bother monitoring. I don't know, but that's what it looks like. Not aliens, I don't think. I can't tell that weapons were used."

The two men moved deeper into the building. The lobby was just a staging area, a place for guests to wait once they landed for the shuttles to take them through the mountains to Royal City."

"Strange that they kept this so far from the city," Ben said. "I guess the guests didn't want to be bothered by the noise of ships landing and taking off."

Magnum shrugged. The ways of the wealthy were alien to the two men from Torrent Four. They kept searching and eventually found the communications center. It was smashed. Whoever had led the attack on the guests had made sure that no survivors could radio for help.

"I guess that's why they didn't respond to our hails," Ben said.

"Should we leave?" Magnum asked.

"Not yet," Ben replied. "There might still be survivors. Let's look around a bit more."

They checked the offices and the utility rooms. The welcome center seemed to be vacant, until they found the small dining facility. It was a utilitarian space, mainly for feeding the workers who serviced the welcome center and ferried people back and forth Royal City. Ben was just about to leave when he heard a whimper in the pantry.

"You hear that?" Ben asked Magnum in a whisper.

He nodded, and they headed over to the large pantry. It had a heavy-looking door, which was locked, and also a pass-through with thin doors that slid apart to form a window. There were scuff marks on the pass-through ledge, and the doors didn't close all the way. Ben looked through the crack. The pantry was dark, but he could see the frightened eyes of children staring back at him.

"Don't be afraid," Ben said. "We're here to help."

Magnum moved to the other side of the pantry window as Ben slowly opened the thin doors. They were on a tandem and pulling one made both retract into the wall. Light from the kitchen shone into the pantry, where four frightened women huddled with over a dozen children.

"Who are you?" one of the women asked.

"My name is Ben, and this is Magnum. You can come out of there. We've searched the place and there's no one else here."

"You were a worker?" another of the women asked.

Ben noticed the fine cut of their clothes, which were wrinkled and soiled. The women all looked haggard, and the children were frightened. He guessed they had been guests when the attack occurred.

"Actually, we are crew members on a ship," Ben said. "The *Modulus Echo*. We helped the Royal Imperium get troops on the ground. They're in the city. We can take you back there if you want."

"We want off the planet," the first woman said. "Can you do that?"

"Not right away," Ben said. "I guess you know about the aliens."

"Jen, let's not talk about all this in front of the children," one of the other women said. "I'll take them out the side door."

"I'll go with them," Magnum said. "Just in case."

Ben nodded. "Go ahead and have Kim land the ship."

Magnum nodded and Ben turned back to the woman named Jen. She was older than he was. He guessed early forties, but it was hard to tell for sure since she had been hiding for a while. She leaned onto a stainless-steel prep counter and watched the children go outside. Two other women stayed close. They were quiet, but Ben could see the fear and distrust in their eyes.

"So what happened?" Ben asked.

"After the royal family was evacuated, we waited, expecting more news once they were safe," Jen said. "Then the satellites began picking up alien ships, and there were rumors on the networks about an invasion. Eventually, the workers here stopped working. Some disappeared. No one could tell us what was happening. There was a fight in Royal City between a group of maintenance workers and the stewards in the hotel. All the guests were urged to pack up and go here to wait for rescue, and only a handful of the workers were willing to help us.

We weren't even here for a full day when the rest of the workers attacked us. They stole everything, all our luggage, jewelry, anything of value. And they beat the guests. Some fled. We took the children and fled in here."

"The children aren't yours?" Ben asked.

"We're nannies," Jen explained. "We traveled with the families to help care for the children."

"And their parents?" Ben asked.

"Gone. The workers went berserk. You saw the bodies, right?"

Ben nodded.

"They were in a rage, screaming about inequality and how arrogant the guests were. I don't know, maybe they were right, in a way. Some of the people here were conceited and treated the help like second-class citizens, but they didn't deserve to die because of that."

"I agree," Ben said, although he wondered what it must have been like for the workers on Gershwin, surrounded by luxury but forced only to serve others and never enjoy the posh living experience of the guests.

"I can't promise when help will come, but you'll be with over two hundred soldiers back in the city," Ben said.

"Why not just leave the system?" Jen asked.

"It's a long story, but suffice it to say that it's not safe."

He led the women through the lobby and out to where the children were boarding a people mover. Kim was bringing the *Echo* in for a landing.

"Is that your ship?" Jen asked.

"Yes," Ben said.

"I guess it's better that you can't rescue us," Jen said.

There was conceit to her tone, which stung. Ben couldn't believe anyone would look down on the *Echo*. It was an old ship, and the mismatched paint gave her a roguish look, but he would never imagine that anyone would look down their noses at the Kestrel class vessel. Especially when they had spent who knew how long huddled in a pantry, fearing for their lives.

"Back in her day, the *Echo* was a luxury vessel," Ben said. "There's food, clean water, showers. But you won't need to be on board that long before you're back in the city."

"Perhaps we never should have left," Jen said.

Chapter 10

"The crown prince," Staff Sergeant Visher said. "You're sure?"

"Positive," Corporal Dial said.

"Well, that changes things," Visher said. "We have to get him out of there. Let's break radio silence."

"What if the aliens pick up the signal?" Corporal Dial said.

"They don't even speak our language," Private Rhoades said. "Who cares if they hear us?"

"It's a chance we'll have to take," Staff Sergeant Visher said. "The general needs to know what we're about to do."

"What if she isn't up there?" Corporal Dial asked. "Our comms will reach orbit, but if those alien ships came back, we could be all alone."

"Yeah, she left Major Le Croix," Corporal Amadi said. "And look what happened to him."

"We're expendable," Visher said. "The crown prince isn't. We'll send word about the mission, but at the end of the day, we'll do what we have to do."

"You really want to take on that entire settlement?" Corporal Miller asked.

"No," Staff Sergeant Visher said. "But I will if I have to."

The other commandos all nodded. Contrary to most people's beliefs about them, the Special Forces commandos weren't anxious to fight unless it was inevitable. The team of specially trained warriors would form a plan to rescue the prince that encountered as little resistance as possible. But at the end of the day, they were ready to fight if the need arose.

Staff Sergeant Visher gave the settlement one last look to make sure he hadn't missed anything. The workers had finished their inspection and closed the doors again. He couldn't see the crown prince, but he trusted Corporal Dial. His biggest fear was that the aliens had wanted them to see Prince Godfred. The odds that spotting the prisoner was actually a setup were very high, but Visher knew he had no choice. As a staff sergeant in the Royal Imperium military, he couldn't just sit back and leave the crown prince to his fate in the hands of an enemy force.

He pulled out the long-range communicator from his backpack. It was a self-contained unit that looked like a box. The tops and sides folded back to create a miniature parabolic dish, capable of sending and receiving radio signals. His personal com-link connected to the long-range communicator wirelessly and boosted the range exponentially. The LRC powered on, and Visher waited for the green light on the side to indicate that his com-link had synced with the device. When it came on, he searched through the frequencies, hoping to hear from the Royal Imperium forces in orbit. There was nothing but static. He would have to send a message and set the LRC for a multichannel broadcast.

"Royal Imperium Fleet, this is Spec Ops Alpha team. Do you read me? Over."

His call seemed to go unheeded. Sending the signal over multiple channels was expedient, but weakened the signal. He would have to go through them one by one. It was possible that the fleet was still in orbit, but there were a variety of atmospheric conditions around the planet that could block their signal. Staff Sergeant Visher spent over an hour working through the various frequencies, hoping to make contact. It was slow, tedious work that didn't yield any obvious results.

Corporal Dial joined him after a while. Visher noted the tension on his friend's face. Staff Sergeant Visher was in charge of the team, but Dial was his second-in-command, and Visher trusted him. Dial could often see the things that Visher missed.

"Anything?" the corporal asked.

"Nope," Visher said. "Looks like we're on our own."

"It's not the first time," Dial replied. "You try all the channels?"

"Everything on the main frequencies," Visher said. "You want to give the emergency channels a try while I start formulating a plan?"

"Sure," Dial said. "The settlement is quiet. Nothing different from the past few days."

"Roger that," Visher said, handing Dial the LRC. "I'll do an equipment check and inventory our resources, then figure out how we'd rescue the prince."

It was a redundant task. Staff Sergeant Visher already knew what they had. Nothing had changed since the ambush in the mountains, except for solar chargers that had replenished the battery packs for the assault rifles. Still, going through their supplies was a familiar task, almost comforting, and it was inspiring as he considered what they might do. The problem with rescuing the prince was twofold. First, they needed to distract the aliens, and second, they needed to get inside their settlement. There were no handles on the outside of the gate, and Visher knew the aliens must have some way to lock it from the inside. They could easily blast a hole in the wooden structure, but that would draw a lot of attention.

He decided they could cut a hole in the wall using their laser rifles with a minor adjustment to the weapon's settings. It would burn through the wood, which was slower but made less noise. The only issue would be the smoke. He was pondering the possibility of attacking at night when Dial waved to him.

"I've got something."

Staff Sergeant Visher felt his pulse quicken. He moved over to where Dial was fiddling with the LRC.

"What are you doing?" Visher asked.

"It's an analog signal," Dial said. "Single sideband, and I'm trying to get it dialed in. There's a lot of static, but there's something there."

"Could be old," Visher said. "Or some kid playing with old tech."

"I doubt there's a lot of old equipment lying around in this world," Dial said. "From what I've heard, the royals only want the latest and greatest."

"Tell that to Prince Godfred. I'm guessing he would settle for anything human at this point."

...at Royal City. The aliens have taken control of the system, and all personnel must report on this analog frequency...

"Just what we thought," Visher said. "Now we're stuck out here."

"Maybe we should hold off on the rescue mission," Dial said. "If we take Prince Godfred, they'll come after us for sure."

"We can't wait," Visher replied. "They could kill him at any time."

"They haven't yet," Dial argued.

"Yeah, well, they didn't have control of the system and now they do. Which means they'll either send the prisoner up or—"

"Send more warriors down here," Dial interrupted. "I get it."

"Can you reply back on the SSB signal?"

"Sure. Their signal seems to be getting through easily enough."

"Tell them where we are and what we're planning. If they can back us up, or better yet, come and get us, that would be golden."

"Roger that, Staff Sergeant," Dial said. "I'll get right on it."

Chapter 11

Kim landed the *Echo* in the open space right in front of the royal palace. She was anxious to leave the planet, but she had to admit it felt good to rescue the group of children. The adults with them weren't as pleasant. One had turned her nose up as Ben herded the group up to the main deck and Kim lifted off in the *Modulus Echo*. She obviously found the ship beneath her standards, but Kim didn't have time for the adults as several of the children gathered around her pilot's chair. She answered questions while flying through the mountain pass. As soon as they touched down, the adults herded the sweet, inquisitive children off the ship.

"Well, that's done," Kim declared.

"I've got a message from Captain Lawrence," Nance said.

"Put it through," Ben said.

The captain's face appeared on the big bridge displays. Kim thought the man was handsome, with some gray at his temples and large green eyes. His square jaw and wavy hair added to his striking looks.

Hello, Ben. Thank you for checking on the spaceport.

"Our pleasure," Ben said.

Kim couldn't help but frown. She was happy they had saved the children, but she wouldn't have called it a pleasure.

We got a message on the old SSB signal. It's from a group of Special Forces operators. We're forwarding you their coordinates now. They're requesting backup and evac.

Kim turned in her chair. Ben looked at her, and while she didn't want to stick around, she knew it was the right thing to do. She gave a little nod, and Ben turned his attention back to the display screens.

"We were hoping to hear from them," Ben said. "We'll head out right now."

Good, Captain Lawrence said. *They're claiming that Prince Godfred is being held captive. I wouldn't waste my time trying to save any of the spoiled royals, but you do whatever you think is best.*

"We'll be in touch," Ben said.

"I'm lifting off," Kim said.

"The coordinates are in the system," Nance said.

"ETA?" Ben asked.

"Are you seriously asking if we're there yet?" Kim teased.

She had taken the *Echo* straight up and then out over the forest. They were well above the treetops and gaining speed as she followed the yellow line on her personal monitor that showed the way. Another monitor showed their speed, which was climbing, the distance to the coordinates, which were halfway around the world, and the estimated time to reach it.

"Six hours," she continued. "If we don't have trouble between here and there."

"Okay," Ben said. "I'm going to check on the professor. We should keep an eye open for any sign of the aliens attempting to make planet fall."

"Roger that, Captain," Kim said with a heavy dose of sarcasm.

"Radar is clear," Nance said. "All systems are in the green."

Kim was acutely aware of the differences between flying in space versus flying in planetary atmosphere. The biggest being gravity's constant fight to pull the ship down to the ground. The *Echo* was a hybrid ship that could fly in atmosphere and in hard vacuum. The engines didn't struggle to keep them aloft, and the ship's airframe was designed to create lift as she moved forward. Still, they burned significantly more fuel flying in atmosphere where gravity and friction fought them at all times. Ben had switched out the Zexum tanks the night before, and she knew there were nearly a dozen more full tanks down in the engineering bay, but it still worried her to spend precious fuel on Gershwin when all she wanted was to get them safely off-world and out of the system.

The ship climbed upward as they went along. Kim's altimeter continued ticking upward, and she hoped they would get close enough to orbit to get a peek at what was happening beyond the blue sky. It wasn't long into their journey before the dark-green forest gave way to golden fields that led to dazzling white-sand beaches. The ocean on Gershwin was emerald green and looked flat and calm beneath them. Kim knew they were much too high to make out any real details. The ocean spread out as far as they could see in every direction, with no sign of people anywhere. It seemed like a wasted opportunity to Kim. So much promise, so much opportunity, all reserved for just a handful of people. On Torrent Four, the Royal Imperium was distant. They governed the planet, but for the people living there, the government was just another constant, like gravity, that couldn't be fought against, only accepted—

and mostly hated. Kim didn't like it, but she didn't have the same animosity as the Confederates who were from worlds where the loss of freedom was felt more acutely.

She thought about the workers who had revolted and murdered the guests left behind when the royal family fled Gershwin. It was hard to blame them for resenting the people they had served. To be so close to the beauty and luxury of a pristine world, yet completely forbidden from actually enjoying it would be a hardship beyond her ability to fathom. Even if one of the service professionals on Gershwin could save every credit they earned for their entire life, it wouldn't be enough to pay for a single night's stay in the royal home world. And Kim knew that having money wasn't the only factor. In the Royal Imperium, whom you knew was equally as important as how much money you had. Power and privilege were entwined with social politics. The upper classes didn't mix with the people they considered beneath them, and they weren't keen on accepting new people, or any change, for that matter. They wanted to keep things just the way they were, and even a poor orphan like Kim knew that it was impossible to keep things from changing. Gershwin was a prime example of that. The planet that had been preserved for the pleasure of a privileged few was quickly becoming the focal point in a galactic struggle that had completely upset the applecart of power. The Royal Imperium had been struck a nearly fatal blow by the flux rocket that destroyed most of their fleet and opened a wormhole to another galaxy. The Imperium had been forced to make peace with the Confederacy of Free Planets, who had been the only threat to their power. And Gershwin, along with several members of the royal family, appeared lost. At least

Kim couldn't fathom how the Royal Imperium could win back the planet.

Unlike Ben, she didn't feel responsible for any of it. She had some guilt over the lives lost when they fired the flux rocket, but she knew that no one on the *Modulus Echo* had expected the tiny weapon to have such a huge, cascading effect. It was the admiral general's fault for summoning so many of his ships to the system in an effort to display his power that had cost them so dearly in the end. Many of the vessels could have escaped if their commanders hadn't panicked. In their haste to escape, they had crashed into one another, their broken ships unable to break free from the growing gravity wave that was fed by the destruction of their vessels until it drew in the entire Royal Imperium military space station. Thousands of military personnel had died. That was a difficult fact to live with, even if she had told herself they were soldiers who knew that dying in the line of duty was a possibility. If they hadn't been in the military, they wouldn't have died, but Kim also recognized that the *Echo* wasn't a warship. They had never actually joined the Confederacy. They were, in the truest sense, outlaws, not rebels. All Kim wanted was the chance to fly, but to get that chance, she had to break the law and align herself with the Confederacy just to get the fuel they needed.

Like every other time she tried to sort her thoughts and feelings about the war and their part in it, she had to give up hope of ever figuring it all out. Who was at fault was impossible to pin down. At first, helping General Pershing seemed like the obvious choice, but eventually Kim felt used. No danger was too great for the general to risk, but Kim hadn't signed on to die in service to the Royal Imperium. For her, working with the general had been a means to an end. All she wanted was the freedom to fly and work with the people she cared about. Eventually, getting away from the general and her war with the aliens was inevitable, but Kim feared that it was, in many ways, similar to the massacre the service workers had committed against the guests at the spaceport. By breaking free, she feared that they had condemned themselves forever.

"Kim, the air is getting pretty thin," Nance said. "Are you planning on breaking into orbit?"

"No," Kim replied. "But I wouldn't mind getting a peek at what's going on out there. How long would you need to get a scan?"

"I've got readings from here," Nance said. "The debris is blocking our radar attempts for the most part."

"So we can't see what they're doing?"

"Not really," Nance said. "Sorry."

"Are we going to be able to get off-world?"

"I think so…" Nance let her thought trail off.

Nance wasn't unemotional, but she rarely let her emotions show. Kim looked over her shoulder and saw her friend staring down at her computer screens intently.

"What is it, Nance?"

"I can't be certain, but it looks like maybe the aliens are trying to clear the debris field," Nance said.

"That makes sense, doesn't it?" Kim said. "They're scavengers. There's no sense in letting usable scrap go to waste."

"That's not what I'm concerned about," Nance said.

Magnum spoke, and what he said made Kim nervous.

"Maybe they're clearing orbit so they can launch a proper invasion," he said.

Kim felt her blood grow cold. Chill bumps rose on her arms, and she let the ship begin a slow descent. She couldn't help but think of the alien ships, each one as big as a battle cruiser. There had been over a hundred of the alien vessels, and each of those could have hundreds of warriors on board. Just one of them descending near Royal City could wipe out the Confederates and slaughter every human being on the planet.

"I think we should tell Ben," Kim said. "We need a plan before it's too late."

Chapter 12

The plan called for them to wait until dark, but the commando team had split into three groups. Staff Sergeant Visher was with Privates Rhoades and Wriggles. Their job was to break into the alien camp and rescue the prince. Corporals Amadi and Miller were on overwatch and would give fire support to the staff sergeant's squad upon their retreat from the alien camp.

Corporal Dial was with Private Felix as they made their way toward the opposite end of the alien camp. They were moving quietly through the forest. Slow and silent, they were like shadows moving between the trees. There was no sign of the aliens who seemed content to stay inside the walls of their camp, but that wouldn't last forever. Dial knew the *Modulus Echo* was on its way, and to him it felt a little bit like home. They had gotten the message over the old SSB frequency, and they knew the Kestrel class ship would arrive shortly before dark. Dial and Felix needed to be in position by then, but they weren't in a hurry. Their job would be to make contact with the ship and direct an air strike on the side of the alien camp opposite from where Dial had seen the prince. Once the wall was down, Dial and Felix would lay down a steady barrage of fire to keep the aliens occupied so that Staff Sergeant Visher could rescue the prince.

It was a daring plan considering the fact that the Spec Ops team of eight was vastly outnumbered. In fact, they had no idea how many aliens were in the camp or what weapons they might have. The staff sergeant would have exactly six minutes to cut his way into the camp, get the prince free of the wooden cage, and escape. After that, if Dial and Felix were still alive, they would run for their lives back along the edge of the mountains, hopefully drawing the aliens away from Visher, who would be evacuated on the *Echo* before the ship changed course and returned to help Dial and Felix.

They stopped at the edge of a stream and took a break. There were still two hours before dark. Dial bent low, scooped up some water, and splashed it onto his face and rubbed his wet hands on the back of his neck. The water flowed out of the mountains in a wide but shallow stream. There were plenty of rocks to use as stepping stones so their boots wouldn't get wet. The water was cold, and Dial took the time to fill a canteen with a biofilter that would ensure that the water was clean enough to drink.

"How far we got?" Private Felix asked.

"Another mile or two," Dial said. "Then we'll find a good place to hunker down."

"Something with clear lines of retreat, I hope," Felix said.

"You worried?"

"Aren't you?"

"A little," Dial admitted.

In fact, he was more than a little worried. He had volunteered for the more dangerous assignment without really thinking about it. It was part of being a Spec Ops grunt—they were trained to run toward danger, not away from it. And it wasn't the fighting that bothered Corporal Dial; it was the unknown. They just didn't know enough about the aliens to know what they would do when the bombs and bullets started flying.

"But we have the upper hand," Dial said. They were whispering just to be safe. "They don't know we're coming, and we'll be ready when the fighting starts."

"I hope it's enough," Felix said. "Six minutes seems like a long time."

"I guess it is," Dial replied, taking a swig of the cold water. "But we've been in worse spots. At least the aliens don't tend to use firearms. That's in our favor."

"That we know of," Felix pointed out.

Dial knew what his companion was thinking. They didn't really know what the aliens might do. In the mountains, when the commandos had ambushed the small party of aliens, they hadn't fought back at all. This time around, Dial knew things would be different. He couldn't help but wonder what Le Croix was up to. What had the traitor told the aliens about the commandos? The entire camp seemed like one giant trap to Dial, and if not for the crown prince being held inside the camp, he would have argued against attacking. But they couldn't walk away if there was still a chance to save the next king of the Royal Imperium, even if they would most likely all die in the attempt. Still, the *Modulus Echo* gave them an edge over the aliens. Dial and the commandos had been watching the camp for days and hadn't seen any sort of mechanized transport. If they had an aircraft, they were hiding them.

"Better keep moving," Dial said.

The two men stood up, stretched, then checked their weapons. It was a habit. Dial saw that his assault rifle was fully charged and currently set on laser fire. Beams of superfocused light didn't have the stopping power of a projectile and burned through the battery power at three times the rate of any other setting, but it was also the quietest firing option they had. With their assault rifles on the laser setting, there was no report when they fired, no recoil, just a gentle hum as the weapon recharged after every burst. If they stumbled upon the enemy, they could shoot without alerting more aliens in the surrounding area.

Of course, that didn't take into account what the enemy might do. And with just two commandos, the chances of taking out an entire party of aliens before they managed to alert others nearby were slim, but it was worth the chance, and the two men kept their rifles set to laser fire. Dial made sure his safety was off and kept his index finger straight across the trigger guard. Once he was certain his weapon was ready, he set off, hopping from stone to stone until he reached the other side of the stream. Private Felix was right behind him.

An hour later, they settled onto a large rock with a clear view of the wooden wall that surrounded the enemy camp. Both men had hidden their backpacks along a game trail that ran away from the alien camp. Once the fighting ended, they would slip off the back of the large boulder and run down the trail long enough to retrieve their packs before moving through the forest or into the mountains.

Dial had four power packs tucked into pouches on his belt. Across his chest were traditional ammo loops. He had three magazines with plasma cartridges and three with depleted uranium rounds. As they waited for the *Echo*, they switched the rifles back to traditional ammunition. Dial would fire the depleted uranium, and Felix would shoot plasma. Both men could hit targets with accuracy at the distance they would be aiming for. When the time came, Dial would roll off the side of the boulder and spread out to mimic a larger group of attackers. Of course, the best-laid plans rarely worked out, and Dial didn't bother analyzing the minute details. If the aliens attacked in an organized group, they would kill as many as possible before getting killed themselves, but they wouldn't retreat until at least six minutes had passed from the initial attack. Other than that one parameter, they could hit the aliens however they wanted.

"Double-check your night vision monocular," Dial said. "Hopefully, we'll be running in the dark."

"Yeah, hopefully," Felix replied.

"Have a little faith, man. It's a good plan."

"If you say so. But it seems like we're all risking our necks for one person who wouldn't spit on us if we were on fire."

"The crown prince? You know him?"

"I know enough," Private Felix said.

"Yeah, well, don't believe everything you read in the tabloids."

"If even a fifth of it's true, we're wasting our time."

"Maybe so," Dial said. "But that's the gig. Where else are you going to have the opportunity to waste aliens and save the galaxy, man?"

"I love what I do. I'm just not so crazy about whom we're doing it for."

"So don't think about the prince," Dial said. "Just cover my six and we'll make it out of here alive."

"You know it," Felix said, but Dial could hear the aggravation in the younger man's voice.

It was a common feeling, even in the military. Most people didn't like the royal family. And the politicians were just as bad. But Dial didn't care about all that. He liked being a soldier. The danger and discipline suited him. And if he was a little scared about the battle ahead, it only meant he was sane. He was even more excited than scared. He had been in firefights before, then afterward felt guilt over the loss of life. Why men felt the need to fight other men was above his pay grade, but fighting aliens seemed right no matter what. These beings from another galaxy had come along, attacked the royal family, and were squatting on Gershwin. Dial had no qualms about taking the fight to them.

Twilight was just setting in when Dial's com-link beeped. He keyed his throat mic and spoke quietly.

"This is Corporal Dial. Go ahead, over."

Dial, this is Ben on the Echo. We're almost at the coordinates you sent us. What's the plan? Over.

Corporal Dial quickly relayed the plan as Private Felix switched on the laser-aiming device that the *Echo* could read and zero in on with their missiles.

"Once you pick them up, you're to swing back and get us. We'll be on the move, but we'll be waiting for your call. You set the LZ and we'll get there. Over."

Got it, Ben replied. *Magnum has the missiles ready to fire. We'll be in position in ninety seconds. Over.*

"Roger that," Dial said. "Ninety seconds and counting. Good luck, *Modulus Echo.* Dial, out."

"It's about damn time," Felix said.

"Shake off those nerves, Private, and trust your training. You know the drill," Dial said. "We hit them hard for six minutes, then run like hell. I've got your back."

"And I've got yours," Felix said.

The light was fading. Dial wasn't sure if he was hearing the distant rumble of the *Echo*'s engines or just the wind through the trees. He could feel his heartbeat in his ears, and his skin tingled. Ninety seconds seemed like an eternity, but when it passed, everything happened fast.

Modulus Echo has a lock, Ben said over the com-link. *Firing now.*

The missile came shooting low over the trees, almost directly above Corporal Dial and Private Felix. Both soldiers closed their eyes and put their faces down close to the rock they were lying prone on. The explosion was incredibly loud. It rumbled through the rock and made Dial clench his teeth as he endured the assault on his senses. When he looked up, the debris from the wall, which was blown apart by the missiles, began to rain down in flaming fragments. The first missile destroyed the wall; the second impacted the ground just inside the compound. A large berm of earth had been thrown up and was smoking.

"Watch for movement," Dial ordered.

He rolled off the stone and slid down to the ground where he knelt for a moment. He could see the gaping hole in the wooden palisade clearly, even in the dim light, but smoke obscured the aliens inside. He could hear shouting in the strange, grunting language the aliens used. He decided to make his move and scrambled around several trees before kneeling behind a fallen log. He propped his assault rifle on the log and searched for any sign of movement, but there was still no visibility through the hanging pall of smoke.

Someone in the camp was barking orders. Dial decided not to wait any longer. His rifle had sixty rounds of depleted uranium, and he flipped the setting to full auto. With a gentle squeeze on the trigger, he fired three waves into the smoke, then ran to a thick tree and hid behind it. There were shouts, roars of pain, and outrage. His barrage had done something, and time was passing quickly. A glance at his wrist link showed a full sixty seconds had passed since the missile strike. His rifle showed thirty-two rounds remaining in the rifle. Leaning out from behind the tree, he raised his rifle. Small bits of wood burned, and smoke continued to rise from the missile strikes. Dial keyed his throat mic.

"Going dark," he said.

"Going dark," Felix repeated.

Dial reached up and flicked down the monocle that was connected to his helmet. It activated and the dim shadows of the forest lit with a green light. Smoke was still rising, too thick to see through at the hole in the wall, but Dial could hear the aliens grunting and barking commands. He wanted to see his enemy, but they were hidden inside the compound. Dial considered firing blind again, but he didn't want to waste his ammunition. With a flick of his thumb, he changed the rifle's setting to three-round bursts and then checked his wrist link again. Almost two minutes had passed and there was no sign of the aliens.

The chatter of Private Felix's assault rifle was a unique sound. Instead of compressed gas that ignited and propelled the depleted uranium rounds, the plasma cartridges were hurled from the weapon using microrails. They popped like bubble wrap when fired, and the cartridges whistled through the air. Dial looked up when he heard his partner firing. He couldn't see the bullets, but he saw the damage. Each cartridge burst apart on impact, the gas inside igniting as it contacted the oxygen in the air and flared to life.

A mob of aliens was running through the hole in the wall. Most had artificial limbs of some kind, and all carried gleaming axes in one hand and what looked like shields in the other. The plasma rounds were impacting on the shields and burning through, but leaving the aliens unharmed. Dial saw several aliens toss their smoking shields aside as they ran forward.

There was nearly a hundred yards between the smoking hole in the wall of the compound and the boulder where Felix was perched on. Corporal Dial was slightly closer and he fired off several quick bursts. The alien shields did nothing to stop the depleted uranium. In fact, the bullets punched through the shields, penetrated flesh, and shot out of the aliens' bodies to impact the warriors behind the first row. They were snarling and screaming as Dial kept firing burst after burst. Private Felix's plasma cartridges were having an impact too. Dial could hear the sizzle of flesh burning and blood boiling over the screams of the aliens. Several threw their axes just as Dial ducked back behind the tree to change the magazine in his assault rifle.

He pressed a button and the empty magazine dropped from the gun. After pulling another from the harness on his chest, Dial rammed it home and pulled back the slide to load the first round. With his weapon ready, Dial dashed back to the fallen log. The aliens were spreading out, but he couldn't see them through the trees as darkness fell. The fires burning around them ruined their night vision, and the forest was a dark morass of death. Dial flipped the selector to single shot and began targeting the aliens. He could see them through the night vision monocle, but it didn't take the aliens long to adapt. They dashed into the forest, using the trees for cover and letting their eyes adjust to the gloom before they attacked. When they did, they targeted the muzzle flash of Dial's rifle. He had to flop to the ground as an alien ax thumped into the fallen log where he'd been leaning.

"How much time?" Dial asked, his voice strained as he crawled away from the log.

"Two more minutes," Felix said.

The space around the boulder was clear of trees, which meant that the aliens had to come out from the protection of the trees to attack Private Felix. He waited patiently and dispatched the fearsome aliens one by one. A few hurled their axes at him, but lying prone on the high rock gave him a perfect vantage point. Perhaps in daylight, with no danger of being shot, the aliens might have hit him with their axes, but they couldn't take careful aim or make a solid throw before his rifle sent plasma hurling toward them. It was a painful way to die. Corporal Dial was gagging on the odor of burning flesh as he rose to his knees and began to fire again.

The aliens were outgunned, but the humans were outnumbered. Dial knew that they couldn't hold out much longer. The aliens were getting closer, and soon they would strike a lucky blow that would injure or kill him.

"Fall back to the secondary position," Dial ordered just before turning and hurling a grenade into the trees. It exploded with a resounding boom and sent soil, rocks, and chunks of wood flying.

"Look out for that tree!" Felix shouted. "It's coming down!"

Dial couldn't wait to see what his grenade had done. He turned and ran. Behind him, the unmistakable cracking and popping of limbs snapping off could be heard as the tree fell. It hit close to Dial but didn't impede his retreat. He jumped over a boulder and slid to a stop before turning back. He hesitated just long enough to identify his partner. Felix was limping. Dial didn't know if he was wounded or had injured himself getting off the big rock he'd been perched on. There was no time to ask. The aliens were green shadows fleeting between the trees. Dial flipped his rifle's fire indicator back to full auto and emptied his magazine in an extended barrage.

There was no time to wait, no chance to breathe. His wrist link vibrated, letting him know that six minutes had passed. They had completed the mission, and the only thing that remained was to survive until they could be rescued. With a flurry of movement, Dial changed out his magazine and flicked the indicator back to three-round burst. He stood up, fired several times into the trees, just as Felix reached his position.

"Keep running!" Dial ordered. "I'll hold them off."

But at that moment, an ax came whirling out of the murky green forest. Dial swayed backward, acting on instincts alone. The ax flipped past so close that he felt the air moving around the weapon. *Chunk!* With a sickening sound, the ax buried itself into Private Felix's chest. The younger man dropped beside Dial, who fired back. The assault rifle chugged in his hands, and a warning in his mind told him to run. He glanced down at Felix. The ax was buried deep in his back right between the shoulder blades. Dial knew the younger man was dead, but leaving him was difficult.

A huge alien came running toward Dial, ax held high as it bellowed a war cry. Dial fired and the depleted uranium tore gaping holes in the alien's chest. It dropped to the ground just as Dial turned and ran down the game trail.

Chapter 13

The explosion from the missiles shook the forest and lit up the night. Staff Sergeant Visher had his trio as close to the compound as they could get without being seen. They were just inside the tree line, and the stout timber wall was only forty feet away. They could have cut through the wood at that distance, but it would be slow and sloppy. The staff sergeant was a firm believer that speed and efficiency were two of the greatest assets in a fight. But he held his anxious soldiers back for a few moments to let the camp focus all its attention on the far end where the missiles had impacted the wall.

"Alright, here we go," Visher whispered. "Move, move, move."

Private Wriggles and Rhoades dashed from the trees. Their weapons were set to continuous laser, which meant that as long as they held down the trigger, the weapon would fire its focused light beam capable of cutting through two inches of solid steel. The rifles would make quick work of the wall, but the tall timbers would still be dangerous. If they fell into the camp, they could hit the crown prince and kill him. And if the soldiers didn't keep a close watch on their weapons, the barrels could overheat and warp. The assault rifles had a safety measure built in, but Visher was an experienced staff sergeant. He knew that, in the field, a soldier couldn't count on anything working the way it should. If something could go wrong, it would, and a wise soldier would have to adapt.

Visher held back, keeping a close watch on the top of the wall. He was responsible for keeping the two privates safe while they cut a hole in the palisade. It was dark enough, after the flare from the explosion had died down, that he flipped his monocle over his right eye to engage his night vision capabilities.

"You're clear," Visher said using the com-link to speak to his subordinates.

"Yes, Staff Sergeant," Rhoades said. "Commencing the cut now."

Visher risked a glance over to the two privates to make sure they were following his orders. They only needed to cut two of the thick logs. And chances were high that they were held together, perhaps with wooden frames or some type of liquid bonding agent. Still, he had ordered them to kneel and cut the wooden poles at an upward angle so that when the logs fell, they would topple out of the encampment and not into it.

Once he was sure they were cutting the poles correctly, he turned his attention back to the top of the wall. There had been two sentries on the wall at dusk, but they left before the missile attack and had not been replaced. From their observation, Visher knew the aliens kept only a few guards watching through the night. He supposed that was because they felt safe behind their walls, and hopefully because they didn't have night vision capabilities. Despite the plan, which should have drawn the aliens to the far end of the camp, Visher knew that his team could run into problems at any second.

"Going hot," Private Wriggles said.

The assault rifles burned through the wood easily and sent copious amounts of smoke billowing upward. Fortunately, the dark hid the smoke, but it only took a few seconds for the smell of the burning wood to reach Visher.

"Let's hope they think that smell is from the missile strike," the staff sergeant said.

The wall had been made from trees cut down recently. They weren't dried or treated with anything, and the response to the lasers was intense.

"I'm through," Private Rhoades said. "It's still standing."

"Hit the seams," Visher ordered.

He looked at his wrist link and saw that nearly a minute had passed since the missile strike and they weren't even inside the compound yet. If the crown prince had been locked in a cage for very long, he might not be able to walk. That would mean carrying him, which would slow their egress significantly.

"Mine's loose!" Rhoades said.

Visher saw the log on the right teeter for a moment. Wriggles finished his upward cut along the seam between his own log and the rest of the wall. There was a crack, as loud as a gunshot report, then the logs were falling. Visher noted that his soldiers had their backs to the wall as the tall logs fell.

"Reload!" he ordered them. "And reset your rifles."

"Yes, Staff Sergeant," they both said.

Visher gave the top of the wall one last glance, then dashed toward the opening. The camp seemed deserted. There was a massive spaceship sitting right at the foot of the mountain, but it was dark. Visher saw no movement or signs of life. The camp was spread along the base of the mountains, and he couldn't see what was happening at the far end. He had to trust that Corporal Dial was getting things done according to the plan.

"Where's the prince?" Wriggles asked.

He and Private Rhoades had moved inside the compound to either side of Staff Sergeant Visher. All around them were large crates and cages with animals inside. The aliens were collecting specimens for strange experiments. Visher saw that many of the animals had missing limbs that were replaced with robotic prosthetics.

"Spread out and check every cage," Visher said.

"What the hell are they doing to these animals?" Private Wriggles said.

"Medical experimentation," Rhoades said. "It's like we're in a bad horror flick."

"Stay focused," Visher said. "We're running out of time."

The staff sergeant went around a large crate and discovered the prince's cage. It was short, only four feet tall, and small enough that Prince Godfred had his feet sticking out through the wooden bars. Visher was about to announce to his companions that he had found the prince when suddenly a dark shape loomed in front of him.

Visher stepped back and started to raise his weapon, but the figure knocked it aside with a powerful blow and grabbed the staff sergeant by the front of his vest. He pulled Visher close.

"Order your men to stand down!"

It was Major Le Croix and he shook Visher hard, like an abusive parent trying to make a baby stop crying. Visher nearly lost his grip on his rifle. His mind was spinning. The figure looked like an alien, it even had a tentacle hanging from its head, but at the same time, Visher recognized the voice.

"Major?" Visher said.

The figure let him go, and the staff sergeant stumbled backward. The night vision monocle worked well in certain settings. Up close wasn't one of them. As Visher moved backward, the figure resolved from a murky green blob, into a man. But Major Le Croix looked more like the aliens than a human. He had robotic legs that made him taller. A band of metal encircled his head and covered his eyes. The tendril hanging from one side of the band looked like a thick dreadlock, but it moved almost like a serpent, as if it had a mind of its own.

"We have to get out of here," Le Croix said. "I've been waiting for this chance."

"What the hell happened t—"

"There's no time for stories," Le Croix growled.

He lifted an ornate ax and brought it down in a savage chop that smashed through the prince's cage. Visher heard a cackle, and his blood ran cold. Nothing was right. He felt as if he was losing his mind. A flash of light from a rifle ripped through Le Croix's arm as he started to raise the ax again.

"Hold your fire!" Visher demanded. He wasn't sure if it was the right order or not, but he didn't want the privates shooting until he straightened things out in his mind.

Le Croix grunted in pain and the ax fell to the ground.

"Damn it! It's me," Le Croix said.

"Maybe," Visher said. "But just get out of the way."

It was Le Croix's turn to backpedal. His heavy, robotic feet thumped on the ground as Visher pulled the splintered bars of the prince's cage apart.

"Prince Godfred?" Visher asked.

The pathetic individual in the cage was on his back. He was filthy and looked half-starved. Visher felt a shiver run down his spine as the prisoner began to cackle again.

"That's him," Le Croix said through clenched teeth.

"Staff Sergeant?" Wriggles said as he approached from the far side of the cage.

"That's him, Private," Visher said. "Pull the prince out of there and let's move. Major, can you walk?"

"Yeah," Le Croix said, his voice full of pain.

"Good, then start moving."

"I need a weapon," Le Croix said.

"Negative," Visher replied. "You stay in front of us and keep your mouth shut or I'll leave what's left of your corpse here for the birds and worms."

"I can't see in the dark," Le Croix said.

"Tough shit, Major. Start moving before it's too late."

Visher heard Le Croix cursing under his breath, but he headed for the break in the wall. A glance at his wrist link showed the staff sergeant that five and a half minutes had passed since the missile attack. They were out of time.

"You got him?" Visher asked.

"He can't walk?" Wriggles said.

"Give Rhoades your rifle and carry the prince," Visher ordered. "Now move!"

They hurried out back toward the wall. They were almost through when a savage cry rang out behind them. Visher turned and saw one of the aliens running toward them along the fighting platforms that lined the inside of the wall. He flung an ax that spun through the air. Visher raised his rifle and fired instinctively. The laser bolt made no noise as it streaked through the air and hit the alien in its broad chest, burning a hole through flesh, bone, and vital organs. The alien tumbled off the fighting platform and fell to the ground with a sickening thump. But as Visher turned around, it was the shock of seeing Wriggles on the ground with an ax in his back while the crown prince of the Royal Imperium laid beneath the soldier's dead body, cackling maniacally, which made the staff sergeant almost vomit.

Visher jumped through the gap in the wall and grabbed the prince's hand. He knew it wasn't proper, and he might even be in trouble for it later, but he dragged the prince from under the dead soldier's body and kept dragging him until they reached the trees.

Le Croix and Private Rhoades were waiting just inside the tree line.

"I can probably carry him," Le Croix said, even though he was bent nearly double and holding his wounded arm tightly against his chest.

"Negative," Visher said, slinging his assault rifle over his back and then pulling the prince to his feet.

He had to hold Godfred, who didn't even try to stand. It was frightening to look into the prince's eyes. They were open so wide Visher could see the whites all around his irises. Drool was dripping from his open mouth, and the prince continued to laugh in a weird, breathy way.

"I've got the prince," Visher said. "Rhoades, take point. Major, you follow him."

He pulled his sidearm and pointed it at the major, who was frowning. Visher didn't know if he was disappointed or just in pain, but it didn't matter. Getting Le Croix back to the

Echo was important, but not at the expense of their primary objective, which was rescuing the prince. He waved the pistol to get the two men moving.

"Let's go," Visher said.

He bent down, pulled the prince onto his shoulder, and stood up. Prince Godfred had always been overweight, and it seemed the aliens hadn't fed him. Visher lifted the half-crazed royal over his shoulder easily. And just as his wrist link buzzed to let him know six minutes was over, Visher followed Private Rhoades and the strange Major Le Croix into the forest.

Chapter 14

"Can't we land?" Ben asked.

After firing the missiles at the alien camp, the *Modulus Echo* had swung around, searching for a place where they could safely bring the ship down on the ground to evacuate the soldiers.

"It's a forest," Kim said. "We can't land on the treetops."

They had flown over a mile before turning to make another pass. Ben didn't want to go too far and force the soldiers to have to travel a long distance for a rescue, but they couldn't land until they found a clearing.

"What about that?" Ben said pointing ahead.

"That's a river," Nance pointed out.

"I know, but we can set down right on the bank," Ben said. "The rear hatch will open across the water and form a bridge."

"If the bank holds up our weight," Kim said. "Don't forget, this girl's got a fat bottom."

"We have to land somewhere," Ben said.

"If the ship is too heavy, we could fall into the water," Nance said. "It could wreck the main drive."

"Just look for a good place to set down," Ben said. "Otherwise, we've come all this way for noth—"

A voice crackling through the ship's speakers cut Ben off midsentence.

Modulus Echo, this is Alpha team. Requesting location for evac. Over.

Ben looked at Nance, who shrugged her shoulders.

"I see a spot," Kim said. "I'll have us down in thirty seconds."

Ben hit the activator for the comms system and spoke into the microphone that was built into his station. "Alpha team, this is the *Modulus Echo*. Stand by for coordinates."

The ship was running dark, with no exterior lights that would reveal their location to the aliens. Ben could only see shadows as the ship descended into a clearing. He cycled through the ship's exterior cameras to see what side of the river they were on.

"I'm sending coordinates to the soldiers," Nance said.

"How far are we from the alien camp?" Ben asked.

"Two miles," Nance replied just as the ship landed.

"See, told you I'd find a place to set her down," Kim boasted. "No problem."

"Except that we're on the wrong side of the river," Ben said.

"How wide is it?" Kim asked, standing up and stretching. "Maybe they could jump across."

"Alpha team," Ben said into his microphone, "did you get our position?"

Roger that, Modulus Echo. We have your coordinates and are en route to your position. ETA, twenty minutes. We have two wounded. Please have medical help standing by. Over.

"Got it," Ben said. "We'll be ready."

"If they have wounded, they'll need help crossing the river," Magnum said.

"We've got some old pallets down in the cargo area," Ben said. "Let's go see if we can find a place to help them cross."

"What about us?" Kim asked.

"You stay where you are," Ben said. "We may have to take off in a hurry. Nance, go get the professor. He'll need to get his supplies ready to help whoever is hurt."

She nodded and hurried from the bridge. Magnum was already bounding down the stairs.

"Should I be worried?" Kim asked.

"Just stay alert," Ben said. "I have no idea what the aliens are capable of. I want us off the ground as soon as the soldiers are on board."

"Works for me," Kim replied.

Ben hurried to the stairs and bounded down to the cargo hold. Magnum came out of the engineering bay with two rifles. He held one out to Ben.

"Better safe than sorry," he said.

Ben slung the Lancet AR over his back and pulled the lever that activated the rear hatch. The forest seemed quiet. It was very dark beyond the ring of light from the open cargo hold. Ben could hear the gurgle of the water rushing over the rocks in the stream.

"Help me with these pallets," Ben said.

They were old, splintery wooden pallets, really little more than a grid of wooden planks reinforced with two-by-fours so that the tines of a cargo mover could slide under. Ben doubted that they would stand up to the heavy weight of moving cargo again, but after having so little on Torrent Four all his life, he was reluctant to get rid of anything. Wood was a cheap material, and brittle by spacefaring standards, but also hard to come by. Ben didn't know what he might use the worn-out pallets for, but he was glad to have them.

He picked one up, careful of the splinters, and carried it down the ramp. Magnum was right behind him with the other pallet. They made their way to the river, which ran between two muddy-looking banks that were easily four feet tall.

"They won't reach across," Magnum said.

Ben saw that his friend was right. The river was just a little too wide for the pallets to serve as a proper bridge. One could possibly be balanced on the large rocks and give the soldiers a quick way across, but it was the banks that Ben worried about. Getting a wounded man down and back up would be difficult. And he was honestly frightened of the dark forest. Anything could be hiding there, waiting for an opportunity to rush out and attack them. The fact that there were aliens nearby only made his fears loom larger.

"What if we do this?" Ben said, holding his palms together and his fingers apart to form a V. "They can scramble down one side and up the other."

"Worth a shot," Magnum said. "Either way, they'll probably need help."

"I wish we had night vision," Ben said. "I can't help but feel like we're being watched."

"Too much cover," Magnum said. "Even in broad daylight, we might not see them coming."

"Alright," Ben said. "Let's get these pallets in place. We'll just have to hope that the soldiers get here before the aliens do."

Magnum set his pallet down into the river first. It reached from the middle of the stream, almost to the top of the bank. He used the platform first, testing its strength. The wood creaked but didn't break. Ben handed him the other pallet, which Magnum set against the other bank. It was a crude bridge, but Ben felt confident the soldiers could cross it at speed. At least much faster than flailing through the mud.

Magnum climbed up the other side and stood on the far bank. Ben tapped his com-link and spoke in a quiet voice.

"How much longer?"

"It's been fifteen minutes," Kim said. "No word from the soldiers."

"What about the professor?"

"He and Nance are gathering supplies. Did you get a bridge across the river?"

"Sort of," Ben said. "I think it will work. Can you stand ready with the ship's running lights?"

"Sure, I can control it from the pilot's seat, I think," Kim said.

"Good," Ben said. "I want it on when the soldiers arrive. If the aliens are following them, we need to be able to see them."

"Okay, Ben. Are you okay?"

"Sure," he replied.

"You sound nervous."

"We feel a little exposed out here," Ben said. "Try to raise the soldiers on comms. They should be getting close."

"Alright, hang on."

Ben hoped that was all they needed to do, just hang on a few more minutes and then they could dust off. He would feel safer in the *Echo* with plenty of distance between them and the aliens. It felt a little too much like they were poking their enemy in the eye, and that made him uncomfortable.

"Ben," Kim said over the com-link. "They're almost here. Be ready."

"Okay," Ben said. "Did they say anything else? Anything about the aliens?"

"They haven't seen them, but they can hear them," Kim said.

"Great," Ben said. "Activate the lights and make sure the engines are hot. I want to lift off the second we set foot on board."

Chapter 15

Staff Sergeant Visher was bringing up the rear, and he felt as if the aliens were right behind him. He could hear footsteps and heavy bodies brushing against the trees, but whenever he turned back to look, all he saw were murky shadows. His night vision capabilities were limited to a set distance, and there were so many trees that it was impossible to see far into the forest.

Corporals Amadi and Miller had joined their race to escape the alien camp. They worked together to carry Prince Godfred. Thankfully, the rescued prisoner had stopped laughing. His head drooped and his feet hardly touched the ground. Staff Sergeant Visher feared that the heir to the Royal Imperium might be injured or sick. The rescue might have come too late and the strain of rushing through the forest at night could have done him in. But there was no time to stop and check on Godfred. Not with the sound of movement so close behind them.

Lights suddenly flared to life ahead of them. Visher instinctively closed the eye that looked through the night vision monocle and followed the rest of his team out of the shadowy trees into a clearing. He saw the river and the ship on the far side. Someone was even waving to them.

"Go! Go!" Visher shouted. "Get on board."

The big man—Visher forgot his name, but he looked as if he belonged more to their commando team than to the crew of the *Echo*—lifted his rifle and pointed it straight at Visher. The staff sergeant's heart was pounding hard from their run, but he didn't waver. Instinct told him to dive into the stream, but he could hear the water rushing over the rocks. If he fell onto those stones, he'd be lucky to only break a few bones. And as long as the prince made it to safety, nothing else mattered.

The flare of laser light from the assault rifle in the big man's hands forced Visher's eyes closed, and he felt the heat on his face and neck as the laser bolt shot past him. There was a grunt, then the sound of a heavy body hitting the ground behind Visher, but he didn't slow down or look back.

Private Rhoades was the first across the makeshift bridge. He bounded down and back up quickly and easily. Visher was close enough to see that wooden pallets had been used to make a bridge and he was thankful, knowing that climbing down and back out of the river bed without it would have made them vulnerable.

Major Le Croix was next. His heavy, robotic legs smashed through the wood. He tried to break free but couldn't.

"Go around him," Visher ordered.

Miller and Amadi carried Prince Godfred around Le Croix. Ben from the *Echo* helped pull them up the other side.

"Get to the ship!" Visher shouted.

"Down!" Ben's big companion demanded.

Sergeant Visher was used to giving orders, and the big man wasn't even a soldier, but years of discipline caused an involuntary reaction to the order. Visher dropped, rolled over one shoulder, and let his feet slide down the pallet. Above him, the big man fired several quick shots. Visher recognized the sound of the Lancet AR. It fired heavy beams that carried a stronger laser than their standard-issue military assault rifles.

Six aliens were chasing them. Visher saw them running from the trees as the big man fired. Four were hit before one finally flung his ax. The big man dove to the ground, and the ax went spinning over him and—*thunk!*—slammed into the far bank.

Visher raised his rifle and fire two quick shots. One hit the alien who had thrown his weapon. It dropped the alien immediately and left a smoking hole through his chest and out his back. The other was hit in the shoulder. He bellowed in pain, stumbled, but kept his balance and kept running. As Visher prepared to fire again, the alien flung something at him. It flew across the air in a blur and Visher fired again, taking the alien down for good, just as he felt something impact his body with a dull thump. Visher turned toward Le Croix, and a wicked, searing pain erupted in his stomach.

"Staff Sergeant," Le Croix said. "You're hit."

There was no time to worry about injuries. Visher lowered his gun, switching the power to low, and cutting Le Croix's leg free.

"Get to the ship," he shouted, but his voice sounded funny. It was high pitched, and there was a slight gurgle to it.

Le Croix pulled his leg free as the big man from the *Echo* slid down the bank. Visher turned toward the ship and took a step up the far side of the pallet bridge, only to find his strength giving out on him. His leg cramped suddenly, and he felt himself starting to sink onto his knees.

"I've got him," the big man said.

Visher turned, tried to ask whom he had, but the big man grabbed the staff sergeant's arm and dragged him up the pallet and onto dry ground. Visher dropped his rifle, his hands felt numb, and for some reason, his legs felt slow and weak. It was like running through mud that was clinging to him, pulling him down. But the big man's grip was like iron. Somehow, he ran, carried Visher with one hand, and fired the Lancet rifle with the other.

Le Croix was behind them. Visher could hear the major's heavy, robotic legs thumping. One second they were on the ground, and the next they went up the ship's open rear hatch.

"We're on board," Ben shouted. "Take us up."

Visher saw Ben pull the lever to close the rear hatch. The ship engines roared, and Visher finally looked down. There was a strange-looking object sticking out of his stomach.

"Medic!" Le Croix shouted.

"See to the…" Visher meant to order the prince seen to, but his voice faltered. It was suddenly hard to breathe, and the lights were dimming. He wondered briefly if the ship was under attack, but he was struggling to think clearly.

"Get him to the sick bay."

Visher heard people talking, but his body had no strength left. He sagged toward the deck but was scooped up. His head rolled from side to side as the big man carried him across the crowded cargo bay and up the metal steps to the main deck.

"How are we looking, Kim?" Ben shouted as he followed them.

"We're clear," the pilot said.

"Radar is active," Nance added. "There are no other vessels in the area."

"Good, get us moving back toward the mountains. Let's reestablish contact with Corporal Dial.

Visher felt a wave of appreciation. The crew members of the *Echo* weren't military, but they were honorable. He felt that his team was in good hands. The only question that remained was about the crown prince. Was he alive? Was he hurt? Visher wanted to know, but he had no control of his body, not even to ask a question. He was carried into a narrow room and set onto a table. Light flooded his eyes, and he closed them to block out the glare. It felt good to close his eyes. It felt better to let everything go. He was floating, weightless. The pain was distant, and his mind was retreating into itself. His struggle was over and he had won. There was no reason to fight anymore. There was a sharp stab in his arm, and then everything faded away.

Chapter 16

Ben felt a surge of relief as the *Echo* lifted into the air, but it was quickly swept away when he returned to the cargo bay and Prince Godfred, whom Ben had only seen on holovids, started laughing. The rescued royal couldn't even stand up, and the stench coming off him was sickening. Ben could understand the joy of being freed from captivity, but there was no joy in the crown prince's laughter.

"What's wrong with him?" Ben asked.

"Don't know," Private Rhoades said. "He's been doing that since we broke him out of the cage they had him in."

"The animals probably tortured him," Corporal Amadi said.

He and Corporal Miller were supporting Godfred as they headed for the stairs. Ben wanted to sag onto one of the pallets of supplies that lined the cargo hold. Firefights made him tired once all the pent-up fear and surging adrenaline had suddenly drained away. But there was work to be done. Ben went into the engineering bay and began checking the ship's vital systems.

"Ben, can you get up to bridge?" Kim said over the com-link.

He tapped his com-link as he started trudging up the stairs. "Sure, what's up?"

"I don't know, but I've got multiple contacts on radar," Kim reported.

Ben's plodding shifted into frenzied movement as he dashed up the final few steps and darted around the soldiers carrying Prince Godfred toward the med bay.

"They launched ships to pursue us?" Ben asked.

"Actually," Kim said, "these are coming down from orbit."

Ben dropped into his seat and started hitting keys to bring up the ship's radar.

"Where's Nance?"

"The professor needed an extra set of hands," Kim explained. "She and Magnum are helping. What happened out there?"

"They were pursued by the aliens," Ben said. "Magnum took out most of them, but not before one got some kind of weapon past the staff sergeant's defenses."

"How bad is it?"

"I don't know," Ben said. "But we can't worry about that right now."

He finally got the radar up on his console screen and saw what Kim had been talking about. Over forty blips were on the screen, all breaking orbit. Most, it seemed, were heading for the alien camp.

"They must have called for backup," Ben said, "when we attacked their camp."

"How did that many ships get through the debris field?" Kim asked.

"I don't know," Ben said.

"I told you we should have left while we had the chance."

Ben ignored her and brought up the communications controls. He hit the send button and spoke into the mic at his console.

"Corporal Dial, do you read me?"

There was no response.

"We should leave," Kim said. "Fly low and maybe we'll blend into the ground clutter."

"We can't leave the soldiers behind, Kim," Ben replied.

"Why not? General Pershing did."

"And we're not her," Ben replied, before keying his mic again. "Corporal Dial, this is the *Modulus Echo*. Do you read me? Over."

For a second, there was no reply, then the corporal's breathless voice boomed over the speakers.

I read you...Modulus Echo... His voice dropped to a whisper. *I'm being pursued...heading into...the mountains. Private Felix...didn't make it.*

Ben felt a stab of grief. He hadn't really known Private Felix, but the fact that he had been killed touched a nerve.

"We are moving in your direction," Ben said into the communications system. "Turn on your evacuation signal and we'll come to you."

Roger that...Modulus Echo...turning the signal...on now.

"Sounds like he's running hard," Kim said.

Ben wondered how hard one of the commandos had to run to sound so winded. He didn't like the thought of losing Corporal Dial. The man had been friendly to Ben, unlike some of the other soldiers who thought of them as rebels.

"We have to help him," Ben said. He tapped his comlink. "Magnum, send Corporal Amadi to the bridge."

"I've got the tracking signal," Kim said. "Corporal Dial is in the mountains. I'm not sure where we can set down that he could reach any time soon."

"You need me?" Amadi said, as he came out of the medical bay and turned onto the bridge.

"Corporal Dial is running," Ben said. "And we've got ships descending from orbit."

"Oh shit," Amadi said.

"Time is of the essence," Ben continued. "And there's no place to set the ship down close to Dial."

"What about Private Felix?" Amadi asked.

Ben shook his head.

"Damn," Amadi continued. "Alright, well, if it's just one man, we could hang a line. This ship hovers, right?"

"Yes," Ben and Kim said at the same time.

"Good, I'll hook up a harness and we can drop a line somewhere in front of him. We're trained for emergency air evac. Dial will know what to do."

"Just tell me what you need," Ben said.

Five minutes later, Ben was in the cargo hold. They had to open the rear hatch to lower the black rope with a harness at the end for Corporal Dial, since the air lock couldn't have both doors open at the same time. They were near a cliff, hovering a hundred feet above the ground with mountains looming around them. Ben was hopeful that the rugged mountain peaks towering around them would give the ship some cover from the alien invasion. There was no other way to describe what was happening. And it made Ben worry that perhaps the aliens were putting ships down all over, including close to Royal City.

"Alright, stand by," Amadi said as he looked out over the edge of the open hatch.

Ben was at the end of the rope, which was fed through a series of pulleys in the engineering bay. As soon as Amadi gave the word, Ben would relay it to Kim via their com-links and start hauling Corporal Dial in. At the same time, Kim would begin a sweeping maneuver meant to keep them out of harm's way without swaying Dial too much.

"He's almost there," Kim said, her voice small and almost robotic over the little com-link speaker pinned to Ben's collar.

"We're ready," Ben said.

They were running dark. All the exterior lights on the *Echo* were turned off, as were the lights in the cargo bay. Suddenly, Amadi waved to Ben.

"I see him!" Amadi shouted. "Almost there."

Ben tapped his com-link to the on position and took hold of the rope with both hands. There was a tense moment as he waited. Not being able to see what was happening below the ship was agonizing, but he wasn't near a display that could show the video feeds from the ship's external cameras.

"Now!" Amadi shouted. "Go! Go! Go!"

"We've got him," Ben said, just before he heaved the rope.

With the ship's artificial gravity, Ben couldn't feel the movement of the ship, but he felt the increased pressure on the rope. The pulleys made it possible for Ben to haul Corporal Dial up, but he could feel the strain as gravity made his job harder. Ben worked the rope hand over hand. He knew that they were a hundred feet above the ground when Corporal Dial had hooked onto the rope. Amadi stood ready to help the commando over the end of the open ramp, but he couldn't do that until Ben pulled Dial up to the ship.

"We're clear," Kim said. "Let me know when you've got that rear hatch closed."

"Okay," Ben said, his chest heaving with the effort of pulling on the rope.

His hands were aching, and the muscles in his forearms, shoulders, and back felt like they were on fire, yet he kept pulling.

"Got him!" Amadi shouted. "He's in."

Ben dropped the rope and turned toward the rear hatch. He could see Amadi pulling Corporal Dial across the metal of the hatch. Ben jogged over to the controls and pulled the lever that began closing the ramp. Then he bent over and put his hands on his knees, panting for breath.

"Thanks," Dial said as soon as Amadi pulled him across the hinges of the ramp.

Ben could see the sweat, dirt, and what looked like blood on the corporal's fatigues. His skin was pale; his hand shook as Amadi handed him a canteen.

"Are you hurt?" Ben asked.

"Negative, that's not my blood," Dial said.

The hatch closed and the light on the controls switched from red to green. Ben tapped his com-link and gave Kim the go-ahead to get moving.

"I'm glad you're okay," Ben told Dial as he and Amadi helped the exhausted commando to his feet.

"Me too," Dial said. "Did we get the prince?"

"He's on board," Amadi said, "but I'm not sure he's okay. The professor has him in the sick bay. We lost Private Wriggles."

"Damn," Dial said, looking down at the deck. "Two good men died. The prince better be worth it."

"We got more than that," Amadi said. "Staff sergeant came out of that camp with Major Le Croix too."

"Let's go check on them," Ben said. "You look like it wouldn't hurt for you to get checked out when the professor is through with the others."

"Great," Dial said. "Stairs."

Ben and Amadi helped Dial, who had pushed himself well past the limits of his strength and stamina, up the stairs to the main deck. At the door to the med bay, Ben could see that the small room was crowded. Amadi helped Corporal Dial into a chair as Magnum moved toward Ben. It was the first time Ben had laid eyes on Major Le Croix. He had heard the reports of the commandos, but seeing the major towering above everyone, even Magnum, on the robotic legs that the aliens had created for him, seemed strange. He stood in the back of the med bay, holding his arm close to his chest. Ben could see the black blistered flesh around the hole in his forearm.

"The staff sergeant is stable for the moment," Magnum reported. "But he lost a lot of blood."

The big man held up a weapon with four curved blades protruding from a small disk. It was stained with blood, and Ben recognized it as the weapon that had taken Staff Sergeant Visher down.

"It cut through his armor," Magnum said, handing the weapon to Amadi.

"It's got to be some type of molecular blade, then," Corporal Amadi said. "I guess they throw it."

"I saw a few of those," Dial said. "Although they were whipping past my head at the time."

"It cut through the muscle and lacerated some of his small intestines, but the equipment General Pershing brought on board included a surgical bot," Magnum said. "They stopped the bleeding and got everything sealed up with flesh glue."

"He's tough," Amadi said. "He'll be up and around in no time."

"I hope so," Ben said. "The aliens are making planet fall as we speak. I should go help Kim."

"We've got this," Amadi said. "You guys do your thing."

"Let's keep Le Croix in here," Ben said. "I don't feel good about him roaming around on the ship."

"Roger that," Dial said.

Ben left the room with a glance at the crown prince, who was sedated on the second examination table. Professor Jones was running a scanner over the prince's body. Ben left the med bay and went back to the bridge, where Nance had returned to her station. On the big displays, Ben could see that the ship was racing over the treetops of the forest.

"Have they seen us yet?" Ben asked.

"The aliens?" Nance confirmed. "There's no indication that they have."

"But that could change at any moment," Kim said. "A few have begun to land, but some of them are hovering at around twenty thousand feet."

"What do you think they're waiting for?" Ben asked as he sank onto his seat. He was thankful to finally be off his feet, but the fear of being caught was beginning to wear on his nerves.

"Hard to say," Nance replied. "Orders, maybe?"

"Or they're looking for us," Kim said. "There's no way they just happened to come down right after we attacked their settlement."

"Yeah," Ben said. "Odds are, that wasn't a coincidence. At least they haven't seen us."

"For now," Kim said. "But we need to get out of this system. Our luck is going to run out eventually."

"Are we headed back to Royal City?" Ben asked.

Nance nodded. "ETA is five and a half hours. It should be dark the entire way."

"Let's hope that plays in our favor," Ben said.

"Let's hope there's a Royal City left standing when we get there," Kim said.

Chapter 17

"You want to take my ship?" Admiral General Dietz said.

"We need all the firepower we can get," Pershing declared. "With only the *Tradewind*, the *Eclipse,* and the Confederate vessels, we can't keep the aliens pinned in the Celeste system until we have enough ships to smash them for good."

"And what will I do?" Dietz asked.

"You shall coordinate all our efforts from here, sir," Pershing said. "We can't have the admiral general on the front lines. You're too important."

"I couldn't agree more," Dietz said. "But it won't do to be left on a territorial station. The *Everest* is a proper ship for the commander in chief."

"She's the only battleship we have, sir," Pershing argued. "How can we harass the enemy with two Corvettes and a handful of rebel ships that are nothing more than converted commercial ships?"

"So don't go," Dietz said. "No one is forcing you."

"I'm sorry, sir. You don't seem to understand the predicament we're in. The Krah don't just want the Celeste system. They want the entire galaxy."

"Careful," the admiral general said, waving a finger in the air. "You mustn't let your emotions get the best of you, General Pershing. Discipline is the key. We're officers in Her Majesty's military, never forget that."

Pershing's temper was spent. She wanted the *Everest*, but it didn't surprise her that the fool Queen Ultane had installed as admiral general cared more about appearances than actually winning the war. The fact that he was calling the Royal Imperium military Her Majesty's revealed just what the two of them were up to. It had nothing to do with the crisis to the galaxy caused by the opening of the wormhole or the alien ships currently occupying the Celeste system, but was focused more on restructuring the Royal Imperium's chain of command. With her husband and son missing, Queen Ultane was desperate to hang onto power, and she had her new admiral general spreading her propaganda for her.

"Sir, as you know, I've interrogated the prisoner," Pershing said. "And if nothing else, it's clear that the Krah intend to strike hard and spread fast. I'd rather not give them that opportunity."

"If they do, we shall crush them piecemeal," Dietz said. "One ship at a time if we have to."

"Very well, sir," Pershing said. "With your permission, I'll move aboard the *Tradewind* and command our forces in the Celeste system from there."

"I want regular reports, General," Dietz said. "And don't waste our resources. There's been enough of that at the hands of my predecessor."

Pershing saluted even though it felt as if she were mocking the strict discipline and honor that she felt the Royal Imperium military stood for. Dietz was a political appointee, which wasn't unusual. She had hoped that the royal family who had survived the invasion by the Krah would see reason and let someone with actual military experience lead the war effort.

And while Dietz was a craven fool in Pershing's opinion, his one redeeming quality seemed to be that he would let her do almost anything she wanted.

He returned her salute, but with very little enthusiasm. It was clear that he was tired of dealing with her and just wanted to be left alone so that he could continue to court Queen Ultane. Perhaps he believed that she could fall in love with him and make him king, even though Duke Simeon was clearly next in line to the throne. In politics, Pershing thought to herself as she left the admiral general's lavishly furnished salon on the *Everest*, rules were made to be broken. But Pershing knew that Ultane had no desire to share power. She would use Dietz as long as it suited her, then cast him aside for someone else who could do more for her cause.

Duke Simeon was waiting for her just outside the admiral general's salon. He leaned against the wall of the ship's main corridor. He was a dashing figure, tall and lean, with piercing blue eyes and roguishly handsome features.

"I just got back," Simeon said. "Your prisoner is on the *Tradewind*, although Captain Davis wasn't pleased."

"She's a stern woman," Pershing said. "Not a political appointee."

"Which is why she only commands a midsize ship?"

"Unfortunately, that is the case."

"But you rose to senior command," Simeon pointed out, "and you are not a political appointee."

"I'm the highest-ranking officer of the Royal Imperium Army, which is the stepchild of the military even though we do the bulk of the fighting. The truth is, command of a capital ship is more of a prestige posting that an actual position. Like the

Everest, the officers operate the vessel, while the commander takes credit for their work."

"Why?" Simeon asked as they walked side by side down the long corridor. "It seems like the more I learn about the Royal Imperium, the more I realize how broken the system really is."

"And this surprises you?"

"It does. I was under the impression that we were loved by the people and that the government was a masterpiece of political science."

Pershing couldn't hold back the laughter, but she got herself under control quickly. Duke Simeon looked chagrined, and she decided it was time to placate him.

"If it makes you feel any better, you can't take the credit or the blame for how the Imperium has turned out," she said. "Perhaps in the past, strong kings had taken the reins of power and made the galaxy a better place. But since winning the Great War to unify the galaxy, the royal family has given more and more power to corrupt political appointees and self-serving politicians. They have wrecked the system. The only crime your family is guilty of is apathy."

"That will change once I'm king," Duke Simeon said.

General Pershing didn't have the heart to tell him that he would never be king as long as Queen Ultane had her say. Pershing wasn't political, but she understood the landscape. And it didn't take political savvy to see the greed and desperation in the queen. She would murder to stay in power. Pershing didn't think Duke Simeon had the drive to stick it out in a prolonged fight with her. Nor did he have the political contacts to sway what remained of the Royal Imperium leadership to support him.

"I'm glad to hear it," Pershing said. "Shall we go across?"

The *Everest* was docked at Mersa Station, which was a military space station that housed the system's patrol craft. It was also used as a refitting station for other military vessels. The *Tradewind* and *Eclipse* were also docked at the station. Pershing and Duke Simeon crossed through the air lock from the *Everest* onto the station.

"Actually," Duke Simeon said, "I want to join your armada officially."

Pershing stopped and looked at the duke. She had no idea what he was talking about, but there was an unmistakable twinkle in his eyes.

"What are you on about?" she asked.

"I've ordered a ship. The *Hyperion* has just come into the system. She's armed and I've added an entire array of surveillance equipment."

"I don't know if I have the people to spare to crew another ship at the moment," Pershing said, hoping to dissuade the duke.

"There's no need. She's top of the line. Practically flies itself. I'll crew her on my own. I understand I'm a novice, but I can't just stand around and watch any longer. I need to contribute."

Pershing understood the feeling. There were times as a commander when she missed being in the field with a weapon rather than making decisions on a capital ship. But that was leadership. Her job was to empower others, to bring out the very best in them, so that they could do the work that needed doing. Perhaps giving the duke some small responsibility would help him grow.

"I can't guarantee your safety," she said.

"Of course not. This is war. But I won't be the kind of ruler who sits by and lets others do his fighting for him. The Krah want our galaxy, and if I'm to be king, then I want to fight for it. I want to fight for the people."

Pershing didn't think Duke Simeon would be much use in a fight. Nor did she think he wanted to save the people. Impress them, win their loyalty, maybe. But he wasn't a fighter. Still, he had taken initiative and was doing more than she expected. She needed ships even if it was nothing more than a show of force. Having one more vessel in her flotilla would help.

"Very well," Pershing said. "You follow orders, though. Even if the order is to retreat."

"I will," Duke Simeon said.

Pershing nodded, and like a child given permission to play, the duke ran down the corridor. General Pershing watched him go, wishing that the officers of the Royal Imperium military had half as much enthusiasm.

It took ten minutes to reach the *Tradewind*. She was a sleek fighting vessel, built for speed and loaded with firepower. The main difference between the Corvette class ships and the larger battle cruisers was the lack of fast-attack squadrons. The Corvette had no other ships on board, but she had a solid crew. Captain Davis was waiting when Pershing crossed through the air lock.

"Orders, General?"

"Rendezvous with the *Eclipse, Hyperion,* and the Confederate ships," Pershing ordered as the two women walked toward the bridge of the *Tradewind.* "We leave for the Celeste system at once."

Chapter 18

"Royal City, this is the *Modulus Echo*. Do you read me? Over."

Ben waited several seconds, then keyed his mic again. They were less than fifty miles from the city and at the edge of normal communications range.

"Commander Lawrence, this is Ben on the *Modulus Echo*. Do you read? Over."

"Any chance the aliens are blocking the signal?" Kim asked.

"I'm not picking up anything," Nance said.

"We don't even know if they can," Ben said. "It would have helped if the professor hadn't given Le Croix that sedative. Maybe we would have some answers."

"He was in pain," Professor Jones said. He had only come out of the medical bay a few minutes earlier. He was clearly exhausted. There was blood on his wrinkled clothing, and his eyes were bloodshot. "The first rule of medicine is do no harm."

"It wouldn't hurt him to talk," Kim said.

"You're not that kind of doctor, are you?" Ben asked. "I mean, you didn't take an oath or anything, right?"

"It is a point of professional pride," Jones replied. "But if I had known you wanted to speak with him, I could have waited."

"It doesn't matter," Ben said. "We're all just on edge."

"We haven't seen an alien ship in hours," Nance said. "There's no reason to believe we're in danger."

"But no proof we're not," Kim said. "I'd feel better if the city was still intact."

Ben hit the transmit button again and spoke into the mic. "Royal City, this is the *Modulus Echo*. Do you read me? Over."

Modulus Echo, this is Royal City. We read you loud and clear. Over.

Everyone on the bridge of the *Echo* breathed a sigh of relief. Professor Jones got to his feet and started for the med bay.

"I'll let the soldiers know," Jones said.

"Thanks," Ben replied.

"So what's our plan?" Kim asked. "Drop off the soldiers and Prince Godfred with the Confederates and get out of the system?"

"Let's see what they know first," Ben said. "Then we'll make a plan."

"This isn't our fight," Kim retorted. "I'm just saying."

"We could all use some downtime," Nance said. "Maybe we could take a break for a few hours once we reach the city."

Ben keyed the microphone again. "Royal City, we're forty miles from your location, coming in with precious cargo. What's your status? Over."

We have visitors in the neighborhood, Modulus Echo. Multiple contacts touched down overnight. We are on high alert. Over.

"What does that mean?" Kim said. "Multiple contacts? They have alien ships nearby?"

"At least within radar range," Nance said. "I don't know what their system is like, but even a rudimentary radar setup should cover a hundred miles in every direction."

"Will the mountains block that signal?" Ben asked.

"Probably, but it depends," Nance replied.

"If there are aliens nearby, I don't want to stay," Kim said. "We can rest once we make the jump to hyperspace."

"If we can get out of the system," Ben said. "There's still a lot of variables to consider."

Modulus Echo, what's your ETA? Over.

Ben keyed his mic and replied. "Fifteen minutes, Royal City."

Commander Lawrence is requesting that you do a flyover. We're sending you coordinates now. We need to see what the aliens are doing. Over.

"Are you kidding me?" Kim said. "We're taking orders from the Confederates now?"

"No," Ben said. "But it's not a bad idea. If the aliens are moving toward the city, we can't leave the soldiers and Prince Godfred there."

"This is really starting to chap my hide," Kim said.

"I've got coordinates," Nance said. "Three separate locations."

"Royal City," Ben said into his microphone, "we have the coordinates. We are altering course and checking those landing sites. Over."

Roger, Modulus Echo. Your help is appreciated. Royal City, out.

"Thanks for asking," Kim said as she turned the ship in a slow arc toward the first of the coordinates. "I need to take us up if we're doing this spy job, and that means we'll show up on their radar."

"That's a chance we'll have to take," Ben said. "It's not like they're unaware of Royal City."

"All the more reason to get as far away as we can," Kim said.

"We're coming up on the coordinates," Nance said as she changed the bridge display screens to show the video feeds from the bottom of the ship.

Ben activated the ship's intercom function and called for Corporal Dial to join them on the bridge.

"They aren't wasting time," Kim said.

The first landing site was in a clearing near the convergence of two rivers. Ben saw one ship, not as large as the alien vessels near the mountains where the commandos had rescued Prince Godfred, but large enough to shuttle over a hundred of the aliens. Around the landing craft were machines and dozens of the spidery worker aliens.

"What are they doing?" Nance asked.

Ben could see that trees were being cut and put through some type of milling process using the machines the workers had set up.

"Looks like they're milling lumber," Ben said.

"For what?" Kim asked.

"That's a good question," Ben said.

Corporal Dial's face was puffy from sleep, but his eyes were alert as he walked up to the bridge and stood beside Ben's console.

"You need me?"

"We're taking a look at some of the alien landing sites near Royal City," Ben said. "I thought you might have a better idea of what they're up to."

"I don't know," Dial said. "They used timber to build things at the other settlement. The wall, the fighting platforms, crates and cages for the animals they caught. They also built fires."

"So this might just be what it looks like," Ben said. "They're harvesting resources."

"Looks like it to me," Dial replied.

"Alright, let's move on," Kim said.

"Gershwin has a number of indigenous arbors," Professor Jones said. "Timber is still used for furnishings and decorations on a number of planets."

"There was plenty of it in Royal City," Ben said. "The buildings are all steel and glass, but I saw furniture, bar tops, wall paneling, and even sculptures carved from wood in the hotel."

"Well, at least the soldiers at Royal City don't need to worry too much about that group," Kim said.

It took ten minutes to reach the next landing site. The *Echo* was flying at over forty thousand feet and used the ship's computer system to digitally zoom and enhance the video feed from the exterior cameras. The aliens had landed on what looked like a massive stone butte in the middle of a wide expanse of grassy plains.

"That's got to be a watch station," Ben said.

The alien ship was much smaller, and while there were workers setting up equipment of some kind, Ben also made out several warriors.

"It's not large enough to be an invasion force," Kim pointed.

"Can you tell what they're building?" Ben asked.

"It looks like some sort of transceiver," Nance said.

"At least this group isn't a threat to the city," Ben said. "Let's go."

Kim accelerated and the *Echo* flew on toward the third landing site.

"Two out of three seem safe," Kim said.

"It's possible the aliens don't want to fight," Ben said. "Maybe they just see an unpopulated world and are laying claim."

"The Royal Imperium will never stand for that," Corporal Dial said.

"They may not have a choice," Kim said. "The aliens are taking all the strategic locations."

"It's much harder to remove ground-based forces than those in space," Magnum said.

"Yeah, just ask the Confederates about that," Kim said.

"The old king would have obliterated the planet before he let someone take it from the royal family," Corporal Dial said.

"Speaking of the royal family," Ben said. "How is Prince Godfred?"

"I don't know," Dial replied. "He was sleeping."

"Does being captured by aliens make him unfit to rule the Royal Imperium?" Nance asked.

"Why should it?" Dial said.

"They might have infiltrated his mind," Kim said. "He might wake up and decide to give the galaxy away to his new friends."

"He wasn't being treated like a friend," Dial said. "They had him locked in a cage that was four feet tall, like he was an animal."

"But Major Le Croix wasn't," Ben said. "You reported that he was working with the aliens, right? And he's got their technology, the robotic legs, the strange tendril on that band of metal covering his eyes."

"True," Dial said. "We'll have to question him about all that."

"The point being," Kim said in a loud voice, "is that we don't need to be here. This planet is contested ground, and I vote that we leave the system as soon as possible."

"We can't," Professor Jones said. "Not yet. I am close to solving the wormhole problem. We cannot leave before that is accomplished."

"First, we have to deliver the prince to whoever is best suited to deal with him," Ben said. "And the commando team needs to be able to recuperate somewhere they can make contact with their superiors."

"So we drop them off at Royal City, and then we get out of here while we still can," Kim said.

"What if Royal City isn't the best place?" Ben asked.

"I don't care where we take them," Kim said. "As long as it's not here. We've done enough."

"Maybe she's right," Nance said.

"We broke our deal with General Pershing," Magnum pointed out.

"But we've gone above and beyond down here," Kim said. "We saved the Confederates and the crew of the *Plato*. We even rescued the crown prince. That's got to be worth something."

"Only if we deliver him safely," Ben said. "Once we assess the last landing site, we'll find out what's happening in Royal City, then make our plans."

"Finally," Kim said. "I thought you'd never see reason."

"Is that what you call agreeing with you?" Ben asked.

Kim smiled. "Of course," she said in an exaggerated tone. "Everyone knows that."

Their conversation was cut short when they came within sight of the third landing. It was an open field and there was no mistaking the landing craft. It was a transport ship large enough for perhaps two hundred of the aliens, but only a few were visible.

"Where are they?" Nance asked.

"Maybe they're still in the ship," Kim said.

"That seems unlikely," Ben said.

"It's an army," Corporal Dial said. "They're marching to Royal City."

"How can you tell?" Ben asked.

"It's a hunch, but it makes sense."

"Okay," Ben said. "Take us down, Kim. If there's an army marching toward the city, we have to find it."

"Aye, aye, Skipper," Kim said.

"Magnum, how many missiles do we have ready to fire?"

"Four," the big man said. "And the lasers."

"Alright, let's find the best place to use them. And we need to contact Royal City again. They need to know what's coming."

Chapter 19

The *Tradewind* dropped out of hyperspace inside the shadow of Chopin, one of three gas giants in the Celeste system. The planet was unique in that it had over twenty moons. Some were large, almost the size of a planet, but most were smaller. General Pershing was hoping that the sheer number of moons would allow her to drift around the planet and observe the Krah without being seen.

The rest of her flotilla appeared from hyperspace behind the *Tradewind*. They were a motley band of ships that had almost nothing in common except for the fact that they were armed to the teeth. Pershing was confident that they could overpower the Krah in an even fight, but they would be outnumbered. And until she could get more ships in system to help her destroy the Krah, all she wanted to do was harass them when the opportunity presented itself. Until then, the most important thing she could do was to keep tabs on the aliens.

"Orbital speed?" Pershing asked.

"We'll make a complete circuit around Chopin in just under ten hours," the officer at the helm said.

"Very good. Have the *Eclipse* wait for five hours, then begin their orbital run at this same speed," Pershing ordered. "Let's prepare for long-range surveillance as soon as we make the curve around the planet. Comms, please patch me through to the Confederate ships."

"Roger that, General," the communications officer said.

"General, should we prep the long-range laser cannons?" Captain Davis asked.

Pershing nodded. "Have them ready, but let's keep our fingers off the triggers. We don't want to draw the aliens into a fight if we can help it. Surveillance is our top priority. We'll send the rebels out to fight if they send ships this way."

Pershing knew the captain was merely looking for something to do. Unlike a political appointee, Captain Davis wasn't used to stepping aside and letting someone else make the decisions on her ship. Pershing could relate, but for the time being, the *Tradewind* was her flagship, and the crew would have to adapt to her way of doing things.

"General," the communications officer said. "I have Commander Holt standing by."

"Very good," Pershing said. "Holt, are your people ready?"

"As ready as we'll ever be," came the surly reply.

"I want you to divide your forces and send them to each of the planet's poles. They're to stay there, out of sight of the Krah forces near Gershwin, until needed. I'll leave the logistics up to you."

"Roger that," Holt said. "Confederate squadron is moving into position and standing by for further orders."

"General," the navigation officer said. "We're beginning the first turn. The aliens should be in visual range momentarily."

"Captain, release the communications satellite," Pershing ordered. "Is it preprogrammed to reach the optimal position?"

"Affirmative," the captain replied. "We have two communications birds painted all black and set to reach fixed positions on either side of the planet."

"Alright, we only get one shot at this operation, people," Pershing said. "If the Krah are monitoring the system, they might spot us spying on them. Shut down radar and all running lights. I want zero emissions that might be picked up on radar. Get those cameras at maximum zoom, but I want everything else dark."

Captain Davis began snapping orders while Pershing sat back and waited. There was nothing more she could do until the *Tradewind* rounded the curve of the gas giant they were hiding behind and they got a look at the wormhole. She had done her homework. There were no planets between Chopin and Gershwin. The two planets were millions of miles apart, but for the next few weeks, they would be at their closest point in their respective orbits. Her plan was to orbit Chopin and spy on the aliens. She couldn't keep them from coming and going throughout the galaxy, but she hoped that their attack that drove the alien fleet out of the system had been enough to warrant them keeping a large force near the wormhole.

There were worrisome issues at work as well. Chieftain Grubat revealed that the aliens had access to the Nav Net. With that information, they could not only efficiently travel through the galaxy, but they could also choose the most prime targets for their needs. It was frustrating, and she had her doubts about their ability to tap into the closely guarded network, but the majority of that effort had taken place on the Royal Imperium space station that was destroyed when the wormhole was opened. With those resources gone, Pershing doubted that the network was being monitored. Keeping the aliens out of it would be difficult.

The fact of the matter was they needed to close the wormhole. Or, at the very least, drive the Krah out of the Celeste system and control any traffic through the portal to their alien galaxy. That thought led to her curiosity about the *Modulus Echo*. Did the little ship survive? She hadn't expected their betrayal. It angered her and, at the same time, she blamed herself. She should have used more caution with Ben and his crew. They were outlaws, after all. It was through their carelessness that the wormhole had been opened in the first place. She had shown them mercy because she felt that fighting the Krah was her destiny, but they would pay for their constant betrayal. Their carelessness would catch up with them soon, and she vowed to be there—that is, if they were still alive.

"Crossing the boundary," the helmsman said.

Pershing focused her attention on the large holographic projection from the ship's external cameras. Unlike the video feeds on the *Modulus Echo*, the *Tradewind* had proper holographic capture devices. They created an exact replication of the area they were focused on. Gershwin was almost in line with the wormhole, and they would get a better read on that section of the system as the ship moved around the gas giant they were orbiting, but Pershing could tell at a glance that more ships had entered the system through the wormhole.

"Start visual marking of the alien ships," Pershing said. "We need to know how many they have and have some way to keep track of each."

Her job was nearly impossible without more ships. And she could only hope her interview with Chieftain Grubat was enough to stir the Royal Imperium forces into action. From her limited field of view, she guessed the aliens had already doubled their number of ships in the system. If the war lingered, how many more might pass through the wormhole? She could only imagine, and that thought frightened her more than anything.

Chapter 20

Ben stretched in his seat. Fatigue was catching up with him. He couldn't remember how many hours he'd been awake, but his body was telling him he needed rest. Of course, he knew it was worse for Kim. Flying the *Echo* had to be taxing, and she had been awake as long as he had.

"Radar is still clear," Nance said. "No sign of incoming ships."

"So maybe they prefer to stay on the ground," Ben said.

"There could be thousands of the aliens hidden in this forest," Kim said. "The trees are too dense to see anything."

"I can switch to thermal imaging," Nance said. "But you'll have to get lower."

"What choice do we have?" Ben said. "Take us down, Kim. How close are we to Royal City?"

"Forty-two miles," Nance said.

"How far are we from the alien ship?" Corporal Dial asked.

"Twenty-six point four," Nance replied.

"If they're down here," Kim said, "moving on foot, they've covered a lot of territory."

"Maybe that's not unusual with those robotic legs," Ben said. "Have you seen them on Major Le Croix?"

"Maybe," Dial said. "But not all had legs like that at the camp we were watching."

"Either way," Kim said, "they're making good time. We should have seen something by now unless they're still ahead of us."

"Are there any other targets they might be marching for?" Magnum asked.

"I don't think so," Ben said. "Royal City is the only town, except for the village where the workers lived, and that's only a mile or so away. Close enough for the workers to walk back and forth."

"What do they do in bad weather?" Dial asked.

"There's an underground shuttle that goes back and forth from the village to the city," Ben said. "But I can't imagine the aliens would care about the village. The Confederates sealed up the tunnel to the village as soon as they took control of Royal City."

"Maybe they're a recon unit," Magnum said.

"You mean spies?" Kim asked.

"Sure, that makes sense," Corporal Dial said. "Only, they didn't try to hide their landing."

"Maybe they thought, with so many alien ships making planet fall, it wouldn't matter," Ben said.

"They could surround Royal City and gather intel," Magnum said, "before a proper invasion."

"Either way, we need to warn the Confederates," Ben said.

"What we need is a way off this rock," Kim said.

"If they sent ships down, it must mean they've cleared a significant portion of the debris field," Nance said. "Maybe we could get away."

"And leave the Confederates behind?" Dial asked.

"Captain Lawrence has over two hundred men," Ben said. "Even if we emptied the cargo bay, we couldn't get that many people on board."

"So how'd they get here?" Dial asked.

"That's it!" Ben shouted. "The *Plato*. How far is she from here?"

"Hang on," Nance said as she worked at her station for a moment. "Eight miles. I'm bringing it up on the plot now."

"Got it," Kim replied. "We'll be there in a minute."

The view on the bridge displays were blobs of yellows and greens. Occasional small dots of orange and red flashed by, but nothing that would indicate an army.

"What are you thinking?" Corporal Dial asked.

"The *Plato* isn't the only target," Ben said. "Not to the aliens. They salvage ships in space. It makes sense that they might want one on the ground too."

"Secure the downed ship, then turn to the city?" Dial asked.

"It's the easier target. I don't think the commander left any of the crew behind to guard it."

"But it can't fly," Kim said. "It's no good in atmo. She sank like a stone. It's a miracle they got the ship down in one piece."

"It still has tech they might want or need," Ben said. "They aren't building robotic legs with wood and stone."

Kim slowed the *Echo*. Ben couldn't feel the ship slowing, but the images on the display screen passed more slowly until they came to a complete stop.

"We're only a half mile from the clearing," Kim said.

"That's too far for thermal imaging," Nance said.

"Switch it back to normal," Ben said. "Kim, take us just high enough to see down into the clearing."

"You read my mind," Kim said.

The display screen changed back to a normal video feed. The trees were just below the ship, their thick leafy tops swaying in the breeze. They looked bright green in the bright sunlight.

"Zooming in now," Nance said.

The picture on the bridge display shot forward, and Kim raised the ship slowly. Soon they could see down into the clearing. The *Plato* had crash-landed on the far side, and four groups of alien warriors were visible in front and on top of the vessel.

"Would you look at that," Corporal Dial said.

"I count sixteen," Ben said.

"What are they doing?" Nance asked.

"Standing guard," Dial said.

"Shouldn't there be more?" Kim asked.

"Yeah," Ben said. "But they've been here and moved on."

"First target, secure," Dial added. "The rest are probably headed straight to Royal City."

"That's a long hike," Magnum said.

"We have to head there now," Ben said. "Kim, go as fast as you can until we find the aliens."

"You got it," she replied, already turning the ship.

"Switching the cameras back to thermal," Nance said. "You want me to contact Royal City?"

"Not yet," Ben said. "Let's find that army first."

It only took a few minutes before the thermal imaging picked up large amounts of heat. The display began showing large blobs of dark red. Nance switched back to normal on the ship's cameras, but it was impossible to see through the canopy.

"There's no way to tell how many there are," Ben said.

"Too much cover with the trees," Magnum agreed.

"It won't do the Confederates much good if we can't tell them how many aliens are headed that way," Kim pointed out.

"I'm open to suggestions," Ben said.

"I have one," Corporal Dial said. "Put my team on the ground. We'll recon the alien force and radio in. We might even be able to flank them once the shooting starts."

"Good idea," Ben said. "Only, there's no place to land."

"We can rappel down," Dial said. "I'll inform the others. We're shorthanded, but Amadi, Miller, and Rhoades can join me. Just get us ahead of the aliens."

"How far?" Kim asked.

"At least a mile," Dial said. "We'll need a few minutes to get into position to watch them without being seen."

"Alright," Ben said. "Let's do it."

Kim accelerated away from the aliens, and Dial gathered what remained of the commandos. Ben and Magnum went down and opened the rear hatch. Wind whipped through the cargo bay for a minute, then everything settled down as Kim hovered just over the trees as Dial and his companions arrived carrying heavy black ropes.

"Once you're down there, we won't be able to get you out," Ben said.

"That's okay," Dial said. "We can hike out."

"How far to Royal City?" Corporal Amadi asked.

"Six miles, due north from here," Ben said. "But only half that distance is forested."

"Roger that," Corporal Miller said. "But our radios may not reach that far."

"We'll stay closer," Ben said. "And relay your info to the Confederates. Good luck."

Magnum helped the commandos secure their ropes to the walls of the cargo bay. The soldiers hooked the ropes through harnesses that were built into their fatigues and then jumped out the open hatch. Ben waited at the edge of the ramp, looking down. When all four commandos were on the ground and had removed the ropes from their harnesses, they gave him a thumbs-up.

"Alright, pull up the ropes," Ben told Magnum before tapping his com-link. "Kim, they're on the ground. Take us halfway to Royal City."

"Yes, sir," she replied in a mock military salute.

The ship began to glide upward. Ben helped Magnum pull up the last of the ropes. Once they were inside the cargo hold, Ben pulled the lever to close the rear hatch. Then he headed up to the main deck where he could contact the Confederate force waiting in Royal City.

Chapter 21

"What are they doing?" Pershing asked.

"It's hard to say for sure from this distance," Captain Davis said. "There's too much activity around the planet."

General Alicia Pershing couldn't agree more with the ship's captain. There was a flurry of activity around the planet. She knew that the debris field surrounding Gershwin was substantial, but in her gut she knew the aliens were doing more than removing the orbiting junk created by her first battle in the system.

"Is it possible they're landing ships on the planet?"

The question was from the tactical officer, a tall man with broad shoulders. He was older than most of the other officers. Pershing had guessed that he wasn't intelligent enough to rise higher in rank than first lieutenant, but she had to admit that maybe she'd been wrong.

"Anything is possible," she said.

Of course, she agreed with the tactical officer. There were far more ships in the system than when the Krah had pushed her tiny group of Royal Imperium ships out. And it only made sense that they would begin landing larger groups. There were hardly any humans on the planet, certainly not enough to stop a proper invasion. Gershwin was a rare prize—an uninhabited planet capable of supporting life. The Krah would have been insane not to land as many of their people on the planet as possible. And it would make rooting them out of the system almost impossible.

"If they're occupying the planet, they mean to stick around," Captain Davis said.

"Indeed," Pershing agreed. "This isn't just a run on our resources. They mean to make the Celeste system their new home."

But Pershing was determined to stop them, and she just needed a way to do it. An entire battalion of Royal Imperium battleships would be outnumbered by the Krah. The crew of the *Tradewind* were doing all they could to count and catalog the alien vessels, but it was like trying to count ants on the ground from the top of a tree. Even with their long-range optics, it was an uphill battle. What they needed was a full radar sweep, but that would give their position away. The only thing that had gone right in the entire war so far seemed to be that the Krah hadn't noticed them spying from the orbit of the gas giant Chopin.

The key to the war was finding a way to close the wormhole. It was the simplest of strategies—cut off your enemies' line of supplies and they will wither away to nothing. The Krah already had a fleet of ships in the Celeste system to rival what the Royal Imperium could field. But the human vessels had far greater firepower. As long as the aliens couldn't spring a surprise on them or continue to bring vessels from their own galaxy into the fight, Pershing was certain she could win the war. It might take a long time, and indeed, the Celeste galaxy could be lost in the process, but it was winnable. Gershwin had the unfortunate luck to have been infested with the Krah. That might require slagging the entire planet, but one way or another, the aliens would be killed, every last one of them.

"We're approaching the curve, General," the helmsman said.

"Still no indication that we've been seen," the tactical officer added.

"Very well," Pershing said. "Prepare to launch the communications satellite. We're in a marathon here, people, not a sprint. Our job is to stay on station and keep an eye on the enemy."

Pershing stood up, stretched, then watched as the ship crossed the horizon and lost sight of the aliens near Gershwin. She felt a cold shiver run down her back. Not being able to see what the aliens were up to played on her worries. Pershing reminded herself that even if she could see them, even if her ship were right in the middle of their fleet, she wouldn't really know what they were doing.

"Launching the communications satellite," Captain Davis said. "Any other orders, General?"

"All officers should rotate watch while we're on the dark side of Chopin," Pershing said. "Get some rest and be back on the bridge before we make the far curve. Comms, get me Duke Simeon's ship. Push it through to my quarters."

"Roger that, General," the communications officer replied.

Pershing heard the captain giving her crew orders. That was her job and she was good at it. Pershing didn't worry about the ship and focused instead on the larger strategy of the Royal Imperium Fleet. Her berth on the *Tradewind* was a tiny temporary cabin, barely wider than the bunk, and with no bathroom. Her spare uniforms were rolled up and stored in the overhead bins above the bed. It had a built-in data display on the wall opposite her bed, and when she sat down, the icon on the screen blinked to let her know that the duke was waiting.

She tapped the icon, and the duke's handsome face appeared. He looked well rested and happy. Serving in her flotilla had given him something to do, a sense of purpose, and it agreed with him. Pershing only hoped her next orders would continue to build his confidence.

"General, you look tired," the duke said.

Commenting on her looks was out of line, especially as she was serving as his commander, but she let the faux pas slide. He was a royal, after all, and next in line to the throne.

"We have news for the admiral general," Pershing said as she tapped a few commands into her display. "I'm sending you a report now. I assume your ship is fast?"

"The fastest," Duke Simeon said. "State of the art, really. I got her—"

Pershing held up her hand to halt his speech. She didn't care about his ship, only about the messages she needed to deliver and receive.

"I need you to take that report back to the Mersa system," Pershing told him. "Deliver it to Admiral General Dietz. And bring me any news, specifically, what ships have arrived in the system and what the AG is doing with them."

"Okay," Duke Simeon said.

"Don't get bogged down with the queen," Pershing warned him. "Until we know more, you're going to be a runner. I need you back here to deliver the news in the Mersa system to me."

"Roger that, General," Duke Simeon said.

"Very good. You're a vital link to what we're doing here, Your Grace. Watch your six and stay safe."

"Of course," he replied. "I'll return as quickly as possible."

He signed off, and Pershing tapped her display screen. She brought up a timer that showed how much time before they reached the far curve and the aliens came back into view. She had enough time for a short four-hour nap. It was enough to recharge her body, then she could get a shower and a quick meal before returning to her station on the bridge. Pershing knew the routine would become her entire world for the foreseeable future. Her stomach rumbled, but she didn't bother with food. Sleep was more important at that moment. When she woke up, she could eat, and she would have some food brought to her berth at the end of every orbital cycle. That way, she could eat a snack before catching a few hours of sleep.

The bunk was narrow, the pad was so dense it felt hard, and the sheets were stiff and scratchy. Despite it all, her body was relieved to stretch out, and as soon as she closed her eyes, she fell asleep. The lights in her cabin dimmed, but the numbers on the display screen continued counting down. They glowed an ominous red, as if they knew of the danger that lay ahead.

Chapter 22

"Alright," Kim said. "We're holding steady at ten thousand feet."

"Corporal Dial, what have you got down there?" Ben asked over the com-link.

We're in position, Echo. No sign of the aliens yet. Over.

Kim thought the commando sounded nervous. She thought she would be terrified. The four soldiers had spread out through the forest and taken to the trees. But if one of the aliens looked up and saw them, there was no chance of escape.

"We've warned Royal City. They're prepared," Ben said. "We're holding here to pass along whatever you find, then we'll swing around and pick you up on the edge of the forest."

Roger that, Echo. Corporal Dial, standing by.

"What do you think the general would do in this circumstance?" Ben asked.

The bridge was quiet. Professor Jones had gone back to the med bay and was checking on his wards. Magnum sat ready at the fire control console. He had the missiles primed and ready. Not that Kim expected them to need the weapons. So far, they had been lucky and the aliens weren't using atmospheric craft, which meant the *Echo* was safe as long as they were in the air. Unfortunately, they were burning through a lot of their Zexum supply. Kim would have preferred getting off-world and conserving their fuel until they found some friendly ports and got a few jobs under their belts. Ben was sure they had plenty, but Kim didn't think that was possible.

"Who knows?" Kim said. "She isn't here. And the last battle was a success because of your plan, not hers."

"The missiles will make a difference," Magnum said.

"But we've only got so many," Ben said. "And dozens of ships were coming down from orbit. There's really no telling how many aliens are on Gershwin. We won't be able to keep fighting for long."

"We shouldn't be fighting," Kim said.

She firmly believed they had done more than their share in the battle with the aliens. Yet she also felt responsible for the commando team. They were risking their lives in the forest, and she didn't relish the idea of leaving the planet without them.

"Maybe we can hold out until help arrives," Magnum said.

"We need to get word to the Royal Imperium or whoever will listen about the aliens making planet fall," Nance said.

"Best way to do that is in orbit," Kim said. "We might be able to tap into the communication network once we're up there."

"I think you're probably right," Ben said. "Once we have the commando team on board, we'll do what we can for the Confederates at Royal City, then make for orbit."

Kim couldn't hold back a smile. "Well, it's about time," she crowed.

Modulus Echo, this is Commando team. Do you read? Over.

"Loud and clear, Corporal," Ben said. "Go ahead."

We've got a lot of movement down here. Rough estimate is above one hundred and fifty alien soldiers.

Kim strained to hear the corporal's whispered report.

They're carrying hand-to-hand weapons. No firearms that we can make out, which is in line with what we observed at the alien camp. They're moving at a steady clip. I'd say seven miles an hour. Over.

"Man, they're really moving," Kim said.

"Yeah," Ben replied. "Much faster than a human army moving on foot."

"Maybe they'll be too tired to fight," Magnum said.

"We'll report to the Confederates," Ben said. "Once they get out of the forest, they'll be easy to watch."

Modulus Echo, do you read? Over.

Kim looked at Ben. He blushed, realizing he hadn't replied to the commandos. He leaned into his mic and pressed the activator key.

"Yes, Commando team, my apologies. We read you. Over."

We've got a problem down here, Corporal Dial said with a new layer of strain to his voice. *It looks like the aliens are making camp. Over.*

"Are you in danger?" Ben asked.

Negative, Echo. They haven't spotted us. They're between our position and the edge of the trees. Over.

"Can you get away without being seen?" Ben asked.

Probably, but we should stay and see what they're up to, Corporal Dial said. *They may be rendezvousing with more troops. Over.*

"Wonderful," Kim said.

"We'll let Captain Lawrence know," Ben said. "Let us know when you're ready for evac."

Roger that, Dial said. *Commandos, out.*

"Patch us back through to Royal City," Ben said.

"Why? We don't know what they're doing," Kim said.

"We know they're stopping," Ben said.

"Probably waiting for darkness before approaching the city," Magnum said.

"Make sense," Ben agreed. "There isn't much cover. They probably know we're poking around."

"But we're not waiting, right?" Kim asked. "I mean, I could use a nap, but we should get to orbit, have a look around."

"Even without the commandos?" Ben asked.

"I have Captain Lawrence," Nance announced.

Kim felt as if the stress of their situation would never end. The *Echo* was holding up just fine, but hovering in atmosphere wasn't a simple ordeal. She was constantly battling gravity, and the wind made it difficult as well. But she didn't want to land the ship. That would put them in danger, and she was desperate to escape the planet. It felt like they were trapped in a net that was closing around them.

Ben relayed the information and his hunch that the aliens were waiting for the cover of darkness. Captain Lawrence wasn't thrilled about the numbers.

They can't attack us outright with less than two hundred soldiers, he said. *We could hold off three times that number. We have cover; they won't. We have firearms, and if what you've said is true, all they have are close-combat weapons.*

"Don't underestimate their fighting ability," Ben said. "They may not have guns, but their robotic limbs make them faster and stronger than we are. They ran for miles faster than a professional marathon racer, and through rough terrain."

Roger that, Modulus Echo. Can you provide help? We need your eyes in the sky.

"We'll do what we can," Ben said.

When Ben got off the call to Royal City, Kim decided it was time to speak her mind.

"You know, if we don't leave soon, we won't be able to," she said.

"Just a little longer," Ben argued.

"I feel like a frog being cooked alive," Kim replied. "We all want to help, Ben. But sooner or later, we're going to have to get off this world if we want to survive."

"She's right," Nance said. "I hate to admit it, but she is."

"Thank you!" Kim said, more loudly than she needed to.

"Maintaining a presence in this world is untenable," Magnum agreed.

"I'm not arguing that," Ben said. "I want to get out of here, but those soldiers in the forest are our friends."

"And I'm all for helping them," Kim said. "If we can."

"Why can't we?" Ben asked.

"Because we don't know what's happening in orbit," Kim said. "For all we know, there could be a thousand ships up there. Every second we waste down here, more could be filling the system."

"I know that," Ben said quietly.

"So what are we waiting for?" Kim asked, letting a little compassion into her voice.

"I don't know," Ben said. "I just have this feeling that we're missing something. Or maybe that we're here for a reason."

"That's insane," Kim said.

"Is it? I don't know," Ben said.

"Not knowing is the problem," Kim said. "Let's go up, take a look around, and see what we're dealing with. We can come back down. I promise."

Ben looked uncertain, but he nodded.

"Commando team, are you secure?" Ben asked over the comms channel.

Roger that, Modulus Echo. Over.

"Corporal, we're taking the ship up to orbit to have a look around. We'll be back."

Copy that. Dial, out."

"Alright, Kim, take us up," Ben said. "Let's see what's out there."

"Next stop, low planetary orbit," Kim said.

"I'll get the radar ready, but it won't do much good through the debris field," Nance said.

"I have a feeling that won't be a problem," Ben said. "They couldn't have sent landing craft through all of that."

"You think they cleared it?" Kim asked.

"At least a portion of it," Ben said. "They had to."

"Then we should be able to escape through it," Kim said, feeling a surge of hope.

"Maybe," Ben said.

The word sent a chill of fear through Kim. There were things about Ben that sometimes seemed supernatural, like the way he could find just the right part in a seemingly endless field of junk, or how he knew how to repair a piece of equipment he'd never even seen before. He had a knack for knowing things that he shouldn't be able to know. And Kim was afraid he knew something about the aliens that he wasn't sharing.

Chapter 23

"Ben, perhaps you should come in here for a minute," Professor Jones said.

Ben glanced at the plot. Kim was taking the *Echo* up in a gentle spiral. They would reach orbit in less than an hour, but there was nothing for Ben to do in the meantime.

"Sure," he replied, getting up from his console and walking toward the med bay.

The lights in the long, narrow facility were turned low. There was new equipment lining the walls, compliments of General Pershing. Staff Sergeant Visher was on the far table, with several monitors hooked up and keeping a close watch on his vitals. On the closer exam table, Crown Prince Godfred was sleeping soundly.

"I had to shave his head to get rid of the lice," Professor Jones said. "I hope he doesn't mind."

"I hope he still has a mind left," Ben said. "He seemed on the verge of insanity when they brought him in."

Professor Jones nodded. "I'm keeping him sedated for now. It seemed the best option."

The prince lay under a paper-thin bedsheet. His filthy clothes had been removed, and his body had been cleaned up. Ben didn't think that would have been a fun job. But Godfred seemed more at ease. Ben didn't know if that was a result of the medical care or simply the drugs. They moved past the prince to where Staff Sergeant Visher lay.

"How is he?" Ben asked.

"Stable," Professor Jones said. "We stopped the bleeding. He just needs time to heal. Barring any setbacks, he should be fine."

"What kind of setbacks?" Ben asked.

"Infection is the primary concern. He was wounded with an alien weapon, which could have been exposed to who knows what from a different galaxy. Only time will tell."

Ben nodded. The idea of being infected with germs from another galaxy was horrifying. Humanity had beaten most illnesses and stamped out disease centuries ago, but that didn't mean they were immune to new pathogens. They may have saved Staff Sergeant Visher only to have him slowly waste away due to an alien illness they had no way of fighting.

In the corner, perched on a stool and leaning against the wall, was Major Le Croix. He looked groggy, but he was awake. Ben had seen him take notice of them, but he'd seemed lost in his thoughts since then. Professor Jones approached the big man slowly. Ben couldn't help but admire the robotic legs. They were elegant in their design and made to be large and powerful.

"Major Le Croix," Professor Jones said, "presents a unique problem."

When Le Croix looked up, Ben could see the blisters around the metallic headband he wore. They looked painful and irritated. The former soldier frowned and spoke quietly.

"Good to see you again, Ben," Le Croix said.

"It appears that the major's body is rejecting the prosthetics the aliens fitted him with," Professor Jones said.

"Why don't we remove them?" Ben said. "I'm sure we can come up with suitable substitutes."

"No," Le Croix said. Ben heard a note of panic in his voice. "You don't understand."

"The major's new *enhancements*, as he calls them, are tied to his nervous system," the professor explained. "And, unfortunately, his eyes were removed."

"He's blind?" Ben asked.

"No, I can see," Le Croix said. "But you can't take the enhancements off. They aren't like our prosthetics. They're more like new limbs."

"Removing them would be painful," Professor Jones said, "and debilitating."

"But if his body is rejecting them?" Ben pointed out.

"It's nothing," Le Croix said. "I can live with a little irritation."

"I thought you might want to talk with him," Jones said. "Despite his recent activities with the aliens, he has volunteered to stay here and keep watch on Staff Sergeant Visher and Prince Godfred for us."

Ben didn't think that was a good idea, but he didn't know where to put Le Croix that he wouldn't be a danger to them. If he was set on mischief, the medical bay was the least dangerous option.

"I thought you might want to question him," Professor Jones said. "I'm sure there is much we can learn about the Krah. Am I saying that right, Major?"

Le Croix nodded.

"Yes, the Krah. There is much we can learn about them from our friend here."

Ben looked at the professor, who clapped him on the shoulder and then headed out of the med bay. There was an empty chair in the other corner. Ben was familiar with it, having slept in the chair when Kim was wounded during their escape from Torrent Four. He slipped into the chair and looked at Le Croix. Ben didn't think he'd ever seen a man looking more miserable than Le Croix did.

"You didn't want to leave them, did you?" Ben asked.

Le Croix shook his head without looking up.

"They gave me my life back," he said quietly. "They accepted me, at least they did at first, until Chieftain Grubat was captured."

"Some people will think of you as a traitor," Ben said.

"I did what I had to do," Le Croix replied, "after you all left me to die in space."

"We tried to save you," Ben said. "But the aliens were closing in. If we could have saved you, we would have."

"I know," Le Croix said quietly. "General Pershing did what she had to do. I can't blame her. I wanted to fight when the Krah captured me. I had to get Prince Godfred out of the emergency pod before his air ran out. We were alone, exposed. I tried to fight them off, but he surrendered and we were taken captive."

"What did they do to you?" Ben asked, glancing where the prince lay across the room.

He couldn't help but remember how Prince Godfred had acted. It was as if he had lost his mind, which made Ben wonder what horrors he might have been exposed to. The prince's body seemed intact, and mostly unharmed, but it seemed his mind had been injured.

"At first, they questioned me," Le Croix said. "Then they released me and let me fight for my life against other troopers."

"Troopers?" Ben asked.

"That's the lowest rank of their warrior class," Le Croix said.

"You had to fight them?"

"It's a sign of respect with the Krah. They're a class society, with the warrior class near the top. They saw me as a warrior and let me determine my own fate. I won the fight but was injured in the process. I passed out, and when I came to…"

He waved at his legs and then at his face. The aliens had experimented on him. Ben didn't see how that could be considered a sign of respect, or determining his own fate, not if they performed surgery on him without his permission.

"They gave you new legs," Ben said.

"And new eyes. And some type of neural chip so that I can understand their language. They speak and I can hear it, but I also hear an almost instant translation."

"That's handy," Ben said.

"And when I see their writing, I see an overlay that I can read in our language."

"They must have pulled that from the networks," Ben said. "Instant translation tools are available. It wouldn't take the computers long to work out the kinks."

"I felt whole for the first time in ages," Le Croix said. "I don't feel these new legs, but they respond as if they were flesh and blood. I can see better, not just sharper but also wider. And the tendril picks up on things around me, feeding that information into my neural chip."

"Such as?"

"Such as the tension you're experiencing," Le Croix said.

"It doesn't take alien tech to read that," Ben said.

"True, but this is different. It's like I can smell it."

"That can't be pleasant."

"It's like knowing something, such as when it's time for dinner, even before you realize you're hungry."

"Okay, that makes sense," Ben said.

"I can't tell you how it works. You'll just have to cut me open and see for yourself."

"We're not doing that," Ben said.

"You won't, but the Royal Imperium will," Le Croix replied. "I guess I deserve it. I'm a traitor, right? I told the enemy our secrets, but they didn't ask for much."

"What do you mean?"

Le Croix shrugged his shoulders and scratched at the raw skin on his forehead. "I guess they got what they needed from His Royal Highness."

Ben looked over at the crown prince, who was resting peacefully on the table.

"You think they tortured him?"

"They didn't have to," Le Croix said. "I think he gave them whatever they asked for. He was scared out of his mind that they were going to torture him."

"It must have been a rude awakening to go from the most pampered position in the entire galaxy to being a prisoner and afraid for your life," Ben said.

"I guess so. He gave them access to the Nav Net and probably everything else as well," Le Croix said. "I was accepted as a trooper since the enhancements they gave me seemed to work."

"Did they know you were rejecting them?"

"No, but it was only a matter of time," Le Croix said. "If the general hadn't attacked Chieftain Grubat and my body wasn't fighting these prosthetics, I wouldn't have left."

Ben looked at Le Croix for a long time, neither man speaking. It was rare, in Ben's experience, for anyone to be so completely honest. But he believed Le Croix and even felt that he understood where the former soldier was coming from. To have lost his legs fighting for the Royal Imperium, and then to have been left behind on a mission for them, would test anyone's loyalty.

"We're heading up into orbit," Ben said. "What do you think we'll find?"

Le Croix shrugged his shoulders again. "Beats me. I wasn't included in their planning."

"But you spent time with them," Ben said. "Surely, you have an idea."

"I know they plan to conquer the galaxy, just like they did their own," the major explained. "But they're also taken with Gershwin. Apparently, there aren't any planets that would support their kind in their own galaxy."

"They had to come from somewhere," Ben said.

"They did, but their world was destroyed. Since then, they've adapted to living in space."

"By taking whatever technology they could find and adapting it to their needs," Ben said, realizing why the alien ship operated the way they did. "They capture ships or space stations, rip them apart, and use them to build onto their own vessels."

Le Croix nodded. "They also use it to enhance their bodies. I was told I could live for hundreds of years with the right enhancements. The Krah don't die from natural causes. They've found a way to manufacture life."

"But they can't terraform their own planets to live on?" Ben asked.

"I don't know, but from what I gathered, it's something they plan to steal from us," Le Croix explained. "I'm sure their worker class is studying it from our networks as we speak. But terraforming takes time, and here is Gershwin, ripe for the taking."

"You can say that again," Ben said. "They landed ships all over the place."

"When?" Le Croix asked.

"Last night, just as we began our operation to rescue the prince."

"Then my guess is you'll find more of them in orbit," Le Croix said. "Most of the first wave weren't keen on settling down here. They wanted to be out hunting for our ships and winning glory in battle."

Ben thought about that. It made sense. On the one hand, if a person had lived their whole lives in pursuit of capturing plunder, giving that up to build a new world might not be appealing. On the other hand, Gershwin represented a new home world. They could settle here and then spread through the galaxy. Unless… The thought was terrifying. Unless there were so many of them that one world wouldn't hold them all. One planet would never support all of humanity.

"So what should we do with you?" Ben asked.

"That's your call," Le Croix said. "You hold all the cards, it seems. You have the traitor and the crown prince. You can have whatever you want if you're willing to turn us over to the general."

"General Pershing isn't in charge anymore," Ben said. "The queen named someone else admiral general. Someone called Arnold Dietz."

Le Croix snorted with laughter but quickly regained his composure.

"You know him?" Ben asked.

"I know who he is. He's no military leader," Le Croix said. "Most of the highest-ranking officials in the fleet are politicians pretending to be officers."

"Either way, I don't think we have any friends left," Ben said. "I was planning to leave you and the prince with the Confederates in Royal City."

"You were? What changed?"

"An alien army is marching toward the city as we speak," Ben said. "Well, actually they're camped just inside the forest a few miles from the city, but they're obviously planning some sort of attack."

"I hadn't heard about that?" Le Croix said. "How many?"

"Just under two hundred of them."

"And how many Confederates are in Royal City?"

It occurred to Ben that perhaps there was more to Le Croix than he realized. Maybe the neural chip in his head was transmitting data.

"More than enough to hold the city," Ben said. "I want you to stay in here. Is that going to be a problem?"

"No," Le Croix said. "But I could use some food."

"I'll see to it," Ben said. "Look, Major, I don't know what's going to happen to you. But we aren't in the business of handing someone over to the enemy. If we can get out of the system and somewhere safe, I don't mind leaving you where you can get transport to wherever you want to go."

"Really?" Le Croix asked.

From the look on his face, the major was genuinely surprised.

"Just don't make me regret it," Ben said. "We can always toss you out the air lock if you cause trouble."

"I won't," Le Croix said. "I'll stay here. No trouble."

"Good," Ben said. "Thanks for the info."

"However I can help," Le Croix said. "I mean that."

Ben started to leave, he got to his feet and took several steps toward the door but then suddenly turned back.

"Any chance that the aliens are getting information from you?" Ben asked.

"From me?" Le Croix said. "I don't think so."

"But they put their tech inside you," Ben said. "Chances are, they know where you are and what you're doing. They may even know everything you know. They could be listening to this conversation right now."

The look on the major's face was abject horror and also recognition of the truth. It was an undeniable fact that as long as he kept the alien enhancements, there was a chance they were listening in. It might even be possible that they could take control of his body. Ben could see the anguish on Le Croix's face.

"I'm going to have to give it up, aren't I?"

"It looks that way," Ben said. "I'm sorry."

"Yeah," Le Croix replied. "Me too."

Ben left him but couldn't stop thinking about what giving up the alien technology would cost Le Croix. He would be a blind cripple. Perhaps worse, depending on what it took to get the chip out of his head. It might even kill him. But no one would ever trust him the way he was. Ben certainly didn't. No matter what Le Croix's intentions were, he was just too big a risk to have around. Ben didn't want the aliens following the *Echo* across the galaxy because they were tracking Le Croix. One way or another, they would need to find a way to be rid of the major. It was the type of thing that made Ben feel ill. He had grown up in a world of discarded trash and found a way to turn it into treasure. Now it appeared that he was the one throwing away something—someone, in this case—and it felt lousy.

Chapter 24

"Where are we?" Ben asked as he hurried back onto the bridge.

He was afraid his conversation with Major Le Croix had gone on too long. If Kim was given enough leeway, she might have them on a course out of the system before Ben could stop her.

"Almost to orbit," Kim said.

"Learn anything useful?" Magnum asked.

"Quite a lot, really," Ben said. "None of it makes me feel any better."

"Radar is ready," Nance said.

"I'm at escape velocity," Kim said. "We're just inside the upper atmosphere."

Ben watched at the blue sky faded to be replaced by the darkness of space. It took the ship's cameras a few seconds to adjust, and then they saw it. The orbit around the planet was empty, but the space beyond was lousy with alien ships.

"Would you look at that," Kim said, her voice full of awe.

"More ships have come through the wormhole," Nance said. "A lot more. Do you still want me to fire up the radar?"

"No," Ben said quickly. "Better not to draw attention."

"I told you we should have left when we had the chance," Kim said.

"When was that exactly?" Ben said, feeling a little irritable.

"We're in deep," Kim said, ignoring him. "I mean, I'm not saying we can't get away, but we'd be cooked without that fancy shield."

"Even with it, we might not get far," Ben said. "They can follow us through hyperspace. And we don't have the weapons to fight them. Not successfully."

"I don't know," Kim replied. "We've done it before."

"Only because they underestimated us," Ben said. "They've changed their tactics. I'm not sure how well our shields will hold up against one of those kinetic missiles."

"It worked against the Royal Imperium missiles," Kim said.

"Yes, because they use small rockets to propel powerful warheads. The shield could spin them away because they didn't have much mass. But the aliens don't have warheads. They were basically using large lumps of metal as projectiles. Some of them were bigger than the *Echo*."

"Yeah, well, leave those to me," Kim said. "They aren't missiles and they can't change course. I'll fly circles around them."

"Unless they fire hundreds at once," Magnum said.

"He's right," Ben said. "Man, this is bad. Really bad."

"What are our options?" Nance said.

"We could run for it," Kim said.

"You want to leave everyone behind?" Ben asked.

"I want to escape this death trap," Kim said. "What alternative do we have? We can't ferry everyone off the planet, and I don't see the Royal Imperium coming to the rescue."

"She's right," Magnum said. "They don't have the firepower to put a dent in that fleet."

"So we just run?" Ben said. Even considering the idea made him feel like he was going to be sick. "We leave the system to the aliens? We leave the wormhole open and let them keep coming through until they're an unstoppable force?"

"What other choice do we have?" Nance said. "We can't do anything about the aliens, can we?"

Ben looked at Professor Jones. Soon, the rest of the crew joined him. They stared at the old man, who looked bewildered.

"I can't just snap my fingers and come up with a solution," he said. "I know there is one, but I haven't struck on it yet."

"But you will," Ben said confidently.

"It's possible, yes," the professor said. "But once I work out the science, it will require some type of delivery device."

"I'll build it," Ben said.

"We can do that anywhere," Kim said. "We don't have to stay here for that."

"We have to be here to activate it," Ben said.

"Guys!" Nance said, suddenly waving her arms.

Normally, Nance was calm, even in dangerous situations. She preferred to think like the computers she loved so much. But there was no denying the excitement in her voice at that moment. Ben and Kim, who were on the verge of a shouting match, both looked over at Nance.

"There's a signal!" Nance said. "It's on a strange frequency, not the regular channels, but we're picking it up."

"Where's it coming from?" Ben asked.

"This system," Nance said. "It isn't powerful enough to be coming from anywhere else."

"Maybe it's an old transmission," Kim said.

"Or perhaps from the surveillance buoys," Magnum suggested.

"No," Nance said. "Listen."

...all we can to reach you. Hang on, help is on the way. I repeat, this is Royal Imperium General Alicia Pershing on the R-I-F Tradewind. We are at war with the Krah Empire. Do not attempt to approach the Celeste system. All ships should report to Admiral General Arnold Dietz in the Mersa system. To any survivors on Gershwin, we are doing all we can to reach you. Hang on, help is on the way.

"It's a repeating message," Nance said.

"The *Tradewind* wasn't a ship in her control when we were with her," Kim said. "It's got to be a new message."

"That means she's in the system," Ben said. "Can we send her a message?"

"We can transmit on the same frequency," Nance said. "But there's no guarantee that she'll get it."

"It's worth a shot," Ben said. "Maybe we can get the Confederates off the planet and find a way out of the system."

"Or maybe we should just make a run for it now," Kim said, "before she realizes we're still alive and tries to take us prisoner for leaving her on the *Everest*."

"She won't do that," Ben said. "We have the crown prince."

"I don't trust her," Magnum said.

"No way," Kim agreed. "She'll stick it to us if we let her."

"So we don't let her," Ben said. "But if she knows we have him, she'll have to send a ship. They can rescue the

Confederates and the crew of *Plato*. All we need is a way to shut down the wormhole."

"I'll get back to work," Professor Jones said. "But someone has to keep an eye on the med bay."

"We will," Ben said. "Nance, patch me into that frequency."

Kim looked at Ben, and he could see the concern in her eyes. He didn't blame her. The truth was, he didn't trust the general any more than the others did. And it wasn't just General Pershing he was concerned about. The queen was desperate, and there were powerful people who might not honor Pershing's amnesty offer. He couldn't put the *Echo* in danger, but his conscience wouldn't let him leave the Confederates behind either. He had stuck his neck out to get them and he wouldn't leave them behind on the planet to be enslaved and experimented on the way Major Le Croix had been.

"Don't worry," Ben said to Kim. "I won't commit us to anything. But we have to try."

"Fine," Kim replied. "Just be careful."

"I will be," Ben said. He glanced over at Nance, who nodded at him. Ben keyed his mic and sent his message. "General Pershing, this is the *Modulus Echo* on Gershwin. After helping the *Plato* land safely, we ferried the Confederate soldiers and crew to Royal City, where they are manning a defense of town. We were also able to evac the commandos near the alien settlement after they successfully rescued Prince Godfred. The prince is alive and is in good physical condition, but he's resting after his harrowing ordeal. As you may know, the aliens have begun an invasion of the planet. A large armed group has taken over the *Plato* and is marching to Royal City. I've been told the defense will hold for now, but if the aliens have reinforcements, that could change. We request a full evacuation of the soldiers, crew, and a handful of survivors that remain in Royal City. Professor Forrest Jones is working diligently on the wormhole problem, and expectations are high that he will solve the issue shortly. We will return to the upper atmosphere twenty-four hours from now in hopes of hearing from you. This is Ben Griminski for the crew of the *Modulus Echo*. Out."

Ben let go of the mic and leaned back in his seat. It felt as if a weight had been lifted from his chest. He could breathe easier knowing that he wasn't alone any longer. Even if the general did nothing, he had sent word of their predicament. He had done all he could do to save the Confederates and perhaps turn the tide.

"Alright, let's head back down," Ben said. "We can pick up the commando team and see what the aliens do."

"Twenty-four hours?" Kim said. "I didn't agree to that."

"I don't think things in orbit are going to get much worse," Ben said. "But we may be able to make a big difference below."

Kim didn't reply, and Ben felt guilty for upsetting her. He tried to tell himself that no matter what he did, he wouldn't please everyone, but it wasn't much of a comfort. The net was closing in, and despite his best efforts, the soldiers on the ground might all be lost. He told himself that if that happened, he could live with it knowing that he had done all he could to help them.

"We're forty-one minutes from reaching the ground," Nance said. "It will be dusk when we're back in radio range."

"Good," Ben said. "Then it won't be long before we find out what the aliens are going to do."

He hoped that they stayed put. If they did, it was probably because they were waiting for reinforcements, and that would make any attack on Royal City exponentially more dangerous. But time was key. Time for General Pershing to get his message. Time for the Royal Imperium to respond to his call for help. Time for Professor Jones to find a way to reverse the wormhole. If they could get enough time, Ben felt a spark of hope, they just might make it through. He held on to that hope because it was all he had left, but it felt good just the same. He only hoped that Kim would come around. Nothing was more difficult than knowing she was upset with him. She wanted to leave and he didn't blame her, but they really had no choice. Ben knew if he left without helping or trying to help the soldiers on the ground, he would regret it for the rest of his life. He just hoped that Kim was wrong and that they could escape just as easily in twenty-four hours. Otherwise, things could get very scary indeed.

Chapter 25

"They've been preparing," Corporal Dial said, his finger on the activator of his throat mic.

Do you want us to pick you up?

Corporal Dial appreciated the *Echo*'s crew. He hadn't known what to expect from the motley band. Many people within the Royal Imperium considered them outlaws, or worse yet, traitors. But Dial had discovered that Ben and his companions were bright, adventurous people. And most importantly, they had proven their loyalty. In truth, he never expected to be rescued once the *Echo* left with General Pershing and his team returned to the alien settlement to gather intel. He had been around long enough to know that unless a decisive victory followed such an assignment, the soldiers left behind were often written off.

When the *Echo* left his team in the forest, he once again expected the worst, yet they had returned right at sundown, just as they said they would. He wanted nothing more than to slink away through the dark woods and board the Kestrel class ship, but his sense of duty held him in his current position. He was sitting in the crook of a tree, hugging a thick limb where his assault rifle was propped. Their intel job was complete, but the tactical advantage they held was significant.

"Amadi, you read me? Over," Dial said using the team channel of his com-link.

"Five by five, Johnny. You thinking what I'm thinking? Over."

"We can hit this group hard once they're clear of the tree line," Dial replied.

"I'm in," Corporal Miller said, "and itching for some payback for Wriggles and Felix. Over."

"They'll never see us coming in the dark," Private Rhoades said. "I say we send them all to hell. Over."

"Alright, we wait until they move out," Corporal Dial ordered. "Descend and advance, but stay inside the trees and wait for my signal. I'll have the *Echo* mark an LZ for evac. Over."

The other three commandos all double-clicked their com-links to acknowledge the order. Corporal Dial wasn't used to taking charge of the entire platoon, but with their team down to just four commandos, he was relatively comfortable giving orders. He switched his com-link over to the broadcast channel and activated the mic again.

"*Modulus Echo*, this is Commando team. Do you read? Over."

We're still here, Corporal, Ben said.

"We're going to sting these aliens when they come out of the trees, then retreat for evac. We need you to find a place to set down. You mark it and send us the coordinates. We'll find you once we're done. Over."

Alright, Ben replied. *How long?*

"The aliens are mobilizing now; it won't be long. Half an hour at the most. Over."

Okay, we'll notify Captain Lawrence, then find a landing spot. Stand by for coordinates.

"Roger that, *Modulus Echo*. Commando team is standing by."

The aliens started marching again. They were more of a mob than an army. They started slowly, with no clear formations, just a milling group moving roughly in the same direction. Fortunately for the commando team, that direction was out of the forest.

"Let's move," Corporal Dial said over his com-link. "Switch to night vision."

Again, his companions clicked their replies. Dial flipped the monocle on his helmet over his eye and the dark forest became visible in green light. After slinging his rifle onto his back, he began climbing down out of the tree. His training kicked in hard, and Dial moved with silent grace, like a ghost, from limb to limb until he could drop quietly onto the ground.

He had lost sight of the aliens, but he wasn't worried. Moving forward quickly, he made for the edge of the forest. In the distance, he could hear the thump of heavy feet, and when he reached a large fallen tree at the edge of the forest, the open plain before him was visible.

"Target in sight," Dial said over the com-link.

The stragglers of the alien army were less than a hundred yards out.

"In position," Dial said quietly.

"Ditto," Corporal Miller said.

"I'm set," Corporal Amadi added a few seconds later.

"Locked, cocked, and ready to rock," Private Rhoades said.

"Start with lasers," Dial said. "Let's see how many we can take out before switching to heavy ammo. Fire on my mark — concussion grenades only when we fall back."

"You have the evac coordinates yet?" Amadi asked.

"No," Dial said, "but the *Echo* will come through. Let's do this. Fire!"

With his night vision enabled, Dial saw the laser blast. It looked yellow and glowed brightly as it flashed across the distance. More beams flicked out from the trees on either side of him, and the aliens began to fall. Some were killed instantly, the superfocused beams of light burned through their bodies and vital organs so fast that they never knew what hit them. Others lingered and were able to shout a warning.

Dial depleted his battery pack rapidly, then switched it out, never taking his eyes off the alien army. Those in the rear of their mob had turned to face their enemy, but the commandos were hidden inside the trees. Dial flipped the switch on his rifle and pulled the charging lever that loaded the first of the depleted uranium rounds into the chamber of his weapon.

"Switching to heavy ammo," Dial said.

His finger checked the rate-of-fire indicator. He was so familiar with his weapon that he didn't have to think about it. With just a touch, he knew it was set to single-shot semiauto fire. He raised the sight and fired quickly.

The report of the rifle was loud, and the other commandos quickly joined in. A few of the aliens raced back toward the trees, brandishing their axes and wailing strange war cries. But the majority of the group moved on, increasing their pace to a run, and quickly moving out of range.

"They're running," Corporal Miller said.

"Damn cowards," Amadi said.

Corporal Dial's wrist link beeped. He glanced down and saw that coordinates were flashing.

"Hold your fire," Dial said.

"Why not pursue?" Private Rhoades asked.

"Because that would put us in danger," Dial replied. "Even with night vision, we could run right into an ambush. Besides, I doubt we could keep up."

"You got directions to the LZ?" Amadi asked.

"Affirmative," Dial said. "Let's move out."

He looked across the open field. There were several dozen dead aliens, maybe as many as forty. He did the math in his head as he hurried through the forest toward the coordinates on his wrist link. The aliens had to be down to around a hundred and fifty, maybe even fewer. And they showed no indication that they carried any other types of weapons other than their axes and knives. He wanted a straight-up engagement but knew the Royal Imperium wouldn't even consider it. The shot callers preferred to sit in safety and rely on air superiority, even though their struggles with the rebels had proven that strategy to be ineffective. To really root out an enemy, one needed to get in the dirt with them. Dial was willing to fight the aliens on the ground as long as the Royal Imperium would allow him to, but he also knew that his opinion might change if they could get within range with their fancy axes and knives. The aliens might make short work of him and the other commandos. They were bigger and stronger, but Dial preferred light and fast. Hit the enemy where it hurt, then get clear before they could retaliate. In his mind, that was a solid strategy that had been effective throughout history, and no one had improved upon it.

"How'd we do?" Private Rhoades asked.

"I'd say we took out twenty, maybe even twenty-five percent of their fighters," Amadi replied as the commandos jogged through the forest.

They had instinctively moved closer together. Dial wondered if he should order them to spread out. Clumping made them a bigger target and would allow an enemy to concentrate fire on them. But Dial and his team had watched the aliens all day. The entire group had left the forest together, and he didn't anticipate them doubling back.

"Could have been a lot more if they hadn't run away," Miller said. "Damn cowards."

"It was the right call strategically," Dial said. "By moving out of range, the advantage shifted in their favor."

"We don't have to like it, though, do we?" Private Rhoades asked.

He was younger than the three corporals and had less experience in the field. But he was a natural fighter and never backed down. His courage was an asset, but only if it was combined with reason and sound tactical knowledge. Dial knew that self-control was essential in a firefight. Bloodlust or berserker rage made a person dangerous, both to the enemy and to his brothers and sisters in arms.

"But it's important to learn about our enemy," Dial said. "They aren't mindless fighters, are they? They can think and reason. They strategize and make sound tactical decisions. We have to keep that in mind when we're devising our plans."

"Just point me in the right direction and let me go," Rhoades said.

"The kid doesn't know when to quit," Amadi said.

"That's an asset, until it isn't," Miller added.

"What are you talking about?" Rhoades asked. "You sound like a bunch of old women."

"Being old in this business means you're smart and dangerous," Dial said. "Those two characteristics aren't mutually exclusive."

It felt good to run after the firefight and sit in a tree all day. The tension while they watched the aliens had been high, and then the battle pumped a surge of adrenaline into Dial's system. Stretching his muscles and physically moving away from the enemy felt good, but he was growing tired quickly.

"How much farther?" Miller asked.

"Half a mile as the crow flies," Dial said.

"You think the fighting will start in Royal City without us?" Rhoades asked.

"I hope so," Dial said. "If it's over when we get there, that would be fine with me."

Chapter 26

Another rotation and nothing had changed. General Pershing narrowed her eyes as the *Tradewind* approached the far curve of the planet that would take them out of visual range of the alien fleet. Between their efforts and sharing data with the *Eclipse*, they had marked identifiers on most of the alien ships. The last count showed four hundred and eighty vessels in the system, with more occasionally popping through the wormhole.

The Royal Imperium was outnumbered. Pershing didn't even have the information she needed to know if they could field four hundred vessels in their depleted fleet. Not that every alien ship was an equal threat. Odds were high that many weren't armed, at least not the fashion of the ships that had pushed her small flotilla out of the system. Those ships had fired high-mass kinetic bombs, essentially space junk welded together to form a big missile. The alien fleet had gathered plenty of space junk and debris from the remnants of the first battle where Pershing had used weaponized weather drones to overwhelm the alien ships, but it still remained to be seen if they would continue to use archaic weapons or adapt to more efficient methods of fighting her fleet.

"General," the communications officer said. "I have a message. It's from Gershwin!"

"Put it on the speakers," Pershing said.

She feared it would be a cry for help from the vacationers left behind on the planet. She had no doubt that they were very important people, but she couldn't risk the Royal Imperium Fleet to save a few stranded trillionaires.

General Pershing, this is the Modulus Echo on Gershwin.

Pershing's lips pressed together into a thin line. Ben's voice was easily recognizable but brought her no joy. The only positive in hearing from him was that she no longer had to wonder if the Kestrel class ship had survived the attack.

After helping the Plato land safely, we ferried the Confederate soldiers and crew to Royal City, where they are manning a defense.

More good news, but it didn't help her efforts. She could pass on the message that the Confederate soldiers were safe on Gershwin to Holt and his squadron of converted commercial ships.

We were also able to evac the commandos near the alien settlement after they successfully rescued Prince Godfred. The prince is alive, and physically in good condition, but resting after his harrowing ordeal.

Pershing's frustration grew more intense. She had known that Chieftain Grubat claimed the crown prince was alive, and the news from the *Echo* corroborated his testimony, but it also complicated the political situation and gave the queen more leverage in her struggle to stay relevant. She couldn't help but wonder if Ben was telling the truth. He was a criminal, after all, and had betrayed her trust by leaving the *Everest*. Perhaps he was claiming to have the prince just to force her into doing his bidding.

As you may know, the aliens have begun an invasion of the planet. A large armed group has taken over the Plato and is marching to Royal City. I've been told the defense will hold for now, but if the aliens have reinforcements, that could change. We request a full evacuation of the soldiers, crew, and a handful of survivors that remain in Royal City.

And there it was. She almost chuckled. The gall of some people amazed her. Did he not just say that the aliens were in the middle of a full-scale invasion? How could he even think that she could find a way onto the planet to rescue them? They had made their bed, and now Ben and his crew had no choice but to sleep in it.

Professor Forrest Jones is working diligently on the wormhole problem, and expectations are high that he will solve the issue shortly.

Expectations were a far cry from results, Pershing thought. But if the old man could find a way to close the wormhole, she would do anything in her power to get her hands on it. Closing the portal and shutting off the alien line of supply and reinforcement was her highest priority.

We will return to the upper atmosphere twenty-four hours from now in hopes of hearing from you. This is Ben Griminski for the crew of the Modulus Echo. Out.

"Should we respond, General?" the communications officer asked.

"Negative," Pershing said, standing up. "When was this message sent?"

"Four hours ago."

"Can you locate the point of origin?"

"It appears to be coming from the planet," the communications officer said.

Pershing glanced at the captain, who was watching her intently. There was a pleading look on her face, and Pershing realized that news of the crown prince had swayed her. Perhaps it had fooled them all, the general thought as she glanced around the bridge. Only officers were at their stations, no enlisted personnel. Surely, Pershing thought, they were smart enough to see through Ben's ruse.

"Things are rarely as they appear," Pershing said. "Take their wild claim about the crown prince, for instance. We have no proof that they are telling the truth, only the fact that they are criminals whose primary concern is their own wellbeing."

"But if it is true…" the captain said.

"Only time will tell," Pershing said. "For now, we must assume they're lying. They want off the planet and need our help."

"So we're going to do nothing?" Captain Davis asked.

"We're going to stay the course," Pershing said. "That's our priority. I will respond to the *Modulus Echo* when I'm ready. If they truly have Prince Godfred, we will do our duty. But until that fact can be confirmed, we continue the mission. Is that clear?"

"Yes, General," the captain said.

Pershing nodded, stood, and swiftly exit from the bridge. She went directly to her quarters, perched on the edge of her bunk, and prepared a message for the rebel commander.

"Holt, I have word that we may need to mount a rescue mission on Gershwin. Are any of your ships hybrids?"

She sent the message to the ship's network node, where it was shuttled through the communications satellite and beamed to the Confederate ships. Once she was done, she hurried from her room down to the tiny brig. The containment area consisted of a single room with a long metal bench and several rings set in the floor that shackles could be locked to. Chieftain Grubat lay on the bench, his tendrils drooping to the floor, his skin a grayish color that concerned General Pershing. It looked as if the prisoner was ill and struggling to breathe.

Pershing looked at the guard, who was busy reading someone on a data pad. She frowned and waited, letting the weight of her disapproval settle on the man. After a moment, he glanced up at her, realized she was staring at him, and snapped to attention.

"Apologies, General," he said in a shaky voice. "Can I help you?"

"You're on duty here?" Pershing snapped.

"Yes, ma'am!"

"And you're in charge of the prisoners being held in the brig?"

The man nodded.

"Are you aware that the prisoner is in distress?"

The color left the man's face completely, and he tried his best to look over at Chieftain Grubat without turning his head. The brig had a large window of transparent steel that allowed the duty officer to keep tabs on anyone inside. Pershing watched the man's eyes cut hard to his right.

"He's ill. I should have been notified immediately," Pershing growled as she took a step toward the guard. "That prisoner is our only link to the aliens. If he dies, we lose that link. What do you suppose would happen to the guards assigned to watch him?"

"I-I-I'm n-not sure," the guard stammered.

"This isn't someone being held for a petty crime," Pershing said. "Unless you want to join him in the brig, I suggest you get a medical team down here on the double."

The guard saluted smartly and replied, "Yes, General!"

"But first, open the door," she said. "Quarantine protocol."

General Pershing moved over to the brig's sliding door. It was made of thick steel and had a large locking mechanism on the outside. Just inside the door, a thin plastic partition dropped from the ceiling, and a fan drew air into the room while a series of vents sucked the air from the room, creating negative pressure. The plastic billowed inward around the door, like a solar sail, as the heavy steel doors slid apart.

"Chieftain, are you ill?" Pershing asked.

Grubat turned his head but didn't even try to sit up.

"Hard...to...breathe..." he wheezed.

Pershing had no idea what could be causing the alien distress. "I have a medical team coming."

"Air..." Grubat said. "Need...more...nitrogen..."

His voice was weak, but fortunately the translation device in his headset was loud enough to hear over the quarantine fans. Pershing turned toward the guard. He was looking at her fearfully. Perhaps it was the distress on her face, or having been caught loafing on the job, but he was clearly afraid of her. She hoped that fear would motivate him and not make him freeze up in panic.

"Get someone from engineering up here on the double," she ordered. "Tell them we need a nitrogen canister."

The guard nodded. Pershing turned back to Grubat, but there was nothing she could do for him. The larger ships had a mix of gases that simulated planetary conditions, while smaller ships, like the *Tradewind*, used the pure oxygen outgassed by the fusion of Zexum gas to ensure the crew had breathable air. She wondered briefly how the alien had faired so well on the *Modulus Echo*. It must have been from being on Gershwin long enough to get a mix of gases on board. They simply weren't on the little spaceship long enough to filter out the nitrogen.

It only took a few minutes for the medical team and a pair of engineers to set up a nitrogen feed into the brig. The result was remarkable. As soon as the gas was pumped into the room, Grubat began to breathe more easily. He took great lungfuls of air in, and after a few moments, was strong enough to sit up.

"I apologize for the failure to compensate for your needs," Pershing said. "There is still much we need to learn about one another."

"I concur," Grubat said.

"I have some questions. I would give you time to rest and recover, but that is a luxury I do not have at this moment."

"I understand," Grubat said.

"Your fleet is growing around Gershwin. They have begun an invasion of the planet. May I ask what their intentions will be toward the humans living on Gershwin?"

"We have claimed the planet for our own," Grubat said. "The humans will be conquered and subjugated, unless they can be incorporated into our ranks."

"Incorporated?" Pershing asked.

"Our workers may find your people ripe for enhancement. Some may even be fit to join the worker class or serve as warriors if they can find a chieftain or warlord willing to allow them into their thrall."

Pershing didn't quite understand, but it was plain enough. The humans on Gershwin were in danger. She hadn't really thought they wouldn't be, but she had to know for certain. She nodded at Grubat. "Thank you."

He nodded, his headdress tendrils perking up and beginning to writhe again.

Pershing headed back to her cabin, weighing the possibilities in her mind. If the crown prince was really on the *Modulus Echo*, she could argue that getting them out of the system was her priority. Rescuing the Confederates on the ground would only slow the process down and increase the danger. That was not acceptable with the crown prince of the Royal Imperium in the balance, but she also knew Ben Griminski. He was an idealist, and the crew of the little ship listened to him. He would insist that she save the rebels. It was a tricky situation. The idea itself was ludicrous on its face. There were over four hundred Krah vessels in the system. Any rescue effort was bound to fail, yet she had no choice. Once word leaked out that the crown prince still lived, anything less than an immediate rescue attempt would be seen as treason. Her enemies would seize upon that one fact, regardless of the others, and use it to ruin her career.

When she reached her quarters, she found a tray of food. Protein wafers with nut butter and slices of fresh fruit were spread around a plate in an appetizing pattern. Pershing sat on the edge of her bunk and ate the food without really tasting it. Her mind was working the problem of how to deal with the villainous crew of the *Modulus Echo*. She needed to manipulate them, to make them do her bidding while believing it was their own idea. She had worked with politically appointed superior officers, and eventually the very leaders of the Royal Imperium military itself. That experience served her well as she made her plans. By the time she finished eating, she knew what she had to do. It wasn't a perfect plan, but her resources were limited. She set the tray aside and powered on the touch-sensitive display so she could record a message for the crew of the *Modulus Echo*.

Chapter 27

"The soldiers are all on board," Ben said. "Rear hatch is closing."

"Roger that," Kim said. "I'm lifting off."

The main drive and wing engines were already pointed straight down. Kim pressed the throttle forward with her left hand to bring the Kestrel class ship straight up into the air. There were trees close on every side. The clearing they had landed on was barely big enough for the ship, but it was the closest LZ to the commando team so Kim made it work.

They rose over the leafy upper branches of the trees, and suddenly it was as if the world had opened up to them. The night was dark, but light filtered down from the heavens. Not starlight, but the running lights from ships in orbit around the planet. On the ship's big bridge displays, Kim saw the shadowy forest below, and the grassy plains that led to Royal City. She could even see the dim outlines of the mountain peaks far in the distance.

Ben bounded up the metal stairs to the ship's main deck, then hurried over to his console. He immediately radioed the Confederate troops in Royal City.

"Captain Lawrence, we have the commando team and are heading your way," Ben said.

Roger that, Modulus Echo. We have movement in the green space beyond Grand Avenue, but the aliens don't seem intent on attacking. At least not yet. Over.

Kim flew over the scene of the attack from the commandos, moving slowly and letting the ship's exterior cameras record the carnage. A few of the aliens were wounded and still moving, but most lay dead. Many had gruesome wounds that made Kim thankful it was too dark to see clearly. She flew up a few thousand feet to ensure that they weren't in danger from the aliens on the ground before continuing toward Royal City.

"So what's our plan?" Kim asked. "We drop off the commandos and the prince, then make for orbit?"

"Can't do that," Ben said. "We have to stick around, for a little while at least. The Confederates might need our help."

"Okay, but where?" Kim asked. "I'm not too keen on landing on Grand Avenue between the two armies."

"We don't land," Ben said. "We can circle the city and help them keep watch on the aliens. At dawn we head for orbit to see whether General Pershing has contacted us."

"Fat chance of that," Kim said.

"Someone has to monitor the radar," Nance said.

"And keep an eye on the aliens on the ground," Ben agreed. "I'll take the first watch. Three-hour shifts. You can set the ship on autopilot, right?"

"Autopilot," Kim scoffed. "Sure, whatever."

"You need to get some rest," Ben said.

"We all do," Kim said. "But I don't know how well I'll be able to rest knowing that we could be blown out of the sky at any minute."

"If we get anything on the radar, I'll alert you immediately," Ben said. "I'll wake Magnum in a few hours, and he can wake Nance. Until then, you should all sleep."

"You sure?" Magnum asked.

"Positive," Ben said.

Nance looked uncertain, but she set the radar to display on one half of the bridge screen. The other half showed a thermal image of Royal City below them. When the ship flew out over the green space, tiny red dots began to appear.

"Looks like the skies are clear," Nance said. "And the aliens on the ground are holding their positions."

"Waiting for reinforcements, maybe," Ben said.

"If you need me, just wake me up," Nance insisted.

"I promise," Ben replied.

Magnum walked her to her quarters, and Kim got up slowly from her pilot's seat.

"I could sleep out here, you know," she said.

"You could do anything," Ben said as he stepped close and pulled Kim into an embrace. "You're an amazing woman."

"Stop trying to butter me up, Ben," Kim warned.

"I'm not," Ben said. "Go get some sleep. I've got this."

He kissed her forehead and then steered her toward her cabin, which was on the far side of the atrium behind the bridge. For a moment, he watched her go, then he dropped down into the pilot's chair. He was tired; they all were. It had been a long time since any of them had gotten to sleep.

"You on watch, Ben?" Dial said as he came down the stairs from his quarters.

Ben turned and saw that the commando had showered and changed clothes. He nodded.

"We're going to hold this position tonight," Ben said. "The aliens are waiting."

Dial watched the thermal display. The ship was moving on a long, slow circle several thousand feet above the city. The exterior cameras didn't make out a lot at that range, but when they passed over the green space directly across from the city, a line of red dots appeared.

"Waiting for what?" Dial asked.

"Reinforcements?" Ben said.

"Maybe," Dial said. "That's not a cheery thought. If they get enough soldiers around the city, they could overrun the Confederate defenses."

"Any chance they're just recon?" Ben asked. "Just watching Royal City the way your team did their settlement?"

"No," Corporal Dial said confidently. "There's too many of them for that type of mission. They would only need a handful of soldiers to keep tabs on the rebels holding the city."

"I guess we just have to wait and see."

"Ah, the fun part of war. Long periods of stressful tedium punctuated by short bursts of terror," Dial said. "You mind if I hang here with you for a while?"

"Not at all," Ben said. "But shouldn't you be resting?"

"Can't. I'm too keyed up. I have to wind down for a while before I can rest after a firefight."

"Well, you're welcome here. Le Croix's in the med bay keeping an eye on Staff Sergeant Visher and the prince."

"You think that's a good idea?"

"I don't know," Ben said. "He seems contrite."

"He might be playing you."

"True, and he might just be a pawn. The aliens did things to him. Implanted devices in his brain. They could be getting some kind of audiovisual transmission from him that we don't even know about."

"Damn, this is crazy," Dial said.

An hour passed with nothing new happening. Ben had to stand up and walk around a little while to stay awake once Corporal Dial headed back up to his quarters. The ship was quiet. The cargo bay was dark. Everyone was resting except for Ben. He checked his wrist link and saw that he had over an hour and a half left on his shift. He didn't mind the work and felt no resentment, just fatigue. His body was telling him it was time to rest.

To help pass the time, he ran short diagnostics on each of the ship's systems. Everything was working perfectly; the only question mark was the fusion reactor. They were down to just a quarter tank of Zexum. He was doing the mental math, trying to decide if he had time for some sleep before changing out the tanks, or if he would have to see to it before he finally got a chance to close his eyes, when a new set of red dots appeared on the thermal imaging.

At first, his mind struggled to understand what he was seeing. The ship wasn't even over the green space, but rather the lake that Royal City was built beside. He couldn't understand how he could be seeing red dots that indicated heat. At first, he wondered if perhaps it was some sort of aquatic life, but soon the dots resolved into two separate blobs. They were moving toward Royal City, and he was sure it wasn't fish or some other animal.

He thought about waking the others but decided to do a little work on his own first. He hit a few keys on the controls at Kim's pilot seat, where he was watching over the ship. He could have done the same thing from his own console, but with the ship in flight, he felt safer having the controls close at hand. The autopilot was flying, but Ben could override the automatic controls if he needed to. The thermal image changed to night vision. The lake was like a black hole, just a dark-green shadow that filled the screen. But above the lake, with running lights flashing, Ben saw what looked like two transports.

He keyed his mic to contact the Confederates.

"Royal City, this is Ben Griminski on the *Modulus Echo*. Do you read me?"

We have you, Modulus Echo. Go ahead.

"I'm picking up two vehicles," Ben said. "Moving toward you over the lake. Looks like it might be the resort's passenger transports. Can you confirm?"

A new voice, one with obviously more concern, replied, *Modulus Echo, did you say those bogeys are moving toward the city from the lake side? Over.*

"Yes," Ben replied. "They have running lights on. You should be able to see them."

Stand by, the first voice said.

Ben guessed that a low-ranking soldier was manning the communications system, overseen by a more experienced non-com. And it sounded like the Confederates were concentrating on the aliens across the green space. With their backs to the water, they may not have been looking that direction at all.

He considered and rejected the idea of turning the ship around for a better view of the transports. After warning the Confederates, there was nothing more he could do. If the vehicles approaching weren't human, then surely they wouldn't have their exterior lights on.

Modulus Echo, the gruff voice of what Ben thought was the supervisor said, *the approaching vessels are human. We have the situation under control. Thanks for the heads up. Royal City, out.*

Just another false alarm, Ben thought. Although, the only people with transports on the planet were the resort workers who had slaughtered their wealthy guests. Ben didn't think they were coming out of the mountains for no reason, but he knew that the Confederates would alert him if something was going on that he needed to know. He went back to calculating the odds of running out of fuel before morning.

Chapter 28

The door slid open and light from the atrium made it hard for Ben to open his eyes.

"Sorry, Ben," Magnum said. "But you better come see this."

"Yeah…sure," Ben said.

He was so tired. The chrono display beside his bed showed that he'd been asleep for less than an hour. But that was life on a ship. There were times when days, sometimes weeks, went by that were filled with tedious routine and so much downtime that a person felt like they would go crazy, and other times when just getting an hour of sleep was like a luxury.

Ben crawled out of his bed. He was still dressed, having not bothered to even take his clothes off when his watch ended. He rubbed his face with both hands and stood up. His body was so tired that even stretching seemed difficult, as if his muscles would strain so hard they would snap his bones. Walking was almost painful as he shuffled to the open door.

Magnum had returned to the bridge and was standing near the pilot's seat. He was a big man and made the bulky chair seem small. Ben walked over to the bridge and looked at his console. All systems were green, which was a relief. The last thing he wanted was a mechanical malfunction when the planet was being invaded.

"What's up?" Ben asked.

"Got a message from the Confederates," Magnum said.

He pressed a button and the message played quietly over the bridge speakers.

...the locals report a large group of aliens moving toward our position through the mountains. Captain Lawrence requests a flyover to confirm. Over.

A moment passed, then Ben asked, "Did you respond?"

Magnum nodded. "Told them I'd see what we could do."

"You ever fly the ship before?"

"No," Magnum said. "And I didn't think I could do it and scan for the aliens in the mountains."

Ben nodded. "Good thinking. Kim had some trouble with the winds through the mountains, and we need to stay low to use the thermal imaging. I'll take the controls, you scan."

For a moment Ben considered waking Kim up, but he decided to wait. She needed as much rest as he could give her. Besides, there was a good chance the workers were lying about the aliens in the mountains. They had probably run out of food or fallen to fighting among themselves and needed an excuse to go back to Royal City.

"Did the Confederates say anything else about the workers?" Ben asked.

"Only that they claimed their village was attacked."

"The fact that they had a secret village in the mountains is interesting," Ben said. "I guess the Confederates gave a sympathetic ear to the workers' rebellion."

"They didn't see the murder victims at the spaceport," Magnum said.

"No," Ben agreed.

For a moment, as he turned off the autopilot and brought the ship into a hover over the lake, he considered the situation of the local workers. He had no doubt they had been mistreated in some ways. Ben didn't have much experience around the wealthy, but he could guess just how careless they could be when dealing with the people tasked with serving them. The resort on Gershwin was billed as the poshest luxury getaway in the galaxy. Only the wealthiest with the best connections could even get on the waiting list. On the other hand, no matter how rude or condescending they were, they didn't deserve to be murdered. Ben could understand and even sympathize with the workers to a point. The wealthy didn't deserve to be rescued more than the workers did. And the workers shouldn't have been expected to continue serving the guests once the aliens took over the system. Perhaps the workers had a right to their share of the supplies, including the transports, but they crossed a line, in Ben's mind, when they murdered the unarmed guests.

Still, those types of crimes would have to wait to be investigated. The workers were wrong, but until they were all safely out of the Celeste system, they would have to work together. The Confederates couldn't divide their forces just to keep the workers under arrest. It was a messy situation, and while it made Ben nervous, he had to go along with it. Even changing the *Echo*'s patrol route was costing him the rest he deserved, but it would be foolish not to investigate the claim the workers had made. As long as they were in the Celeste system, every threat had to be checked or it could cost them all their lives.

"If the aliens came down on the far side of the mountains, is it possible that they marched through the passes already?" Ben asked.

"I don't know," Magnum said. "Should I wake Nance?"

"No, let her sleep," Ben said. "Odds are, this is a wild goose chase, but we've got to check it out. You ready?"

Magnum nodded, and Ben pressed the throttle forward. Flying in atmo was challenging. The ship's engines were well designed and could easily keep them airborne, but Ben had to contend with gravity's constant downward pull and the planet's shifting winds. The hard part was not being able to anticipate the wind, which was strong through the mountains. He would need to keep them high enough to avoid the rugged land that rose on either side, but low enough that the thermal imaging worked.

"How high can I get?" Ben asked.

"Three thousand feet, maybe four," Magnum said. "We won't be able to tell much at that distance, but an army should be easy enough to spot."

"Yeah," Ben agreed. "If we find something, we can descend for a closer look."

They moved into the mountains and began to search. Ben was weary, but the strong winds buffeting the ship kept him alert. And it didn't take long to find what they were looking for.

"I've got something, Ben," Magnum said.

"Okay, hang on," Ben replied.

He had to stabilize their hover. Fortunately, they were in a good position between the mountains. There was plenty of space around them, and the wind wasn't too severe. He looked up at the big display and saw a streak of red in a narrow pass. The rest of the mountains were green, yellow, even blue. Ben knew the distance made it impossible to gauge what was approaching through the pass. It might be a herd of animals, or even more workers. For all Ben knew, the heat signature could even be coming from their secret village. The only way to know for certain was to get closer.

"I'm taking us down. You'll need to switch the cameras over to night vision."

"Okay," Magnum said.

"We might want to record it too. Can you do that?"

"Yep, I'm ready."

"Here goes nothing."

Ben pressed the throttle forward, and the ship began moving toward the narrow pass. He didn't want to fly through it; the risk was much too high that he might crash the ship. Instead, he descended slowly and moved toward the red line. He kept a close eye on the ship's instruments. They dropped down to an altitude of only five hundred feet and were as close to the pass as Ben was comfortable with. He could feel the margin of error growing narrower with every second. A strong gust of wind could push them out of position, and he needed space to ensure that they didn't crash.

"Anything?" Ben asked without looking up from his displays that showed the ship's position relative to the mountains and ground.

"I've got to cycle through the cameras," Magnum said. "How does Nance make this look so easy? Okay! I've got them."

Ben risked a glance up at the big bridge screens, which showed a night vision feed from the forward-mounted camera. He could see the shadows of the mountains rising like a V in front of them. Below, a thick forest of evergreens looked almost like pointed spikes waiting to impale them if Ben lost control. But it was the movement that caught his eye. Through the pass, among the trees, there were aliens. They looked almost like humans, except for their robotic arms and legs, which glinted oddly on the green night vision.

"The workers weren't lying," Ben said.

"What should we do?" Magnum said.

It was a good question. They needed to do something, but he wasn't sure what. From the looks of things, more aliens were coming through the mountains than hiding in the green space on the far side of Royal City. Ben pulled back on the joystick and nudged the throttle forward, sending the *Echo* into a slow climb. He waited until they were several thousand feet in the air, with nothing close by to endanger the ship, before returning to a hover.

"Alright, patch me through to Royal City and we'll figure out what we need to do."

Chapter 29

"How many?" Corporal Dial asked.

"Impossible to say for sure," Ben replied.

"More than the last group?"

"A lot more," Magnum said.

"With the right terrain, we could move into position and catch them in a crossfire," the soldier said. "Thin the herd, so to speak."

"Or plant explosives," Magnum said.

Ben shook his head. It was just the three of them brainstorming ideas. Ben had flown the *Echo* back out of the mountains to get a decent radio signal, but they were still waiting for someone to rouse Captain Lawrence and get him to the communications center in the hotel tower.

"I don't want you off the ship," Ben said. "There's a good chance that we're going to need to get out of here in a hurry."

"So what options does that leave us?" Dial asked.

"The ship's missiles," Magnum said.

"It's a start," Dial said. "But a single air strike won't stop them. Not if there's as many as you claim."

"What if we don't target the aliens themselves?" Ben said. "If we could find the right place and blast the mountains, it could start an avalanche."

"That would slow them down," Dial said. "Probably cause as many casualties as actually shooting at them."

"Okay, you two find the right place. I'll let Captain Lawrence know what we're planning."

Dial and Magnum huddled near the big man's console while Ben stayed in the pilot's seat. It had been five hours since he'd sent Kim off to get some rest. He really wanted to give her at least three more hours, but he wasn't sure if they could afford to.

The Confederates were taking their sweet time getting their commander to the radio, and Ben was beginning to worry that something had gone wrong. He was about to test the comms system when a worried and exhausted Professor Jones appeared by his seat. There was something in the old man's eyes that made Ben worry.

"What's wrong?" Ben asked.

"Nothing, nothing," the professor said.

"The prince?"

"He's fine. Staff Sergeant Visher too."

"What about Le Croix?"

"The man has sleep apnea. If not for the sedatives, he would keep our patients awake all night."

"So what's bothering you?"

The professor's face twitched. Ben knew something was wrong and that the older man didn't want to tell him. Still, things were bad on every front, so a little more bad news couldn't be that bad, Ben told himself.

"I have come to a conclusion," Professor Jones said. "Reversing the wormhole is not possible. It could take years to discover a safe way to seal the tunnel, maybe even decades. I just don't know."

"Okay, well, that's not ideal, but we can live with it."

"I did find something," the older man said with a grimace.

"We're in the middle of something here, Professor. Can it wait?"

"Actually, no," Jones said. "It's a solution to the problem."

"Which problem?" Ben asked.

"All of them."

The professor let his statement hang in the air, which suddenly felt cold to Ben. He took a deep breath and did a quick mental calculation. The ship was safe, although running low on fuel. They had time. He didn't think the approaching alien army could get through the mountains before sunup, and then they would have to circle the lake to get to Royal City. He was about to ask Professor Jones what he meant when the comms crackled to life.

Modulus Echo, this is Captain Lawrence. I hope you have good news for me. Over.

"Captain, this is Ben. We found the aliens you were warned about. And there are a lot of them. Several times more than the group poised in the green space. Over."

That's unfortunate. Perhaps we should draw the aliens waiting nearby into a fight, then find a place to retreat to before the others arrive. What do you think, Ben? Over.

"We're looking into a way to slow the second group down," Ben said. "It's the best we can do, I'm afraid. Stopping them completely is impossible. They're too spread out, and there's too much cover in the mountains. Over."

What if we wait until they're out of the mountains? Over.

"Our weapons would be less effective in the open, I'm afraid. My people are formulating a plan as we speak. Once we have it, we'll transmit it to you. We'll hit the aliens, then make a run to orbit to see if we've got any help coming. Over.

Roger that, Echo. Keep us in the loop. We'll begin making plans to evacuate Royal City if it comes to that. Captain Lawrence, out.

"Sounds dire," Professor Jones said.

"It is. Without help, the Confederates are stranded here with no chance of surviving," Ben said, his guilt leaving a sour feeling in his gut. "Tell me about what you've found."

Professor Jones nodded and Ben set the ship on autopilot. He rotated the pilot's seat around to face the professor, who looked frightened. Ben was starting to feel frightened himself.

"Do you know what happens to a star when it dies?"

"Red giant, white dwarf, that sort of thing?"

"Yes, that's correct. Most stars aren't big enough to explode. They grow larger as they use the last of the hydrogen."

"Unstable fusion reaction," Ben said.

"Precisely. But some stars, large powerful stars like Celeste, will burn through their hydrogen and begin burning other elements. Essentially, they explode with more force than anything known to man."

"A true force of nature," Ben said.

"That's right," the professor said. "Exactly. A force of nature so powerful it would obliterate almost everything in the system, then collapse back on its self to form a black hole."

"Okay, but doesn't that take millions of years?" Ben said.

"Yes. Yes, it does. Unless…"

Once again, Professor Jones let his statement hang in the air between them. Ben's heart was pounding. He wasn't sure if it was from exhaustion or the ideas that Professor Jones was expounding on.

"Unless what?" Ben asked.

"Unless the process could be hastened. Ben, I don't even want to tell you the rest, but I have to. Okay, here goes," he said, working up the nerve. "We could build a device, much like the flux rocket that opened the wormhole, only bigger."

"That isn't reassuring," Ben said.

"We would have to get close to the sun, then ignite it," Jones went on, undeterred. "The singularity event would draw away the hydrogen from the sun, only for a few seconds, but if my calculations are correct, it would destabilize the star's fusion reaction."

"And cause a supernova explosion," Ben said.

Professor Jones just nodded.

"How powerful are we talking about?"

"More powerful than you can imagine," Professor Jones said. "The entire system, and everything in it, would be destroyed. Except for the wormhole. I don't think it would close."

"So how does that help us?" Ben asked.

"After the star goes supernova, it would collapse back on itself and form a powerful black hole."

"Powerful enough to close the wormhole?"

"Maybe close it," Professor Jones said. "For certain, nothing that came through it would escape the black hole's gravitational pull. You proved that a black hole is essentially a wormhole, but odds are highly unlikely that such a feat could be repeated."

"So if more of the aliens tried to come through the wormhole, they would be ripped apart by the gravity waves?"

"Probably before they could pass through the portal. I believe the reason your ship managed to succeed where every other ship has failed is that you dropped out of hyperspace right into the eye of the gravitational storm, the center of the swirl, with the crushing force of the gravity waves swirling around you. My research suggests that it is possible to map a black hole and recreate your incredible luck, but even then, the danger is astronomical."

"Tell me about it," Ben said sitting back in his chair. "What would it take to build this star-destabilizing rocket?"

"That's the really frightening part, Ben. We would have to build a gravity shield around it, or it would be incinerated before it got close enough to do its job."

"We can't build another one," Ben said. "We don't have the right parts."

"I know," Professor Jones said in an urgent whisper. "We would have to use the one on our ship."

"You're suggesting that we fly this bomb close enough to the system and start to destabilize it?" Ben asked.

"No, no, no. That would be impossible. Even with the flux shield, we would never get close enough. What we need is a specialized device, housed in multiple layers of heat-shielding material."

"Where are we going to get that?" Ben asked, but even as the words left his mouth, he knew.

"I have no idea," Professor Jones said. "It may not even be possible."

Ben closed his eyes. He knew exactly where they could get everything they needed. The only question was time. Could they build such a device before the aliens attacked and captured or killed them all? If they could build it, how would they launch it? And supposing they could build it fast enough and devise a way to fire it at the sun, how could they hope to get out of the system without the flux shield?

"Okay," Ben said. "Wake everyone up. There's no way I'm making this decision on my own."

Chapter 30

Everyone was on the bridge, waiting for him when he came back down from the galley. He had a tray with energy-boosting shots in tiny disposable containers. He took one for himself and one for Kim, then passed the tray on to Magnum and Nance.

The four remaining soldiers were there, along with Professor Jones. Like Ben, they all gathered around Kim's pilot seat. She was sitting even though the ship was still on autopilot. Ben handed her the energy drink and swallowed his down in three fast gulps.

He felt like an empty glove—still shaped like a hand, but crinkled and hollow. If the crew agreed that Professor Jones's plan was best, he would have a lot of work to do in a very short amount of time. There would be no sleep and almost no rest in the hours ahead. The worst part was that, even if he charged ahead until his body gave out on him, there was no guarantee that he could finish in time or that they wouldn't all die trying to carry it out.

"The professor has a plan. I'm going to let him explain it to you," Ben said.

Jones launched into his explanation of the star disruption device. When he was finished, the questions flew around the bridge like lasers in a firefight. Could it be built? Would it really work? What would happen to the Celeste system? Should they consult the crown prince?

"What we can't do," Dial said seriously, "is let the technology get out. If the Royal Imperium can make a device that destroys a solar system, their tyranny will be out of control."

"Only Ben and I will have that information," Professor Jones said. "I would die before I let someone take it from me."

"To be honest, the only thing keeping the Royal Imperium from forcing us to give them the flux shield technology is the war," Ben said. "They're too busy with the aliens to bother with us."

"For the moment," Kim said. "If this plan works, that all changes."

"If the plan works, a lot of things change," Nance said. "Can we really destroy a solar system just to stop a war?"

"The war will be much more devastating," Professor Jones said.

"So how do we do it?" Corporal Dial asked. "How do you build this device? You have spare parts lying around downstairs?"

"Actually, that's another reason I brought everyone together," Ben said. "For the device to work, it will have to be built in an inverted fusion reactor chamber."

"A what?" Corporal Miller asked.

"A fusion chamber," Ben said. "It's where we burn Zexum to power our ships. And once that's made, it has to be encased in a hull that is covered with heat-shielding tiles and the space between is filled with emergency heat-resistant foam."

"Sounds complicated," Kim said.

"It's not a simple build, but it could be done if we had the parts," Ben said.

"But we don't?" Corporal Amadi asked.

"We have the flux shield, and perhaps the rockets that we could modify to fly the device into the sun," Ben said. "Everything else, we'll have to salvage from the *Plato* if the aliens haven't taken it already."

"Damn, this plan sucks," Corporal Miller said.

"A doomsday device," Kim said, shaking her head.

"We're talking about destroying one of the most expensive pieces of property in the galaxy," Nance said. "Even if we could pull it off, wouldn't the Royal Imperium just lock us up and throw away the key?"

"We should be so lucky," Corporal Dial said.

"He's right," Kim agreed. "They'll need a scapegoat. And we'll be essentially handing all the power right back to the Royal Imperium."

"They promised amnesty," Ben said. "And the opportunity for any world that wants to renegotiate the Imperium's control a seat at the table."

"Doesn't mean they'll follow through," Magnum said.

"No doubt," Kim agreed. "The Royal Imperium has never been known as a fair and honest organization."

"But they're the rightful government," Private Rhoades said. "I mean, the royal family is the sovereign ruler of the galaxy, isn't it?"

Everyone looked at the young soldier. Ben knew he was right and wrong at the same time. Just as the idea of destroying the entire solar system just to shut down the wormhole was both right and wrong at the same time.

"So what are we doing?" Kim asked. "Tell me I didn't get out of bed just to attend a planning meeting."

"First, we have to deal with the aliens coming through the mountains," Ben said.

"We've got a plan for that," Corporal Dial said. "They'll be moving through a narrow pass with a tall overhang. We hit that and it should all come straight down on top of them."

"Will it kill them all?" Nance asked.

"No," Dial said. "I can't promise that. We know they're moving a large group of fighters, and at best we hope the avalanche will slow them down."

"Then what?" Kim asked.

"Phase two is hitting the *Plato*," Ben said. "We need to know if they still have the materials we need to build the device before we present the plan to General Pershing. Plus, we need all the time we can get to build it."

"And if we can get the materials?" Nance asked.

"Then we get back to orbit, alert the general," Ben said, "and hope that help is on the way for the Confederates."

"There's a lot of hoping and guessing in this plan," Kim said.

"Don't I know it," Ben replied.

"But we have to try," Nance said. "Will the Confederates help us take back the *Plato*?"

"They better," Kim snapped. "We've been saving their butts since they got to the system."

"We'll ask," Ben said. "But I wouldn't hope for much."

"Any help is better than none at all," Corporal Dial said.

"Then I'll make the call," Ben said. "As soon as I'm done, we should get into position to attack in the mountains.

We don't want the aliens getting through that pass before we're ready."

"Roger that," Corporal Dial said.

Ben walked over to his console and began his briefing with Captain Lawrence. He decided ahead of time to tell the Confederates as little as possible about the plan.

You want what? Captain Lawrence asked.

"Twenty-five veterans," Ben replied. "We need to get some gear from the *Plato*, but the aliens have it under guard. Over."

I can't possibly spare a single man. Not with an army approaching through the mountains. Over.

"What if we stop that army?" Ben said. "We've got a plan to do just that. We stop the alien army, you give us the soldiers we need to attack the *Plato*…" Ben let the question hang for a moment. "Over."

Eight men, all seasoned veterans. That's all I can spare. And I want them all back just as soon as you're finished in the Plato. Over.

Ben looked at Corporal Dial, who mouthed the word "twelve" at him.

"Make it twelve, Captain, you've got a deal. Over."

There was a pause, then a simple reply.

Done! Lawrence, out.

Ben looked around the bridge. He couldn't help but feel a sense of pride. They had a plan, and if it worked, they might just save the galaxy. It took all his strength not to think of what would happen if they failed, or the hundreds of things that could go wrong along the way.

"The plan is a go, people," Ben said. "Let's make it happen!"

Chapter 31

"General, I have Duke Simeon," the communications officer said.

"Very well, I'll take it in my quarters," General Alicia Pershing said. "Captain Davis, you have the con."

"Aye, General. I have the con."

Pershing left the bridge and went to her tiny berth. The room was starting to feel like a prison cell, yet it was the only place on the ship that she had any real privacy. She could have insisted that the captain give up her quarters, but Pershing preferred not to disrupt the operation of the ship. Ultimately, the captain was in command of the vessel; Pershing's job was setting the general strategy for the group of ships she had gathered in the Celeste system.

All in all, she couldn't complain about their situation. If the Krah knew they were there, circling the gas giant, keeping watch over their fleet, they obviously didn't care. No ship had been sent to investigate. And very few were leaving the system. It seemed as if the Krah were amassing their forces, which allowed Pershing to catalog their ships, but also made her feel as if the Royal Imperium was falling behind. She had been waiting for the duke to return with news from the Mersa system, and it seemed that he had finally done so. Soon, it would be time for the *Modulus Echo* to make contact, and Pershing wanted all her ducks in a row before she spoke to the crew of the Kestrel class ship.

In her berth, she perched on the edge of her bunk and brought up the communication program on her touch screen.

Duke Simeon's face appeared. He looked less dashing and more tired than she expected. The sight made her heart sink, knowing that something had happened. Something had caused the sudden change.

"General Pershing, it's good to see you," Duke Simeon said, trying to conjure up his usual enthusiasm but falling short.

"Your Grace," Pershing replied. "You look tired. Are you well?"

"Fine, fine," the duke replied. "A little harried, is all. Unfortunately, news from the Mersa system is not good."

"Tell me."

"Admiral Gravill of the *Indomitable* has taken control of the system," the duke explained. "He has six battleships with him. I'll transmit some video imagery so you can see them. It's a coup, the admiral general is dead, and Queen Ultane is held captive. The admiral is calling himself emperor. It's very bad business all round."

"They let you pass through the system?" General Pershing asked.

"*Let* is too strong a word," he said with a chuckle. "Once they found out who I was, they did try to detain me, but I was able to get away."

"Admiral Gravill is no fool. What does he plan to do about the Krah invasion?"

Duke Simeon's face twitched. "He's claiming that the footage you transmitted of your interview with the alien is fake, that the destruction of the fleet was a terrorist act, and that you are working in league with the Confederates to destroy the Royal Imperium."

General Pershing wasn't surprised, but she was frustrated by the news. Admiral Gravill was accusing her of doing exactly what he was attempting to do. She had expected petty struggles for power. The absence of the king left a void in the power structure of the Royal Imperium, and nature hated a void. That the admiral was attempting to fill it came as no surprise, yet accusing her of being a traitor made things more difficult.

"So we have no help," Pershing said.

"Not yet," Duke Simeon said. "I could go and drum some up, I'm sure of it. A call to action is what we need. The people need to see and hear me."

"No," Pershing said. "You'll only become a pawn in their power games. Besides, we don't have time and there are very few groups with ships to spare. Even if the commanders spread through the galaxy don't see the Krah as a threat, they'll certainly see Admiral Gravill as one. They'll insist on keeping their ships close. Damn, what a travesty. The Krah are here and we're too busy fighting among ourselves to see the danger."

"So what do we do?"

"That depends," Pershing said. "The *Modulus Echo* has made contact. There's still a chance that Professor Jones can come up with a way to close the wormhole. At this point, that is our highest priority. We have to cut the enemy off, then we can deal with their fleet in smaller engagements."

"I stand ready to help," Duke Simeon said.

"Get some rest, then, while you can. I'll be in touch soon."

"Roger that, General," the royal said in a jaunty tone just before ending the transmission.

Pershing wished she could emulate the duke's enthusiasm. But the truth was, they were a tiny force. Just a couple of second-tier warships and a squadron of modified rebel vessels. It wasn't enough to engage the enemy. Even with superior weapons, they were just too outnumbered to make a difference. And as long as the wormhole remained open, the Krah could always recruit more from their own galaxy.

She stood up, feeling suddenly very tired. It reminded her of action, when all her physical energy had been used up and she had to force herself, and sometimes the soldiers under her command, to keep moving forward solely by the force of her will. She had done it before, and she would do it again. The Krah were here, no matter what Admiral Gravill said or what anyone else believed. She couldn't curb their lust for power, but a good commander uses what she knows about her enemies to her advantage. She couldn't bring the fleet to the Celeste system, but perhaps she could bring the aliens to the fleet.

A plan was beginning to form in her mind. It hinged on factors outside her control, but if they could get lucky, perhaps she would have the help she needed to bring the fight to the Krah. One way or another, they had to get control of the wormhole. She smoothed her uniform and composed herself before leaving her tiny room and making her way back to the bridge.

"General on deck!" the watch officer said as she walked back toward her seat.

"Any news from the *Modulus Echo*?" General Pershing asked.

"We're monitoring all frequencies," Captain Davis said. "So far, nothing."

"How long would it take for a signal to reach us out here?"

"Forty-seven minutes, General," the communications officer answered.

"Alright, let's send them a message. I want the *Modulus Echo* to stay in contact with us if possible."

"Do you have something planned?" the captain asked.

"We can't sit here forever and do nothing," Pershing said. "As things stand, we have no help coming. But we have two imperatives that must be addressed. We need to know if the crown prince is really alive, and we have to convince the fleet that the Krah are the real threat. Establishing contact with the *Modulus Echo* is the first step to addressing these imperatives. Until we do that, we must hold the course."

There was a weight on Pershing's shoulders. The time for bold action was upon her, but she couldn't move in haste. She needed to see the potential outcomes of whatever decisions she made. There were more than just lives on the line. The entire future of the human race hung on the results of what she accomplished in the next few hours. She could scarcely breathe if she let her mind linger on what might happen if she failed. It took all her self-control to put those dire consequences out of her head and focus on the limited moves she could make. That was what really mattered, and that was what she was determined to do.

Chapter 32

"Everything's ready," Magnum said.

The *Echo* was hovering at forty thousand feet, even higher than the mountains. Under the cover of darkness, they had flown through the pass they were planning to target and marked the impact points on the ship's computer. There were two blast sights on either mountain that rose on each side of the narrow trail leading between the massive cliffs. Since then, the sun had come up, and the ship's cameras could focus on the trail.

The first of the alien soldiers were already through the pass. Hundreds more were filling the narrow trail. As Ben saw it, the only real drawback to their plan was that they couldn't get the aliens all together in the danger zone. They would have to settle for what they could accomplish—killing some and blocking the progress of the rest.

"We recording?" Ben asked.

"Yes," Nance said. "All cameras that can focus on the canyon are recording."

Ben glanced over at Corporal Dial. He and the other soldiers were standing behind Magnum, who was sitting at his console. The big man looked almost comical in his tiny chair. Dial nodded at Ben, and he gave the order.

"Fire all rockets," he said.

The missiles shot off in rapid succession. On the big display screens, they watched the missiles streak down toward their targets. One camera was zoomed in on the aliens far below, and Ben saw them look up just as the missiles rammed into the mountainside. Dust and debris shot out, filling the narrow valley with a cloud that blocked the view from the *Echo*. They couldn't see what was happening and couldn't hear the rumble or even the explosion, but they saw the tall shelves of rock above the impact sites give way and begin to tumble down.

"Alright," Ben said. "Take us out."

"Without seeing what happened?" Kim asked.

"It'll take hours for the dust to clear," Corporal Dial said. "Without boots on the ground, there's no way to know how effective the detonation was."

"We'll just have to trust the plan," Ben said. "Hopefully, we've bought ourselves enough time to get what we need from the *Plato*."

"Alright," Kim said. "It's a shame, though."

Ben agreed, but he felt a tinge of guilt as well. The success of their plan resulted in the deaths of who knew how many aliens. It felt wrong to hope for a high casualty rate, and yet that was exactly what was needed to save the lives of the Confederates in Royal City.

The *Echo* flew out of the mountains and across the wide lake. The water below sparkled in the dazzling sunlight, and Ben wondered how they could even contemplate destroying such unspoiled beauty. Royal City came into view, and he was once again reminded of gigantic jewels lined up along the shores of the lake. No resort guests were lounging on the wooden docks or eating in the cafés. The Confederates were completely out of sight.

Ben keyed his mic and spoke into the tall, narrow device. It was old fashioned, but effective, like so many things on the old Kestrel class ship.

"Royal City, this is the *Modulus Echo*, on approach. Over."

We see you, Modulus Echo. We're standing by to board, as soon as you touch down in front of the palace. Over.

"Alright, we'll touch down in sixty seconds," Ben said. "Can we get one of the *Plato*'s engineers to join us? Over."

There was a slight pause, then the communications operator's voice came back.

Affirmative.

Ben felt a sense of relief. He hadn't thought to request the engineer earlier, but someone who knew the *Plato*'s systems would be invaluable to him. And he wouldn't mind some help in building the professor's doomsday device either.

"We're going down to the cargo hatch," Corporal Dial said.

His four-man squad was back in their battle rattle and ready for a fight. They jogged down the stairs to the cargo hold. Ben and Magnum used the ship's cameras to scan the trees, shrubs, and short hills across from the palace. The aliens had spread through the green space but had yet to show themselves. Sniper teams were in place on the building rooftops, but no shot had been fired. Ben didn't think the aliens had weapons that could threaten the *Echo*, but he wasn't willing to risk his life, or his ship, on that belief.

"Open the cargo hatch," Kim said. "We'll be on the ground in five seconds."

Ben pressed an icon on the display screen built into his console. The rear hatch slowly began to open. There was still no sign of the enemy fighters. Ben wondered if they were actually fighters at all. More likely they were just spotters for the army they expected from the mountains. Still, he could feel the tension in the air as the ship settled onto the ground.

From down below in the cargo bay, Ben heard the Royal Imperium soldiers barking at the Confederates. The sound of heavy boots on the metal deck was unmistakable. Ben waited for Dial's signal, a simple mic click on their com-link. As soon as he heard it, Ben tapped the icon to close the rear hatch.

"Closing the rear cargo door," Ben said. "Get us in the air."

"Amen to that," Kim said.

She nudged the throttle forward, taking them in a slow ascent until the rear hatch closed and sealed.

"How do you want to do this, Ben?" Kim asked as she flew away from Royal City and toward the clearing in the forest where the *Plato* had crash-landed only a few days before.

"Can we do a high-altitude flyover?" Ben asked. "I'd like to get the lay of the land before we make our final plan. There might be a place we can land out of sight of the aliens guarding the *Plato*."

"Has it occurred to anyone that the *Plato* might be full of aliens? There could be over two hundred on that ship," Kim said, taking the *Echo* into a higher altitude.

"Yes, that's why we need to do a flyby," Ben said.

"Well, I'm doing it, I just don't want to send you all in there if it's a suicide mission. We could still make a run for it. And it would be a whole lot easier with the flux shield around our ship."

"Ben," Corporal Dial said, coming up the stairs with a thin, redheaded lieutenant. "This is the senior engineer from the *Plato*. Lieutenant Baker."

The engineer stuck out a hand as Ben turned to face him. Ben shook the man's hand, feeling the callouses from years of hard work.

"Call me Mark," the lieutenant said.

"Okay, Mark, glad to have you with us," Ben said.

"What exactly are we doing?" Mark asked.

"We're scavenging some parts for an experimental device," Ben said. "We need to remove the *Plato*'s artificial gravity generator, the emergency heat-shielding foam, and a large section of the fusion reactor housing."

"Good grief, I'm almost afraid to ask what you're building," Mark replied.

"We'll tell you once we get the parts," Ben said. "What we need from you is help getting to them on the ship. Once we've cleared the aliens, of course."

"Well, most of that is easy enough, but I don't have a saw powerful enough to cut through the fusion reactor housing," Mark said.

"I do. We built ours from spare parts and pieces."

"Then I suppose it's all doable. It might take a while, though."

"Time is what we don't have a lot of," Dial said. "Once we hit the aliens, there's no telling how long it will be before they send reinforcements."

"Kim's doing a flyby so we can see what's down there," Ben said. "Let's make a plan."

The first pass was discouraging. There were three groups of the aliens around the *Plato*: one on each side, and one guarding the cargo bay doors near the rear. Not unlike the *Echo*, the cargo bay on the Royal Imperium ship was next to the engineering bay. To make matters worse, there were even more aliens pulling pieces of the ship's hull off her. Dial pointed out that there were at least as many workers as soldiers. And to top it all off, there were no other places to land within miles of the *Plato*.

"So," Dial said. "Looks like we'll have to make a fast landing and hit them hard before they can get into the ship to take cover."

"Is that possible?" Ben asked.

"Anything is possible," Dial said. "But it isn't very likely. Once they're inside, our weapons won't be as useful, and getting them out will take time."

"Are the workers dangerous?" Mark asked.

"I don't think so," Dial said. "But I wouldn't underestimate that possibility. We have to assume every alien down there is armed and dangerous."

Ben suddenly had an idea. "Hang on a second," Ben said.

He left his seat on the bridge and walked over to the med bay. When he opened the door, the first thing he noticed was the smell. Someone had fouled the place up. Ben looked through the rectangular room, to the back where Le Croix was sitting on a stool, leaned against the wall. He stood up and raised his hands, palms up, as if to say he didn't know what was going on. There was a quiet giggle, and Ben stepped into the room. The crown prince was still on an exam table, but he was awake. The sedatives had worn off, and he lay on his back, laughing to himself. Ben saw that the gown Professor Jones had put on him after cleaning the prince was wet.

"Prince Godfred?" Ben said as he slowly approached.

"Yes, yes, yes," the prince managed to say before a fit of giggles took hold of him again.

"Are you okay?"

"Quite," he wheezed. "Never better. Never…"

The giggles overcame him again. The stench of urine was strong, and Ben knew it would have to be cleaned up soon, but he didn't have time for that. Instead, he walked to where Staff Sergeant Visher lay. He was still asleep, peaceful looking despite the nasty wound in his stomach that Ben knew was just below the thin disposable medical gown.

"I gave him another dose of sedatives," Le Croix said. "He was in a lot of pain."

"I can only imagine," Ben said. "What about you? How are you feeling?"

"Like my skin is crawling," Le Croix said. "Almost like I'm coming apart at the seams. I guess I am."

He rubbed his hand across one hip where the robotic leg met human flesh. It was red, inflamed, and covered in hives. Ben thought it looked painful.

"Can you walk?" Ben asked.

"Sure, I'm fully capable. What can I do to help?"

"We're still making a plan," Ben said. "But if you're willing to fight the aliens, we could use you."

Le Croix hesitated for just a second. Then he nodded. "Okay, I'll do it. What do you need?"

"Head downstairs and wait with the others," Ben said. "Once I have things lined up, I'll come down and explain it all."

"A pre-op briefing," Le Croix said. "Can't wait."

He stood up, towering over Ben, and walked easily toward the exit. Ben hurried past the prince, who didn't seem to notice him at all, and back out into the atrium. Dial walked over, his hand on the pistol in his belt.

"You're letting Le Croix out?"

"He's our secret weapon," Ben said.

"What?" Dial asked. "You trust him?"

"No," Ben said. "But we don't have a chance of surprising the aliens. Not really. I can drop your team in the forest, but we would have to be miles away from the clearing or we'd be heard."

"So what are you thinking?" Dial asked.

"You said the aliens are fast," Ben explained. "We'll drop Le Croix off and let him run to the clearing on his robotic legs. Once there, he can draw the aliens away from the *Plato.*"

"Or he can warn them we're coming," Dial said. "It's a bad idea, Ben. We can't trust him. He turned traitor once already."

"True, but we've had some time to talk," Ben said. "Look, I know he's conflicted. He wanted to be part of their culture where being a warrior is honored, but his prosthetics aren't taking. Soon, he'll be crippled again, worse than he was before. He knows there's no future with the Krah."

"So you really think he'll help us?"

"I think if he can draw the aliens away from the *Plato,* then we have a shot of getting down there and taking it from them," Ben said. "If not, if he betrays us, we're not any worse off. I mean, we can call the whole thing off if we need to."

"Alright, so we drop him in the woods, let him go in on foot, and convince the aliens to move away from the ship," Dial said. "What's next?"

"Then we hit them," Ben said. "Kim can bring us straight down with the rear hatch open. We take out the aliens and get into the ship."

"So simple," Dial said with a grin.

"Best-laid plans and all of that," Ben replied. "It's worth a shot, right?"

"Sure, I'm game. But I'm not giving him a weapon."

"Agreed," Ben said.

They headed down to the cargo hold with Lieutenant Mark Baker. Ben explained his plan to the Confederates who were looking at Major Le Croix with unconcealed disgust. The other members of Corporal Dial's team didn't look as though they liked the plan, but none argued. Ben hurried back up to the bridge while they rigged a harness that would fit around Major Le Croix's thick waist.

"Okay, take us down a few miles from the *Plato,*" Ben said.

"There's nowhere to land, Ben," Kim said.

"We're not landing. Major Le Croix is going to rappel down and go in on foot."

"Can we trust him?" Nance asked.

"We're going to find out," Ben said. "If he does what I've proposed, he'll pull the aliens away from the *Plato*. That should give us the opportunity to land between them and the ship."

"So we can be attacked?" Kim said. "I mean, it's a tiny flaw, but one I'm not crazy about."

"No, we'll open the rear hatch on the way down. The soldiers can fire on the aliens while Mark and I get on board the *Plato*."

"What if it's a trap?" Kim asked. "What if Le Croix leaves aliens on board to kill you when you go in?"

"Then you're to take off and get out of the system," Ben said.

"Oh, that's a lovely idea," Kim said. "Why has no one considered it before now?"

"We know the plan is risky," Ben said. "But this might give us our best chance to get what we need."

"I'll go with you," Magnum said. "Just in case."

"I'd feel better if you stayed with the ship," Ben said.

"I could say the same about you," Kim said. "Having Magnum with you will give you a fighting chance if you run into trouble."

"I agree," Nance said, looking over at Magnum. "He should go."

"Alright," Ben said. "If that's what you all want, I'm grateful for the help. Once we're off the ship, you should take to the air again. Keep watch until we get the parts we need."

"No problem," Kim said. "Just make sure you come back again. Alive preferably."

"I'll do my best," Ben said. "I'm going to see Le Croix off, then get my tools together."

He left the bridge and hurried down to the cargo hold. The rear hatch was opening and Ben could see the treetops below them. Corporal Amadi tossed out a rope, while Miller and Dial checked Le Croix's harness.

"You ready for this?" Ben asked.

"Sure," Le Croix said. "Which way is the *Plato*?"

Ben tapped his com-link and repeated the question.

"Four miles, due south," Nance replied.

"I can be there in twenty minutes once I'm on the ground," Le Croix said. "I'll get the aliens to the far side of the clearing if possible. But I can't guarantee they won't take cover in the trees."

"Just do what you can," Ben said. "Try to get everyone out of that ship."

"Roger that," Le Croix said. "See you on the ground."

Without a second's hesitation, he jumped out of the back of the ship. There was a steady whir as the rope slid through the harness. Then the rope went slack.

"Dang," Amadi said from the edge of the open hatch. "That was a fast descent."

"Couldn't get away from us fast enough," Dial said.

"Well, he'll have to prove himself now," Ben said. "If he's a traitor, at least he's off the ship."

The thought of Holt and his treachery of leaving a bomb disguised as Zexum fuel on the *Echo* sent a shiver through Ben. He didn't like the thought of what a saboteur might do to his ship. But he didn't have time to worry about it.

The thought of Zexum made him remember he needed to switch out the fuel tank.

"Mark, give me hand, will you?"

"Sure," the engineer said, following Ben and Magnum back to the engineering bay. "This ship is really something."

"Yeah, we rebuilt her piece by piece," Ben said.

"Where did you find her?"

"In the salvage fields of Torrent Four."

Mark ran a hand across the bulkhead that separated the cargo bay from engineering. "Good bones."

"The best," Ben said. "She's got plenty of life still in her."

With the three of them working together, it only took ten minutes to exchange the nearly empty Zexum tank for a full one. Ben felt better knowing that no matter what happened to him, the girls had plenty of fuel to get off the planet and across the galaxy.

While Magnum broke out weapons from a hidden compartment, Ben retrieved tools for himself and Mark. They each had a tool belt and carried a chest of extra tools between them. Ben tapped his com-link button on the collar of his shirt.

"Are we all online?" Ben asked

"Alpha team reads you," Dial said.

"Bravo and Charlie teams are ready," said a sergeant with the Confederate fighters.

"We hear you too," Nance added.

"We're at five thousand feet," Kim said. "A mile and a half from the clearing. I can see across the top of the *Plato* into the field beyond. Looks like the spider people are building something from the *Plato*'s spare parts."

"Dirty cannibals," Mark muttered.

"Le Croix should be there any minute," Ben said. "Everyone, stand by."

They moved from the engineering bay back to the rear hatch with the soldiers. Ben had a pistol in his belt and a rifle slung across his back. Magnum stayed between Ben and the rear door. It took several more tension-heavy minutes before Kim responded again.

"I think I just saw Le Croix come out of the forest," she said. "It's almost time."

Ben wondered how much time he had left. Their plan wasn't just dangerous, it was practically insane. A device that would destroy an entire system? Who had ever dreamed of such a destructive force? And they might not even make it that far. He might be cut down just trying to get onto the *Plato*. Or overwhelmed and slaughtered while they were gathering the parts they needed on board. Was he breathing his final breaths? Who could say? It made him feel weak and more than a little sick, but he didn't have a choice. He had to go forward. He had to press on and try to do what he could to help humanity before the aliens took over.

He tried not to think about the possibility that their solution might be worse than living with the Krah. Perhaps, even conquered, they would be no worse off than they had been under the dominance of the Royal Imperium. Were they planning to destroy the Celeste system for nothing? He couldn't even let himself dwell on the possibility. Getting the parts they would need to build Professor Jones's device would be difficult enough. And even with all the parts, they might not be able to build the thing, so he decided just to focus on the task at hand. Get to the *Plato*, get the parts they needed, and get back on board the *Echo*—alive.

Chapter 33

Le Croix felt a bittersweet joy as he ran effortlessly through the forest. In some ways, it felt like he was a teenager again: strong, fast, tireless, and free. In other ways, the sensation was like nothing he'd ever felt before. The robotic legs moved at his command, and yet they took no energy. It was like he was riding a strange running machine, rather than striding through the forest.

He wished the run would last forever, that his body wouldn't reject the alien prosthetics, and that he could be a whole man again. But before he knew it, he came to the edge of the clearing. He could see through the trees, across the field, to where the *Plato* lay slightly tilted on the ground. Between where he stood and the ship, dozens of workers were busy constructing something. Le Croix noticed a priest overseeing the construction and guessed that they were building a temple. The Krah had a strange connection to their religion. There were both an homage to be paid and a rank to be gained from the priests. The more a person gave, the greater the odds of being rewarded with a higher rank.

Le Croix wasted no time and went striding out of the forest with his head held high. He walked straight across the field toward the priest and tapped the alien on the shoulder. The priest turned, eyes widening with surprise.

"I have been sent to warn you," he said.

"Warn me of what? Who are you?"

"Trooper Le Croix. Chieftain Grubat is my leader. There are dangers on board that ship."

"Danger? What danger? The workers have said nothing about it."

"The humans can set their vessels to self-destruct," Le Croix said. "We should move the warriors away and I will check to make sure it is safe."

"We do not fear the humans, or their propensity for wastefulness," the priest said. "I see that Chieftain Grubat has been busy experimenting on his prisoners, but only a priest can elevate a warrior in rank."

"Of course," Le Croix said. "High Priest Alwain elevated me to the rank of trooper after I defeated Yarl Cherbak in single combat."

Le Croix made his single headdress tendril wave to the side of his head.

"I have taken this from him but allowed him to live. I have shared many of the secrets of my former people and been given the great honor of enhancement."

"You serve Chieftain Grubat, but you fought Yarl Cherbak?"

"I fought my chief's son because Yarl Cherbak sought to overthrow his father to distance himself from the shame of their defeat before the fleet arrived."

Le Croix could only hope he was convincing the priest that he was telling the truth. The conversation was taking much longer than he'd hoped. Finally, the priest nodded.

"You can isolate and resolve the danger on the human vessel?"

"Indeed," Le Croix said. "But it is dangerous. We should move everyone away until it is safe."

The priest began barking orders. The workers responded instantly, dropping their loads and moving toward the far end of the clearing. Le Croix felt a wave of relief. But that feeling was soon swept away as a group of warriors approached. One of which, a large Krah warrior with a spear instead of an ax, challenged him.

"What lies are these? The human ship is no danger."

"Yarl Bulfor," the priest said. "It does us no harm to make certain the humans have not sabotaged their forsaken vessel. They are known for such actions."

"Bah! Lies," the big warrior said. "I do not believe it. I do not believe you, human dog."

"I am Trooper Le Croix."

"You are a traitor," the big Krah warrior growled.

Le Croix didn't hesitate, despite being surrounded by several Krah warriors. His left hand shot out and struck Bulfor in the throat. The Krah didn't have the same physiology as humans, but it was close. The Krah warrior staggered back, and Le Croix jerked the spear from his hand. He could have stabbed the big warrior in the chest, but instead he stepped back, allowing the big Yarl to regain his composure.

"I challenge you, Yarl Bulfor," Le Croix said with a sneer.

"I...accept," the alien said, his voice rasping from his shocked windpipe.

One of the Yarl's underlings handed him an ax, and the group spread wide. Le Croix peered over the Yarl's shoulder and saw that the other warriors were hurrying to see the fight. There was plenty of space for the *Modulus Echo* to land; all Le

Croix had to do was keep the warriors occupied for a few minutes.

Personal combat was a sacred custom among the Krah. It was a way to settle differences, a way to gain rank and prestige. A warrior of lower rank had two choices in a dispute. The first was to bow to their superior, and the second was to challenge them in combat. But a fight among the Krah was a fight to the death. Although mercy was sometimes offered, such as when Le Croix had fought Yarl Cherbak, more often the contest ended with one warrior dead. If a direct underling defeated his master, he also gained the right to take his fallen leader's place. Often, a new Yarl or chieftain would then have to survive several battles to keep his or her position. Female Krah were just as strong and deadly as males, and many were highly regarded warriors. Le Croix wasn't afraid to fight Yarl Bulfor, but then he didn't need to defeat the alien. Keeping the warriors occupied long enough for the *Echo* to come in for a landing was all that he needed to accomplish. And if he died in the process, then he wouldn't have to watch his body reject the alien prosthetics that would leave him a blind cripple.

"I will rip your throat out, human," Bulfor snarled.

"You can try," Le Croix taunted. "But I have your weapon. Soon I will take your glory and send your body back to the mud."

The alien screamed and charged at Le Croix, who started to bring the head of the spear down, but instead reversed himself and lashed out with the butt of the weapon as he hopped to one side. Yarl Bulfor had too much momentum to change course or stop, and when the shaft of the spear slapped hard against his knee, the alien pitched forward onto his face.

Once more, Le Croix could have continued the attack, perhaps even pinned the Yarl to the ground with the spear through his body, but instead he sauntered away, twirling the weapon.

Le Croix had studied many fighting forms during his years as a Special Forces officer, including staffs and spears. He felt just as comfortable fighting with the spear than he did with a gun in his hand.

"Do you like that dirt, Yarl Bulfor? Better get used to it."

The alien got quickly to his feet and turned around to face Le Croix, who saw newfound respect in the warrior's eyes. Bulfor moved more slowly and was careful. Le Croix had learned that many of the Krah warriors preferred brute strength and aggressiveness over skill and tactics. The two combatants circled each other for several seconds. Le Croix spent the time straining to hear the whine of the *Modulus Echo*'s engines, but the sky was clear and there was no sound of an approaching ship.

Yarl Bulfor feinted several times but couldn't draw Le Croix out. The human was stalling but continued to grin as he taunted his opponent. Bulfor started to his left, then spun right. Le Croix failed to anticipate the move and dodged to his left, which brought him too close for his spear to be of much use. Bulfor swung his ax hard in a short chop. Le Croix was able to block it with the spear's wooden shaft, but the wood cracked. Bulfor kicked out, hooking Le Croix's robotic leg behind the knee and knocking him off balance. The metallic legs were heavy, but not invulnerable. Le Croix stumbled forward and dropped onto his knees. Bulfor followed the attack with a mighty chop that would have sent Le Croix's head rolling across the clearing, but the human dropped to his side and rolled clear.

Bulfor didn't wait for Le Croix to regain his feet, but rushed to continue the attack. The alien had a large section of metal across his chest and right shoulder. His right arm had been removed and replaced with a delicate, yet powerful enhancement. When Le Croix swung the spear at Bulfor, he lifted his robotic arm to block the weapon. The spear shaft hit the metal arm and broke in two. The spearhead continued forward and stabbed Bulfor's face. He jerked backward and wailed in pain. Le Croix, on his back, kicked out hard into the side of Bulfor's knee. The sound of bones snapping and cartilage popping was loud. The Yarl dropped to the ground. When Le Croix got to his feet, Bulfor was struggling to rise but couldn't. His broken leg was a gruesome sight, and there was blood gushing from a laceration down the side of the Yarl's face.

Le Croix cast the wooden butt of the spear aside and bent low to pick up Bulfor's ax. At that moment, the roar of the *Echo*'s engines made the rest of the group turn. Le Croix didn't look up. Instead, he dropped to the ground and covered his head as the soldiers on board the ship opened fire.

Chapter 34

Kim was descending, and while the artificial gravity made Ben feel as though they weren't moving at all, the world outside the ship was rocking slightly. The *Echo* was built for vertical landings. She could hover and slowly descend, but Kim was bringing the ship down faster than normal. The soldiers opened fire while the ship was still thirty or forty feet from the ground. Ben had seen Le Croix and one of the aliens fighting. It was a good tactic to bring the other aliens into a group. They were crowded close to see the action and didn't see the *Echo* until it was too late.

The Royal Imperium Special Forces commandos fired laser bolts from their assault rifles. The Confederates didn't have premium equipment. They were armed with older projectile weapons that boomed as they fired in short staccato bursts. Magnum joined in with the Lancet AR rifle, which was a laser weapon but more powerful. It vaporized flesh and sent chunks of soil flying with every shot, sometimes killing several of the aliens in a single blast.

The soldiers targeted the warrior aliens first. The circle around Major Le Croix was quickly neutralized. The worker aliens had been near the fight but didn't attempt to crowd in close the way the warriors had. Many ran in panic at the first blast from the descending spaceship. Ben saw them disappear into the woods, including a strange-looking alien with a long, pointed helmet of some kind. Unlike the others, the helmeted alien had no robotic prosthetics, although Ben couldn't be sure the helmet itself wasn't an artificial enhancement.

"Confederate team, set a defensive perimeter around the *Plato*," Corporal Dial ordered as the *Echo* touched down. "Alpha team, go get Major Le Croix. I'll stay with Ben and Lieutenant Baker inside the *Plato*. Stay alert, comms on, weapons hot. Any sign of the enemy should be met with deadly force. Now move!"

Ben hustled out of the *Echo* along with the other soldiers. His only weapon was the pistol he carried in a holster slung low on his right hip and fastened with a strap around his thigh to keep the gun from flopping around when he ran. The tools in the heavy belt he wore high on his waist, secured with shoulder straps that looked like old-fashioned suspenders, jingled and clanked as he ran. Ben was breathing hard by the time they entered the rear hatch of the *Plato* even though it wasn't very far away.

"Stay here," Dial said. "Magnum and I will proceed into the ship and make sure it's safe."

"Just use the central corridor," Mark reminded them. "Engineering is the first three doors on either side."

"Roger that," Dial said. "Once we clear the corridor, Ben will come up and hold that position while we check the engineering spaces for any sign of the aliens."

Ben nodded and drew his pistol. Magnum gave him a reassuring nod, then hurried through the open cargo section of the Royal Imperium ship.

Ben could see the empty weapon racks and the scattered debris left behind by the Confederates who had been transported on the ship.

"Were those racks empty when you landed here?" Ben asked.

"Yes," Mark said. "We removed them to ship missiles and torpedoes before taking the rebels on board."

"At least the aliens didn't get them," Ben said.

"From the looks of things, they're only taking the hull plates," Mark said. "Any idea what they're building?"

"No clue," Ben said.

"Corridor is clear," Corporal Dial barked at them. "Ben, you and the lieutenant stay here. If any of those bastards show up down the hallway, shoot them."

"Okay," Ben said, his mouth feeling dry.

Magnum disappeared into one of the engineering bays, and Corporal Dial went into another. The ship's systems were down, which meant that they felt the planet's gravity. The ship was tilted, and everything seemed a bit odd. Ben sat down the crate he was carrying with Lieutenant Baker's help. He checked the safety on his pistol again, ensuring it was off and ready to fire.

"You ever shoot that thing?" Baker asked.

"A few times," Ben admitted.

"You ever…you know?"

"Kill someone?" Ben asked.

Mark nodded. He looked worried, and Ben felt sorry for him. The man was an engineer who had probably joined the Royal Imperium Fleet thinking he would never actually be in danger. Space was dangerous, but it wasn't like being in a fight and knowing someone wanted to kill you.

"I grew up on Torrent Four," Ben said.

"Never heard of it," Mark replied, licking his dry lips and glancing nervously down the corridor.

"Most people haven't," Ben said. "It's a junk world, and the Royal Imperium only police a few major cities. Everywhere else is exactly what you'd expect."

"Not a safe space?"

"No," Ben said with a chuckle. "Just the opposite. But you learn to look after yourself."

"Hence the weapon," Mark said.

"I never had anything this nice on Torrent Four, but we got by just the same."

"You know, I heard a rumor that the Special Forces people had you all on some backwater planet. That they could have taken you out, but the admiral general wouldn't let them."

"Lucky for us," Ben said.

"Is it true?"

Ben nodded. "We went back to Torrent Four to get parts. They had us under surveillance for a few days while an armada gathered in orbit around the planet."

"And the gravity shield? Is that real too?"

"Yes," Ben said. "Professor Jones can explain the science, but basically we use wave generators to stream a swirl of gravity around the ship from the art grav gennie. It's effective against all the weapons your fleet threw at us."

"Wow, that's saying something," Mark said.

Dial returned from the room he was searching. He nodded to Ben. "That one's clear."

"Okay, thanks," Ben said.

"The artificial gravity generator is in there," Mark explained. "I can have it out in fifteen minutes if you like."

"That's perfect," Ben said. "Go ahead. I'll hold this position until the soldiers are done."

A few seconds after Mark left the corridor, Magnum reappeared.

"They've been pulling stuff from that room," Magnum said. "But it's clear."

Ben nodded, a sinking feeling in the pit of his stomach. He had no idea what the aliens were after, or why they might take some things before others. The only thing that was certain was that the aliens were reusing what they salvaged. It made sense that, if they were building most things, the hull plating was the most desirable component from the down Imperium ship. Even if they planned to use the power plant or life-support systems, they would need to build something to house them in outside the ship.

It seemed like an eternity before Dial came out of the room he had been checking. There was no telling what the aliens were up to, or if they might come back. The only thing Ben knew for sure was that he needed to hurry. Getting what they needed was important, but they couldn't take long getting it without running the risk that more aliens would arrive and massacre them all.

"It's clear," Dial said. "I'll stay out here and keep watch."

"Thanks," Ben said. "Send Magnum my way once he's done."

"Copy that," the commando said with a nod. Ben saw him tap his throat mic with one finger. "Alpha team, report."

Ben stepped into the engineering bay and saw large complex machines. Fortunately, the fusion reactor was easy to identify. Much like the one he had rigged up on the *Echo*, the *Plato*'s reactor had a large window where the engineers could observe the burning Zexum gas during operation. Ben didn't need the glass. He needed the thick, well-insulated cladding of the chamber itself. The chamber was listed as tantalum carbide, which Ben knew could withstand temperatures that would melt most metals and incinerate flesh. He pulled a small handheld cutting device. It was a simple angle grinder, but Ben had mounted a larger diamond-edged cutting wheel. With a flick of a switch, the device began spinning, and Ben started cutting into the fusion reactor. The tool made a loud, grinding squeal as it cut the tantalum carbide ceramic. Sparks flew in a dazzling shower around him, and Ben didn't even notice Magnum come up behind him.

The big man waited until Ben finished his first cut before tapping him on the shoulder. Ben jumped, turning with a look of terror on his face that made Magnum chuckle.

"Just me," he said.

"You scared me," Ben said. "I didn't hear you come in."

"I'm not surprised. That thing's loud."

"Yeah, but I can't do anything about that. Why don't you see if you can find their manual fire suppression systems? We'll need three or four tanks moved over to the *Echo*."

"Got it," Magnum said, moving off to search for the tanks.

Ben got back to work. He made one long cut and two smaller cuts on the side of the fusion reactor. He hoped that the device the professor needed would be small enough that they could use just a couple of long pieces cut into smaller sections. If so, he could cut two large sections from the *Plato*'s fusion reactor and get them aboard the *Echo* to actually build the box that would protect the device from the heat of the sun.

"I have the artificial gravity generator," Mark said as he came into the room where Ben was working.

He held up the device. It was a silver ball slightly smaller than his head and mounted on a short shaft. Except for the size, it was exactly the same as the gravity generator on the *Echo*.

"That's perfect," Ben said, doing a quick mental calculation.

He would need a few electrical components inside the device, as well as a power source, but he was fairly confident that the project wouldn't take up too much space.

"We can always use more power cells," Ben said. "And any surplus supplies that may be easy to move."

"Tools too?"

"Always," Ben said.

He went back to cutting. If they had another diamond-tipped cutter, they could work twice as fast, but unfortunately, there was only one. Ben stayed focused, even when he occasionally heard chatter over the com-link. They had been on-site for nearly an hour when he finally finished the second cut. He hefted the large sheets of ceramic metal and hurried back out the door.

"You finished?" Dial asked.

"Yes," Ben said.

"It's about damn time," the commando responded. "Alright, all teams, prepare for evac. *Modulus Echo*, we are moving your way."

"Roger that," Kim replied, her voice all business.

Ben had forgotten that he'd ordered the ship to take off as soon as they had disembarked. Magnum was standing at the rear of the *Plato*, along with the trio of Spec Ops commandos from Dial's platoon. On the deck was a sizable pile of supplies. Ben stepped to the edge of the open hatch and looked up. The sky was dazzling, but he could make out the dark shape of the *Modulus Echo* descending.

"Alright, let's get this gear loaded ASAP," Dial said, taking charge.

Ben didn't mind. He knew their goals were aligned, and the corporal knew much more about leading a military operation.

"I want the Confederate team to rendezvous on my position at the rear hatch of the *Plato*."

"Roger that," snapped a gruff voice over the com-link.

Ben leaned over toward Corporal Dial. "Major Le Croix?"

"He's fine. I had Alpha team escort him here. He's waiting just outside."

Ben felt relieved but knew he couldn't fully relax until they got onto the *Modulus Echo* and were back in the air. The ship came down with a roar and settled on the ground nearby. Ben saw the rear hatch opening, and he bent to pick up his load of large ceramic plating that he had cut from the fusion reactor. He started out of the *Plato* but noticed movement in the trees. He stopped, searching hard for whatever was out there in the shadows of the forest. After a few seconds, Corporal Dial joined him. The Confederates were moving past, but Ben could see a shadowy figure watching from behind the trunk of a large tree. It was the masked alien.

"You see that?" Ben said.

"Yeah, he's been watching us the whole time," Dial replied. "He's not a fighter, though. No weapons that we could see. Corporal Amadi got a good look earlier."

"That's the priest," Major Le Croix said, coming up behind Ben with an armload of surplus metal from the ship. "They aren't a direct threat."

"A priest?" Dial asked. "Is that what they're building out here? A church?"

"A temple," Le Croix corrected him. "The priests are powerful in the Krah culture. They're dependent on the warriors but have the authority to promote them in rank."

"As long as it isn't a threat, I don't care what it can do," Dial said. "Let's keep moving."

"Right," Ben said, stumbling forward again.

His load was heavy and awkward, but he managed to get it to the rear of the *Echo*. Once there, Magnum took the heat-resistant materials from him and carried them up into the ship. Ben waited long enough to ensure that everything was being carried to the engineering bay, then pulled the lever as Corporal Dial's commandos came on board. He also tapped his com-link to activate the device.

"We're all on board," Ben said.

"Outstanding," Kim said. "That was a lot easier than I expected."

Almost too easy, Ben thought to himself. He looked over at Major Le Croix, who was leaning against a crate of food. They had gotten what they needed to build the professor's doomsday device, but Ben wasn't confident that the major wasn't playing them for fools. He wanted Le Croix back upstairs and safely away from the work he was about to begin.

Ben leaned close to Dial. "Can you have your people take Le Croix up to the galley and keep him occupied up there?"

"That shouldn't be a problem," Dial said.

The corporal rallied the other three members of his team and casually suggested to Le Croix that they get some grub. He seemed happy to comply, and Ben watched him go up.

"What now?" Magnum asked as he came out from the engineering bay.

"If you have time, I could use your help laying out the components of the professor's device," Ben said.

"Sure," Magnum replied.

"Kim," Ben said into his com-link. "Can you send down the professor?"

"Sure, he's on his way," Kim replied.

"What's our ETA on reaching orbit?"

"An hour," Nance said. "All systems are good."

"We'll call if we need you," Kim said. "The girls have this covered."

"Alright," Ben said. "Talk to you soon."

Ben walked over to the stairs where Professor Jones was coming down from the main deck.

"Did you get what we need?" Jones asked.

"I got the main components, but I need you to show me exactly what you need built," Ben replied.

"I have a rough sketch," Professor Jones said holding up a data pad.

"Care if I join you?" Lieutenant Baker asked.

"The more, the merrier," Ben said, leading the way in the engineering bay to start working on what he was thinking more often of as the doomsday weapon.

Chapter 35

"Almost to orbit," Kim said. "Better call Ben and Magnum up."

She could have tapped into the com-link herself, but they were very close to breaking orbit. The blue sky seemed thin, and Kim knew that at any second it would fade, revealing outer space and the hundreds of Krah ships in the Celeste system. She wanted all her focus on flying the *Modulus Echo,* and even something as simple as tapping her com-link controls was a distraction she didn't feel they could afford.

"I'm on it," Nance said.

Kim liked just the girls on the bridge. She and Nance were more than capable of flying the ship and overseeing all the systems that were necessary for the crew. It was empowering to realize that she and Nance were more than just crew members, but women with essential skills they were using to make the *Modulus Echo* one of the most famous ships in the galaxy. Still, without Ben and Magnum on the bridge, it sometimes felt as if something was missing. Kim felt better knowing they were behind her, doing what they could to ensure the ship was safe and their mission was successful.

"Scanning comms," Nance said. "There's a lot of interference."

As if to illustrate what she had said, the sky faded from blue to black and Kim saw dozens of clusters of ships in orbit above them.

"Too many ships blocking the signals?" Kim asked.

"Actually, I think their radio waves are crowding out our own signals."

"Do we have something?" Ben said as he came bounding up the steps from the lower deck.

"I'm working on it," Nance said.

"Can those ships see us?" Ben asked Kim.

"I don't see why not," Kim replied. "We're high enough. And with this many ships in the system, they have to be using radar just to keep from having accidental collisions."

"Maybe that's what's muddying our comm feed," Nance said.

"Hopefully, we're just another blip on their screens," Ben said.

"Should we ask Le Croix what their capabilities are?" Magnum said.

"I'd rather not," Ben said. "I'm still not fully convinced the aliens can't see and hear what he does. Plus, he never left the planet with them. He may not know much about their vessels or their technological capabilities."

"I've got something, but it's rough," Nance said.

...confirmation...the Crown...Godfred...

Static made the message almost impossible to understand. Nance kept working with the signal. The only thing that was clear to Kim was that whoever was sending the message wanted to confirm that they had the prince on board and that he was alive.

"Great," Ben said. "They want to see the prince."

"Is that a problem?" Nance asked.

"No, not entirely," Ben said. "He was awake earlier. But he's not himself yet. For all I know, he may never be completely sane again."

"Are any of the royal family sane?" Kim asked.

Magnum chuckled at her joke.

"Well, that may be true, but they don't normally wet the bed. Our man has. I'll see what I can do. Nance, see if you can isolate where that signal is coming from. I'd prefer to do a tight-beam broadcast, just in case the aliens can intercept our transmissions."

"Working on it," Nance said. "We should be able to encrypt the message too. That should at least slow things down."

Kim worked to keep the ship right at the edge of orbit. If she wasn't careful, there was just enough gravitational pull to drag them back down where the planet's atmosphere could reflect the communication signal before it reached them.

"I think I've got something," Nance said. "The signal is getting clearer. Hold this course, Kim."

"Roger that," Kim said. "Steady as she goes."

Ben came out of the medical bay with the crown prince in tow. Godfred shuffled slowly, wearing a paper-thin medical gown. Kim glanced over her shoulder and saw that he'd been cleaned up, but his hair was still greasy and sticking out from his head. The skin on his neck, cheeks, and even his arms looked baggy, as if he were wearing a sweater from Nance's wardrobe. He even chuckled a little as Ben sat him down at the engineering console.

"Anything?" Ben asked.

"Yes," Nance replied. "It's a repeating message coming from farther out in the system. There must be a Royal Imperium ship out there somewhere. I've just about got the entire message downloaded. One more second."

"Very good," Ben said.

Kim thought he was starting to sound like General Pershing.

"Here goes," Nance said.

General Pershing's voice came through the bridge speakers, surrounded by thick static. Still, it was much clearer than before, and Kim didn't struggle to understand it.

Modulus Echo, this is General Pershing on the R-I-F Tradewind. We are in orbit around Chopin and stand ready to assist you if possible. Please confirm that you have the Crown Prince Godfred on board your vessel, as well as an assessment of his wellbeing. Please transmit a full sit rep and any update you have on Professor Forrest Jones's work regarding the wormhole. We stand ready for your transmission. Please regard the time lag, but stand by for further instructions.

"The message repeats after that," Nance said.

"They want us to stick around in orbit?" Kim said.

"How long will it take for a message to reach Chopin?" Ben asked.

"Just under an hour," Nance said.

"I don't want to stick around that long," Kim said. "An hour for our message to reach them, and another for their reply to come back, all the while we could be attacked by the aliens? No, thank you."

Professor Jones came slowly up from the lower deck, assisted by Lieutenant Mark Baker. Kim saw the older man and felt a pang of empathy for him. He looked much older, and more haggard, than she remembered. She knew he was working hard around the clock, driven by his guilt over the flux rocket. In her mind, he wasn't to blame, none of them were. They didn't know the experimental device would suck most of the Royal Imperium Fleet into the swirling vortex of crushing gravity waves or open a wormhole to another galaxy filled with hostile aliens. Yet that was what happened, and he felt responsible, so he pushed for a way to fix the problem. And it probably didn't help that the solution was a devastating one.

"Professor," Ben said. "We need to send a message to General Pershing. Do you have a summary of your plan?"

"I can get it," the older man said.

"Please do. I'll record a message with the crown prince, and Nance can package and encrypt it."

"You know that if the aliens intercept the message, they will know what we're trying to do," Kim said. "Is it worth running that risk?"

"Maybe not," Ben said. "But if we set off the device, it's going to kill anyone still in the system. We owe it to the general to give her fair warning."

"And what if she tells us not to use it?" Magnum said.

"Then we won't," Ben replied. "We'll do what we can to help the Confederates and then flee the system. This isn't our mess to clean up if the general doesn't want our help."

"Yes!" Kim said. "Finally, some clear thinking on this ship."

The truth was, Kim didn't feel like they owed the general—or anyone else, for that matter—but she loved Ben's compassionate heart. Maybe it got them into a little more trouble than they needed, but it was something that made him who he was. And she had no desire to change him; she only wanted the time and space to love him.

"General Pershing," Ben said, and Kim knew that he was recording a video message.

It was old-school tech, but sometimes that was the best. She tapped a button that allowed her to see the video being captured. Ben stood directly behind the crown prince, who seemed enraptured by seeing his face on the screen. He was pooching his lips out and poking his cheeks like a child staring into a mirror when they thought no one was watching.

"As you can see, we have the crown prince. Physically, we've found nothing wrong with him, but as you well know, our medical facilities are limited. He was captured by the aliens shortly before the emergency pod he was sheltering in ran out of air. Major Le Croix surrendered to the commando team as well and is on board.

Professor Jones has a solution to the wormhole problem, but as you will see, it is an extreme response. We have the materials necessary to build the device, but it is untested and highly theoretical. It also requires that you find a way to evacuate the Confederate soldiers on Gershwin, along with some civilians.

We cannot maintain this position safely, so we will return to orbit ninety minutes after you receive this message. Please outline your plan and what you would like for us to do. If we don't hear from you in that time frame, we'll assume you've been pushed out of the system or this message has been intercepted. In that case, we'll do what we can."

"Your Highness, do you know your name?"

"Me?" Godfred said with a giggle. "Yes, of course. It's a wonderful name, really."

"Can you tell us what it is?"

The prince burst into peals of laughter. "Who doesn't know my name? What a silly game you're playing."

"It's no game," Ben said.

Kim had to admit it was funny. The poor man was completely bonkers, in her opinion, but how much he had changed was uncertain. It was possible that being the heir to a galactic empire had caused more damage than the aliens who took him prisoner.

"Very well," Godfred said, clearing his throat and suddenly trying to look regal. "I am Prince Godfred, heir to the throne of the Royal Imperium."

"That's very good," Ben said.

"Was it? Oh, I do hope so. I want to be good. Mommy says I'm bad sometimes, but I try, I really do."

He began to frown and then suddenly started weeping and asking for his mother.

"We can cut this part out, right?" Ben asked.

"Yes," Nance said. "As soon as the professor returns with his research, I can send it."

"Come with me," Ben said, pulling the weepy prince from his seat. "Let me get something to help you rest."

"Yes, I need to rest. I'm quite exhausted."

Kim felt a lump in her throat. The prince was completely mad, and what would happen to the people on Gershwin if General Pershing decided he wasn't worth saving? He was really their only chance of rescue, and Kim didn't know if there was a safe place on the planet since the aliens had invaded. The *Modulus Echo* could make a run for safety, but it would probably kill Ben to leave the Confederates behind.

"Well, that was something," Ben said.

"How is the work coming?" Kim asked.

"We have it all laid out," Ben said. "A few hours to build the device. It's pretty simple, really, when you don't have to worry about anyone's safety. I'd say a few more hours to build the housing around the device, which we can't completely do without setting a timer. And then we have to launch it at just the right moment. If we're too early, it will get too close to the sun and burn up despite our efforts to protect it from the star's heat."

"And if we're too late?" Kim asked.

"It will go off too far from the sun to have the desired effect," Ben said. "That's all supposing that it actually works the way the professor predicts."

"It will work," Professor Jones said, slowly descending the stairs with Lieutenant Baker.

"I have no doubt that it will do what we build it to do," Ben said. "But destabilizing a star is a massive effect. If your calculations are off even a tiny bit, it might not go supernova for hundreds of years."

Kim felt a sinking feeling in her gut. Were they pressing their luck? She was sure of it, but they had been lucky in the past. It was lucky that they got the old Kestrel class ship working. It was lucky that they survived the flight through the black hole. It was lucky that Ben and the professor came up with the flux shield just in time to save them from the Royal Imperium Fleet. Perhaps they would be lucky again, but she didn't like it. She wanted to fly away, far away, and let someone else worry about the aliens.

"The message is ready," Nance said.

"Send it," Ben said. "And set a timer for two and a half hours."

"Where are you headed?" Kim asked as Ben, the lieutenant, and Professor Jones started for the stairs.

"Back to work," Ben said. "If the general wants to use the device, it needs to be ready."

"If you say so," Kim said. But she wasn't convinced. Not even close.

Chapter 36

General Pershing was tired of waiting, but patience was the greatest virtue in any military campaign. Haste was the ruin of many great armies, and she was determined not to let her desire for action cause her to make a stupid mistake. Still, she felt certain they should have heard something from the *Modulus Echo* already, which meant that something had happened. It could be anything, from a mechanical malfunction to a problem with the signal, but she feared it was something worse. Perhaps the ship had been attacked and destroyed. Worse still, perhaps the crown prince was dead. Even if she defeated the Krah and closed the wormhole, if the heir to the throne died on her watch, she would never live it down. She would be the general who let the most important man in the galaxy die. It would be all she was ever remembered for.

"General, I have an incoming message," the communications officer declared in a loud voice. "Tight-beam transmission from Gershwin."

General Pershing wanted to declare that it was about bloody time they responded, but she didn't want the other officers to see how desperate she was.

"Very good," Pershing replied calmly. "Can you put it on the screen?"

"It's encrypted," the communications officer explained. "It will take several minutes to decode."

"Fine, I'll take it in my quarters, then," Pershing said. "Captain Davis, you have the con."

"Roger that," the captain replied. "I have the con."

Pershing rose to her feet slowly and calmly left the bridge. Her quarters weren't far away. The ship wasn't all that large to begin with, and most of it was weapons and racks of ammunition. The Corvette class battleships had oversized power plants that could fire the largest laser batteries made by the Royal Imperium. The crew quarters in the center of the ship were actually only a fraction of the vessel's size. Pershing's temporary assignment to the ship and refusal to push Captain Davis from her quarters left her with one of two tiny guest cabins. The room was beginning to feel more and more like a prison cell. Pershing chuckled at the irony that her captive, Chieftain Grubat, actually had more space in the brig than she did. When she last checked on the Krah warrior, he was pacing back and forth the long, narrow room, still chained to the pipe beneath the bench that ran the length of the brig.

As she sat on her bunk, waiting for the message from Gershwin to be decoded, she reached out and touched the walls on either side of her room. She couldn't walk past the bunk without shimmying sideways. The bunk could fold into the wall and had a support underneath that doubled as a stool, but she found sitting on the bunk with its thin mattress more comfortable.

The display screen suddenly showed a video message. Pershing calmly touched the control to play the message. She recognized Ben, but it was the image of Prince Godfred that shocked her. He looked unwell and acted as if he hadn't seen himself in a mirror all his life. She was not political and had never been invited to meet the royal family in person, but she had seen enough holographic recordings to know that the prince was vain. There were rumors that he spent hours staring at himself in mirrors, making tiny adjustments to his clothes and hair. The man on the screen looked like the prince, but his hair stuck out from his head, and the flesh hung from his cheekbones as if he hadn't eaten in weeks. There was even a strange look in his eyes, as if he didn't comprehend what he was seeing.

Until he proclaimed who he was, General Pershing believed the man was an imposter. But when he said his name, his old pride and pompousness returned. There was no mistaking who the man was, only what he had become at the hands of their enemy. That fact, even more than all the news from Gershwin, including the fact that Professor Jones had a solution to the wormhole, was of utmost importance. She had to ensure the safe return of the crown prince. Once that was done, however high the cost, she could focus on destroying the Krah.

She pressed another icon to open the files sent by Professor Jones. The description of his idea was straightforward however difficult to believe. Once she had sifted through the materials, she scooted back on her bunk and considered what Ben and his tiny crew were proposing. Perhaps it shouldn't surprise her. General Pershing had been one of the few witnesses to the destruction of the Royal Imperium Fleet. That incredibly destructive action hadn't been too ghastly for the tiny crew of outlaws, so why should they hesitate to destroy an entire system?

Pershing hated the idea. What she wanted was to defeat the Krah in a decisive battle, push the survivors back through the wormhole, and gain control over the portal to another galaxy. What if there were treasures beyond human comprehension in that foreign corner of space? If Chieftain Grubat was being honest, the Krah had found the key to incredibly long life, perhaps even immortality, with their mechanical enhancements. Could she really just throw the possibility of that away to defeat her enemies?

Not that the battle plan was bad on its face. The destruction of Celeste, if it truly happened as quickly as the professor calculated, would strike a blow unlike anything humanity had ever seen. Hundreds of alien starships destroyed in an instant. The wormhole rendered impassable. It was a giddy thought, without a doubt, but was it feasible, moral, or wise? She couldn't say for certain. That type of power was more than a person deserved. If the technology got out, it would shift the tides of power. How many trillions of lives would be lost if the rebellion could destroy an entire solar system?

There was only one thing that Pershing could say for certain: No one from Gershwin could live. The professor might have passed on his knowledge of this ultimate weapon, for surely that was what this device was—a weapon of unrivaled power to anyone on the planet. And the planet happened to be filled with aliens and a rebel army, neither of which could be trusted with the knowledge that a weapon of such destructive power even existed. In fact, Pershing couldn't even share the news or the entirety of her plans with the crew of the *Tradewind.* Fortunately, she had the problem contained. In her mind, only the *Modulus Echo* had the technology to get out of the system. Pershing had no qualms about letting the Confederate squadron make a rescue attempt on Gershwin. Some of them might even get to the planet's surface if her diversion was strong enough. But only the *Echo* had the shielding necessary to get clear of the system. They could set off their weapon, then flee with the crown prince to where Pershing was waiting for them. She would take the heir to the throne and then make sure the crew of the *Modulus Echo* was killed before destroying their little ship.

The aliens could be blamed for the destruction of Celeste and most of their own fleet. Pershing would then mop up the few survivors and return the crown prince. If the galaxy hailed her as a hero, all the better. She felt a sense of satisfaction. The crew of the *Modulus Echo* had been a thorn in the side of the Royal Imperium long enough. Their fate was no less than they deserved, and Pershing felt a sense of justice would be served by finally taking them out of the equation. No more Kestrel class ship to worry about, no more betrayal or secret weapons. Balance would be restored, and she could fulfill her destiny as one of the greatest military minds in the history of the human race.

Chapter 37

"That's it?" Lieutenant Mark Baker asked.

Ben shrugged his shoulders. The gravity generator was mounted on a plate of hexagon metal grids, like a board of honeycomb. It was light but sturdy and would hold the silver ball-shaped gravity generator upright so that the wave generator could spin around it.

"Everything is in place," Professor Jones said.

Ben couldn't help but look at the small wave generator. He wondered where it had come from. What machine had been salvaged to get the finger-sized component to him on board the *Modulus Echo*? Now it would be sent to destroy a star, which would, in turn, destroy an entire solar system and countless aliens. He felt a little sick to his stomach just thinking about it.

"In record time," Ben said.

Mark Baker was indeed a talented engineer. Using some of the tools they had salvaged from the *Plato*, he'd been able to help with the soldering. They used a small fist-sized battery that would run current through a simple circuit board that would activate the artificial gravity generator and spin up the wave generator to produce a flux shield. Ben had built in a power breaker that would keep the flux shield from collapsing on itself. Instead, it would shut down the wave generator while switching on the singularity device.

Essentially, heat from the sun would cause the device to implode, but unlike the flux rocket, which had plutonium to fuel what Professor Jones had hoped would be a wormhole to another part of space, the doomsday device was using a special mixture of chemicals that would disrupt the star's natural fusion process. Where the professor had obtained the substances, Ben couldn't say, but he was happy for one less hurdle to leap over.

"What now?" Mark asked.

"Now we find out what General Pershing has to say about our plan," Ben said. "You could go up to the galley and get a snack if you like."

"I wouldn't say no," Mark said. "What about you, Professor?"

"It would be an honor," he said, but his voice was ragged.

Ben wasn't sure if the professor was just tired or if there was something wrong with him. Once there was enough time, Ben planned to put the older man through some medical testing. The scanner in the med bay could do more than just check for broken bones, and if the older man needed medical attention, Ben wanted to see that he got it.

They walked slowly back up to the main deck. Professor Jones looked at Ben. There was sweat on the older man's forehead, and one eye seemed to be drooping.

"May I suggest," he said, panting a little, "the next project be an elevator?"

"I'll keep that in mind," Ben said. "Are you feeling okay, Professor?"

"Right as rain, my young friend. Just a bit fatigued, is all. Getting old is not for the faint of heart."

Ben nodded, and Mark helped the older man up the next flight of stairs.

"Where are we?" Ben asked as he turned to the bridge and made his way over to his console.

"Just below orbit," Kim said. "The air's so thin up here it's like being in a boat during a thunderstorm."

"Thank goodness for artificial gravity," Ben said. "I don't want to solder in a thunderstorm."

"Three minutes until prescribed contact," Nance said, her voice so even it almost sounded robotic.

"How's the science experiment going?" Kim asked

"It's ready to be set," Ben said. "We still need to calculate the time and finish the hull, then add the timing mechanism and some sort of propulsion. Part of me hopes we can junk the whole thing."

"Who says we can't?" Kim replied. "We don't answer to the Royal Imperium. Let's drop the prince and the soldiers at Royal City, wish them all the best of luck, and make tracks out of this system."

"Let's see what the general says first," Ben said. "I can do the work if she's willing to come get the Confederates."

"Do you trust her?" Magnum asked.

"He's got a point," Nance said. "We betrayed her when we left the *Everest*. What's to keep her from double-crossing us?"

"Nothing," Ben said. "We should be ready for that."

"Ready how?" Kim said.

"Once we drop that bomb, we need to go fast, but not where she's expecting."

"Do you have a place in mind?" Nance asked.

"No, but it should be out on the fringe somewhere—multiple jumps, someplace where she won't find us. We need to just disappear."

"Amen to that," Kim said. "We could go right now. Drop our passengers somewhere on the way, hit the hyperdrive, and never look back."

"It's time," Nance said.

"Take us up," Ben said to Kim.

"Up and away?" Kim asked.

"No, just up. Let's see what the general has to say before we make a decision. While we're up there, Nance, why don't you calculate an escape trajectory? I want to know how difficult getting out of here is going to be."

Ben sat back in his seat, watching the view on the large bridge display screens. The sky went from blue to gray to black, and he could see stars between the clusters of alien ships. They scanned the skies, watching for any of the alien vessels to notice them.

"You know what I think?" Kim said. "They can't come after us because their ships aren't atmospheric."

"How'd they invade the planet, then?" Ben asked.

"Maybe they have transports to take them down, but their main ships can't get too close to atmo. Those big vessels might get caught in the planet's gravity and get stuck, or worse yet, fall into a decaying orbit."

"You might be right," Ben said as he scanned for a message from General Pershing.

"Of course, the better explanation is that they just don't care about us," Kim went on. "I mean, I'd rather they not chase us out of the galaxy."

"We should load the last of the missiles," Magnum suggested.

"We will, once we figure out if we're firing the professor's device, and if so, how we're going to make her fly."

"Didn't you say if there wasn't an answer, we would assume they had been run out of the galaxy or destroyed?" Kim said. "If there's no message, we should warn the soldiers in Royal City and then get out of here while we still can."

"They have almost as many ships as the Royal Imperium Fleet had," Nance said.

"Wouldn't it be nice if they all went raiding other systems?" Kim said. "Then we could stroll out of here as easy as you please."

"Would it be worth destroying the system if they did?" Magnum asked.

Ben couldn't answer that question. The truth was, he didn't want to have anything to do with the professor's device. Destruction of that magnitude wasn't meant for mere mortals, and what he hoped was that General Pershing would reject the idea outright.

"Wait a second," Ben said. "There it is. Message received."

He hit a few buttons on his console, and a status bar appeared on the display screen. It was mostly opaque, and they could still see the alien ships through it, but they could also track the status of the decryption being done on the general's message.

"Should we stay in orbit?" Kim asked.

"Might as well," Ben said. "She may want a reply."

The bridge fell silent, each person watching the ships around them—some seemed to move, while others seemed stationary. Gershwin was spinning below them, the wormhole's fiery ring glowing in the distance. It all felt surreal to Ben. How could they even contemplate destroying a solar system? Yet, if there was ever one to be destroyed, it had to be the Celeste system. It was home only to the royal family and the servants they employed to wait on them hand and foot. The Royal Imperium Fleet was already reduced to less than half its strength. Their massive headquarters complex, one of the largest space stations in the galaxy, was already destroyed. The planet Gershwin was worth saving, but it was no longer the pristine, untouched marvel it had once been. Removing the aliens would take years and cost trillions and the lives of countless men and women. Then what? Would the royal family simply take possession of it again? If so, was it really worth saving?

The progress bar filled up, and the message from General Pershing appeared on the screen.

Modulus Echo, you have surpassed my expectations. We will, of course, assist you in the evacuation of Gershwin. Your friend Holt and his squadron of Confederates are here in the system and will proceed to the planet to remove the soldiers and civilians. The Alpha team of commandos are to stay with the crown prince at all times. I suggest that they transfer to the Hyperion, which is piloted by Duke Simeon, before you leave Royal City on your mission.

Concerning Professor Jones's device, I order you to proceed. In exactly ten hours, I will create a diversion that should allow the Confederates to jump from our position to

Gershwin or as close as the navigational computers on their ships will get them. They may not all survive the trip, but enough should get through to evacuate their comrades. Once that's done, you may set off your device and leave the system. We will rendezvous at the following coordinates.

Ben's mind checked out at that point. He knew Nance would take down the coordinates, and he was left the task of building and setting off a device that would destroy the system. It was a ludicrous plan, yet in many ways it had been his own. He hadn't dreamed up the device, or put together the strategy for getting the innocent away from Gershwin so that it could be utilized, but he might as well have. If he had listened to Kim from the beginning and left the system when they had the chance, none of it would be on his shoulders. He could have lived with the guilt of losing two hundred innocent lives more easily than living with the knowledge that he had been instrumental in destroying another fleet and the entire Celeste system in the process. Yet, what choice did he have?

"Want me to acknowledge the general's orders?" Nance asked.

Ben looked up and saw the faces of his friends. They were all looking at him. He managed to nod, then left the bridge, knowing he was going to be sick.

Chapter 38

Pershing was in the communications room on the *Tradewind*. It was a small room, not much larger than her berth, but it was the only place on the ship where she could teleconference with the commanders of all the ships in her small armada at once.

"Our mission has changed," Pershing said. "We are going to attempt a rescue operation on Gershwin."

There was plenty of muttering and head shaking from the Confederates. They may have had experience in fighting, but they had no discipline and very little respect for the chain of command.

"That's impossible," Holt declared. "You can't get to the planet through all those alien vessels."

"There are two hundred Confederate soldiers in Royal City," Pershing said. "If we don't get them, they're dead. It's only a matter of time. The Krah have invaded the planet en masse. The city has already come under attack. For the moment, they're safe, but that won't last. They need to evacuate and we're the only ships capable."

"You mean *we're* the only ships capable," Holt grumbled. "I don't see the *Tradewind* or the *Eclipse* sticking their necks out."

"The *Hyperion* stands ready," Duke Simeon said. "I can get two dozen passengers aboard comfortably. Twice that if necessary."

Holt rolled his eyes, and General Pershing had to stifle a grin. The dashing royal, seemingly so full of courage, had no idea how dangerous the mission would be. She would have kept him from it if possible, but she wasn't sure how she could.

"The *Tradewind* and *Eclipse* will engage the Krah and attempt to draw their attention away from the planet," Pershing said. "We're all taking risks, Holt. None more than others, but we have different objectives. Yours is getting to the planet. Once the diversion starts, your squadron will make a microjump that should put you just outside Gershwin's orbit. From there, you will make your way into atmo. The alien ships can't follow you down. Their vessels aren't made for atmospheric flight."

"We're safe inside atmo?" asked one of the Confederate pilots.

"That is correct. We've been in contact with the *Modulus Echo*. There are aliens on the ground, but the skies are clear. Once you pass through orbit and enter the planet's upper atmosphere, you'll be safe."

"Suppose you're right and we make it to Royal City, how are we getting out?" Holt asked.

"That will be up to you, but should the *Tradewind* and *Eclipse* survive the first encounter with the Krah fleet, we will again attempt to draw them away from your position. Once the diversion begins, you'll have to move fast. Set timers for three hours, get the soldiers and civilians in Royal City, and return to orbit before the time runs out so that we can coordinate our efforts. Otherwise, you'll be completely on your own."

"Sounds like we're pretty much on our own anyway," Holt complained.

"If any of you do not wish to take part, that is your choice. But the *Modulus Echo* cannot save the Confederate soldiers on Gershwin. If you choose not to engage, they will be left on their own."

There was more muttering. Most of the Confederate ships had multiple crew members, but Pershing couldn't see them. Only the vessel commanders were included on the conference. She waited a few moments, then pressed a few buttons and added her final orders.

"Once you are off-planet, rendezvous at the coordinates I've just sent out. You should be able to make the jump to hyperspace quickly upon reaching outer space. Bear in mind that the aliens can follow us through hyperspace, so going anywhere other than the rendezvous is dangerous. We will stand ready to defend you from whatever ships might follow. That is all."

Pershing didn't wait for replies. She hit the button that ended the teleconference and took a deep breath. Captain Davis waited just inside the room, leaning against the bulkhead near the door.

"What are the odds they'll succeed?" Captain Davis asked.

"It's impossible to calculate," Pershing said. "We have no idea how the Krah will respond to our attack."

"That many ships, I can't see them all being drawn away," the captain said.

"Be that as it may, we have to try," Pershing said. "The crown prince is on Gershwin. Our top priority is his safety."

"And the rebels?"

Pershing held back the smile that wanted to spread across her face. She didn't want to seem cruel or heartless, but the truth was, the more ships that came out of orbit, the better the chances that the *Modulus Echo* could slip away, fire the singularity weapon, and escape the system.

"We can't just leave them to die down there," Pershing said.

The truth was, she didn't care about the rebel fighters. Her commandos could survive on their own for months if need be, and she wouldn't risk fleet resources to save a few lives. Only the crown prince and the weapon mattered. After that, she would tie up any loose ends—be they Krah or Confederate, it made no difference to her—so that she could spin the story to her benefit.

No one knew about the weapon. Pershing had made the executive decision to keep that to herself. If it worked, it would effectively end the war. But given time, the fault for destroying an entire star system might blowback on her, perhaps even taint her legend after she was dead. It was better, she reasoned, to let humanity believe that the aliens had destroyed the system and that Pershing was the great military strategist who had halted their invasion of the galaxy.

"Send all officers to their quarters for the next six hours," Pershing said. "I want them fresh and alert when we engage the Krah."

"Yes, General," Captain Davis replied.

They moved out of the small communications room and walked down the ship's central corridor together.

"Make sure all weapons batteries are fully charged, armed, and crewed," Pershing went on. "We'll make two microjumps so we can draw the Krah away from the planet. I'll transfer all relevant coordinates to the *Eclipse* so they can mimic our moves. We go in weapons hot and show the Krah what we're capable of, then jump back out of the system."

"They'll follow us," Captain Davis said.

"Of course they will, but we'll be ready for them. Once we've mopped up whatever ships are foolish enough to follow us out of the system, we can prepare to go in a second time."

"From the opposite side of the system?" Davis said.

"That's correct. We'll keep them guessing and hopefully give the rescue ships time to escape."

"It's a solid plan," Captain Davis said.

"The best we can do with so little resources," Pershing replied. "Once we have the crown prince, the rest of the fleet will have no choice but to acknowledge the Krah and follow us into battle. The *Tradewind* will go down in history as the ship that turned the tide in this war, Captain. You can count on that."

Pershing saw the question on her subordinate's face. She didn't understand how saving the crown prince would turn the tide in a war, but then she didn't have all the facts. Pershing sent the ship commander off to make the arrangements. Meanwhile, Pershing returned to her tiny quarters.

It was a good plan, but a feeble one. Odds were almost overwhelmingly high that none of the rebel ships would even make it to the planet. The *Modulus Echo* had a better chance of surviving with its gravity shield, but even that was not a given. And the weapon it was building was an even bigger question mark. Would it destroy the system and the Krah fleet along with it, or would the entire operation fall to pieces? Pershing couldn't know.

She could return to the Mersa system and beg for more ships. The knowledge that the crown prince lived and needed rescue might sway a few more commanders to her cause, but many would rather see the entire royal family dead. The crown prince would just be a challenge to their desperate striving for power. Even if they all followed her back to the Celeste system to engage the Krah, the Royal Imperium forces would still be outnumbered. A toe-to-toe battle would not win the day. Pershing needed a decisive victory, one that drove the alien fleet away from the system or closed the access to the wormhole permanently. Even with hundreds of ships, the Krah couldn't survive for long in a galaxy filled with humans. They would be hunted down and exterminated.

She sat back on her bunk and considered the alternatives. The Krah weren't unreasonable, and perhaps a diplomatic solution could be reached, but that would only delay the inevitable. Alicia Pershing was a military commander, not a politician or a diplomat. She would take the fight to the enemy and carve her name in history. It was her destiny, and she would run to it.

Six hours of sleep, then final preparations could begin. History was waiting, and she would not be forgotten.

Chapter 39

The device was ready. Ben had installed a remote detonator, which put the ship in more danger but gave them flexibility in setting off the device. It was sealed inside the fusion reactor housing, then surrounded with a foot of heat-resistant foam. A simple hull made from a dense metal alloy was then covered with ceramic heat-shielding tiles.

"What's next?" Mark asked.

They were still in the engineering bay. The *Echo* had returned to the circling pattern above Royal City after dropping off the Confederate soldiers. Soon they would need to land to load the missiles to the ship's wings. Their attack in the mountains had slowed the alien army and reduced their numbers, but the fighters continued on. The alien army had almost reached the far shores of the lake and would almost certainly attack the city before help arrived.

The Confederates were making their preparations, and the *Echo* would do what it could to help, but their priority was getting the singularity device ready before the evacuation, and they still hadn't figured out how to propel the blocky device toward the sun.

"We have two extra missiles," Ben said. "We'll remove the warheads and program their guidance systems for the coordinates Professor Jones established."

The professor had finally agreed to rest and was slouched in a chair just inside the recreation area, sleeping peacefully. Ben guessed that it was extreme exhaustion, not a clear conscience, that allowed the older man to sleep so soundly.

"Can we mount the device to the rocket launchers?" Mark asked.

"No," Ben admitted. "We'll have to eject it out of the air lock once we're able."

Mark raised his eyebrows. Tossing things as important as the singularity device out an air lock certainly wasn't normal. It would never pass regulations within the Royal Imperium Fleet, but Ben knew the plan was sound. The vacuum of space would suck out the heavy device and Ben could engage the rockets remotely, sending the device hurtling toward the sun.

"Is that really feasible?" Mark asked.

Ben didn't want to explain that he'd used the method before with excellent results. Instead, he just nodded.

"You remove the warheads," Ben proposed. "I'll set up the targeting coordinates, then we'll figure out how to attach the missiles to the device."

His com-link beeped, then Kim's voice came out of the tiny speaker.

"Ben, the aliens have moved out of the mountains. You should see this."

"Let's take a break," Ben told Mark.

"No argument here," the engineer said.

Mark stretched his back, then headed to the recreation room. Ben would have liked to stretch out on a sofa, or better yet, take a turn in his bunk, but there was no time. He went bounding up the stairs, his breath short by the time he reached the main deck, but it was what he saw on the big bridge display screens that really took his breath away.

"No," he whispered.

"It's a sight to see," Kim said. She was standing up behind the pilot's seat.

"Better get the commandos down here," Ben said.

"I already called them," Kim said.

On the far shore of the lake, beyond the dazzling water, well over a thousand aliens were marching. Ben felt weak. What little contact he'd had with the aliens was enough to know that they were ferocious fighters. If they could get close enough, they might overcome the Confederates' superior firepower.

"How long until they reach the city?" Ben asked.

"Rough estimate is three hours," Nance said.

"The sun is going down," Kim said. "It'll be dark by then."

"Great," Ben said. "That means they'll have another advantage. How long before General Pershing's diversion?"

"An hour and forty-seven minutes," Nance said.

"Alright," Ben said.

He was about to start giving orders when Mark came slowly up the stairs.

"Ben, a word," he said.

There was something about the lieutenant's tone that made Ben pause. He walked over to where Mark waited by the stairs. The lieutenant lowered his voice when he spoke.

"It's the professor."

"What about him?" Ben asked.

"He's not asleep."

"Okay. Well, I'll be down to help in a few minutes. I've got a few other things to take care of first. Tell him to hold on."

"No, Ben. He's not awake, he's…"

Realization dawned on Ben just as Mark finished his explanation.

"…dead."

Grief, fear, exhaustion, and despair all seemed to fall on Ben at once. Professor Forrest Jones was gone? It didn't seem possible. The man was older, but he was a force of nature. A genius who never got the respect he deserved.

"You're sure?"

Mark nodded. "I'm sorry."

Ben took a deep, shaky breath as tears filled his eyes.

"Okay, just give me a minute," Ben said. He walked slowly back to the bridge. Kim and Nance were staring at him. Magnum and the three corporals came down from the galley, their heavy boots thumping on the metal stairs. Ben felt as if he could hardly breathe.

"Ben, what's wrong?" Kim asked, a note of true concern in her voice.

"Yeah, what's happening?" Corporal Dial said. "This place is starting to feel like a funeral parlor."

Ben felt a flash of anger, but it passed just as quickly as it appeared. A tear tumbled down one cheek as Ben looked up at Kim. He wiped it away.

"The professor," Ben said softly. "He passed away."

"What?" Kim asked.

"He's down in the rec room. We thought he was sleeping."

It felt like the air had been sucked out of the room, and Ben let them all feel the weight of their grief for a moment. Corporal Dial looked down at his boots, clearly embarrassed.

"Alright," Ben said. "We don't have time to grieve. Kim, find a place to land so we can load the missiles. Someplace where we could see an enemy coming. We need to get it done before we lose daylight."

"Okay," Kim said softly.

"Corporal Dial, can two of you help Magnum and me load the missiles while the other two stand guard?"

"Sure," Dial said. "Sorry about that wisecrack. I didn't mean it."

Ben nodded. "The professor was a great man. Unappreciated in his time, maybe, but he saw the validation of his theories. We'll carry out this last concept for him. It's the least we can do."

"Forty-two minutes until sunset," Nance said, her normally calm voice husky with emotion.

"Once we get the missiles loaded, we have to make orbit," Ben said.

"What about that army?" Corporal Amadi asked. "Shouldn't we try and slow them down or something?"

"We have to direct whatever ships come to rescue the soldiers in Royal City," Ben said. "The Confederates will have to hold until then."

"Maybe the rescue ships can help fight off the aliens," Kim said.

"Let's hope," Ben replied. "For now, we do what we can, but we can't be in two places at once. Mark and I still have to figure out the propulsion system for the device."

"We'll see to the missiles," Dial said. "You keep working on the professor's project. That's the most important thing."

"He's right," Magnum said.

"Okay," Ben replied. "Let's get it all done and get off this rock. The sooner we're out of the system, the better."

"Ain't that the truth," Kim replied.

Ben bent over, his hands on the back of his console chair. He wanted to give in to the sense of despair, but he knew he couldn't. The weight of responsibility was solely his to live with for the rest of his life. The professor was gone. Nothing would bring him back. Ben took a deep, shaky breath, wiped the tears from his eyes, and stood up.

Kim and Nance were both looking at him. The others found something else to occupy their focus, trying to give Ben the space he needed.

"Alright, I'm ready," Ben said. He gave Kim and Nance a reassuring nod, then walked back to where Mark was waiting for him.

The lieutenant patted Ben's shoulder, then he headed downstairs. Ben followed. The doomsday weapon was waiting. Perhaps it was humanity's last hope, Ben couldn't say for sure. All he knew was that the one man he believed could find a different solution was gone. And that meant his options were down to just one course of action. He had to prepare the device and use it. Perhaps finding a way to close the wormhole, working tirelessly to find the best solution, hadn't cut the professor's life short, but Ben couldn't help but believe that it had. And the only way he had left to honor his friend was to use the device the professor had built. He couldn't think about whether it was right or wrong. He just had to make sure it had a chance, then get the rest of the people he cared about away from the Celeste system as fast as he possibly could.

Chapter 40

"This is it," General Pershing said.

They had already made the first jump out of the system and were now preparing to jump back in to engage the Krah.

"Remember, our shields won't stop their kinetic torpedoes," Pershing continued. "We make a scene, hit as many of their ships as possible, and hold on for as long as we can. But I want us ready to jump back out of the system as soon as possible."

"We're ready," Captain Davis said.

"Alright, signal the *Eclipse*. Then take us in."

The bridge of the *Tradewind* was suddenly busy. The officers called out orders and reports. Unlike the *Echo*, there were no wall screens that mimicked windows. Instead, in the center of the room was a holoprojector that showed the space all around the ship. It spun into a glowing tunnel as the ship jumped into hyperspace.

General Pershing could feel her heart rate speeding up and tiny beads of sweat sliding down the center of her back. Her arms and legs felt heavy, and her breath came in fierce puffs. It was the prebattle jitters. She had felt it before sparring sessions and on missions where she led small teams of special operators against rebel forces in a variety of worlds. Ideally, as the mission commander, she could coordinate the battle from a safe distance where she could see all of her forces and the alien fleet arrayed against them. But she didn't have that luxury with her tiny force, and for that she was grateful. Nothing compared to being in the thick of the fighting. She felt more alive than she had in years.

"Dropping out of hyperspace in five, four," the helmsman counted down, "three, two, one."

The familiar feeling of time slowing pulled at General Pershing's stomach, which was knotted into a tight ball. The holoprojector flickered into focus. They had dropped out of hyperspace on the edge of the Krah formation, if it could be called that. The aliens were clustered all around the planet. It felt to Pershing as if they had just stepped out of the woods and into a massive clearing where a huge herd of game animals was grazing.

"Fire, fire, fire!" General Pershing ordered.

The weapons on the *Tradewind* belched out flame and dazzling bolts of light. Each gunner across the ship was focused on a different target, and the Krah were caught completely off guard. They may have just taken note of the two Royal Imperium ships dropping into the system, but not one had moved to attack positions. Their long, articulated grappling arms had not launched from their bulbous alien vessels. Each shot from the *Tradewind* and *Eclipse* was a hit. Lasers scorched holes straight through the hulls of vessels, some even penetrating completely through to the other side. The missiles and torpedoes took longer to reach their targets, some a few seconds, others even longer. But they all hit their marks, impacting with massive explosions. Space was lit with bright beams and spectacular explosions.

"Slow reverse," General Pershing ordered. "Watch for debris."

"Aye, General. Slow reverse."

"They're waking up," Captain Davis said.

"Enemy ships, moving to attack positions," the radar operator called out. "Looks like they're preparing to fire."

"I want lasers prepared for point defense," Pershing ordered. "Nothing gets through."

"Aye, point defense," the tactical officer echoed.

"Captain Davis, see if you can catch sight of the rescue squadron," Pershing ordered. "We'll stay as long as we have to, but once they make it through orbit, I want to know."

"Yes, General," Captain Davis said.

"Tactical, target the ships closer to the planet," Pershing ordered. "Let the *Eclipse* deal with the ships moving against us. We need to draw more of their vessels into the fight."

"Aye, General. Resetting target priorities."

Waves of space debris formed a wall of sorts between the alien ships and the Royal Imperium vessels. Some of the alien ships hurled long, torpedo-shaped kinetic weapons, but many had no projectiles and attempted to close the distance between the human vessels and their long, waving, grappling arms. The weapons officers on the *Tradewind* and *Eclipse* had made good use of their downtime, and the crews manning the ships' weapons were efficient and deadly. Dozens of enemy ships were destroyed in the first few minutes of fighting. Unlike the Krah, the humans destroyed their enemy vessels, disabling some and blowing others to pieces, which streaked across space like comets.

General Pershing had a good view of the holographic projection that showed the Royal Imperium battleships and the Krah vessels moving toward them. Some were moving directly at the two human spacecraft, but dozens more were circling wide, trying to look as though they were avoiding the deadly fire, but in reality they were attempting to circle and flank them. The *Tradewind* and *Eclipse* were long, narrow ships bristling with weapons. As soon as they came out of hyperspace, thrusters sent the ships on a slow rotation right down the center axis. The first weapons to fire did so, then as the ship rotated away from the fight, they cooled down, recharged, or reloaded depending on what type of ammunition was being used.

"General Pershing, the Confederate ships have just come out of hyperspace," Captain Davis said.

"Just in time," Pershing replied. "Fall back to our default position."

"Aye, falling back to default position," the helmsman called out, already engaging the ship's thrusters to move them back from the approaching Krah ships.

"Continue firing," Pershing warned. "They'll intensify their attack if they think they've got us running."

"General, the lane of escape will be blocked in twenty seconds," the navigation officer called out.

"Roger that, nav control," Pershing snapped. "Helm, prepare to jump to hyperspace in ten seconds."

"Aye, preparing to jump to hyperspace on your command, General."

Pershing watched as the Krah vessels moved in concert, like a giant net collapsing around two ferocious fish. They fired over and over, some shots aimed at the enemy, but others concentrated on the kinetic torpedoes of the enemy or on large chunks of debris flying toward the human ships.

"Now, helm," Pershing called out. "Jump to hyperspace."

"Aye, General," the helmsman replied.

The holographic plot swirled into hyperspace around the *Tradewind*, and everyone took a deep breath.

"We did it," Captain Davis said.

"We drew first blood," Pershing said. "Let's hope it was enough for the rebels to get through the alien ships in orbit. For us, the fight has just begun. How long until we reach the rendezvous point?"

"Eighteen minutes, General," the navigation officer replied.

"Get the weapons reloaded and recharged," Pershing barked.

"Aye, weapons teams are preparing," the tactical officer replied.

"Navigation, as soon as we drop, I want an emergency jump point calculated," General Pershing said. "Coordinate with the *Eclipse*. I don't want her left behind if things go bad and we need to run."

"Aye, General," the navigation officer said.

"Captain, what was the last thing you saw from the rebel ships?" Pershing asked.

"It was hard to make out," Captain Davis said. "The enemy was moving to intercept. I couldn't tell if they were going to make it or not."

"We'll just have to wait and see," Pershing said. "Alright, people, let's get ready for round two."

Chapter 41

Getting the missiles loaded had gone as smoothly as they could have hoped for. Kim had found the perfect spot, a wide-open plain with short grass. If the aliens had tried to attack, they would have been easily spotted, but none did. Magnum and the commandos, including Major Le Croix, had loaded six missiles, three under each wing in less than half an hour.

Ben was busy down in his workshop with Lieutenant Mark Baker. Nance was at her station, helping to keep watch for any sign of enemy movement. And once they finished with the missiles, Kim had taken them up toward orbit. It took time to claw their way out of the planet's gravity, but eventually they reached the final barrier between atmosphere and outer space.

"When does the diversion start?" Kim asked.

"Any minute," Nance said. "Should we call Ben up?"

"Nah, let him work. He's got enough on his mind," Kim said.

The commandos were back upstairs. Magnum was at his station, fully armed, with a Lancet AR slung across his back and a pistol on each hip. Kim wished more than ever that the professor hadn't passed. He was the only person qualified to act as the ship's doctor, and the possibility that someone might get hurt in the next few hours was uncomfortably high. Staff Sergeant Visher remained in the med bay, but the crown prince had been locked in the crew's lounge. Kim hoped he wasn't relieving himself in the corners, but they would have to deal with his insanity later. She hoped it would be somewhere far from the Celeste system when they could feel reasonably sure they were safe.

It had been so long since Kim felt safe that she had forgotten what it was like. It seemed at every turn they were facing impossible odds and the fear of being caught by whatever enemy they happened to be up against. Kim didn't mind excitement or adventure, but she was tired of living with fear as her closest companion. She wanted some space to breathe and a little time to let go of the stress. It felt like her body was becoming rigid with worry and fear, as if her muscles, under the constant strain, were hardening into something she didn't want to be. Life had been hard on Torrent Four, but she was beginning to miss it. At least there she felt like she had a fighting chance.

"Taking us up," Kim said.

She increased the ship's power and brought them into the lowest possible orbit. The fighting was visible immediately. Flashes of light bright enough to rival the planet's star could be seen in the distance.

"Looks like the general is causing a ruckus," Kim said.

"Scanning for the rescue ships," Nance said.

"Won't that attract attention?" Kim pointed out.

"Probably, but as long as the aliens are looking at us, or General Pershing, maybe they won't notice the rescue ships."

There were still hundreds of ships not affected by the fighting, but the idea was to distract the enemy, not draw the entire fleet away from Gershwin. That would never happen, not unless the general had rounded up hundreds of Royal Imperium vessels to engage the aliens with.

"There they are," Nance said.

"Dang, they could have dropped out of hyperspace a little closer," Kim said.

"They're forty miles and closing," Nance said.

Kim watched, barely breathing, as a motley band of ships raced toward orbit. She scanned the nearest alien vessels. Most weren't moving, and she guessed they were too busy watching the battle. But two of the alien craft turned, extending their long grappling arms.

"Can we warn them?" Kim said.

"Comms are open," Nance said.

Kim hit a button on the armrest of her pilot's chair. "Watch out for those alien ships," Kim said.

"We see them," came a gruff but familiar voice.

"Holt, I should have known," Kim said. "It looks like the duke came through with those new ships."

"Was there ever any doubt?" came the duke's unmistakable voice.

Kim felt a shiver as she watched the ships spreading out. Most would make orbit with no problem. That much was clear, but three or four were in real danger. The pilots were all talking over one another on the communication channel. All Kim could do was watch and listen.

The closest alien ship reached out and snagged one of the Confederate vessels. It was small, a light transport. The ship didn't fight back, and Kim saw the pilot eject. The ship was drawn in by the alien vessel, but as soon as the Confederate ship was close, it exploded and sent the larger vessel tumbling toward the planet.

The other alien ship worked to catch two different Confederate vessels, but the aliens were learning. Instead of grappling onto the ships, the alien swatted at them. The first evaded successfully, but the second Confederate ship wasn't as lucky. It was a blocky freight ship and wasn't as nimble as some of the other ships. The grappling arm ripped across its hull and sent it spinning away.

"We're hit!"

Kim heard other pilots urging them to eject, but the Confederate vessel exploded too quickly, consumed in a ball of flame. The other Confederate ship thought it was safely out of reach, but the alien ship's reach was longer than they expected. It caught the ship from behind, wrecking its main drive and setting the ship adrift. The rest of the ships, ten in all, made orbit, and the alien craft pulled back.

"Peters, Rollins, stay up here and see if you can pick up the survivors," Holt ordered. "Everyone else, follow the *Modulus Echo*."

"Next stop, Royal City," Kim said.

She pressed her toes forward and sent the Kestrel class ship diving back toward the surface. The ship began a slow but rocky spiral down through the planet's atmosphere.

"What's the situation down there?" Holt asked, his voice booming over the bridge speakers.

"Not great," Kim replied. "The aliens were closing in when we left. Do you boys have any guns on those ships?"

"We're packing," Holt replied. "I'll command the battle from above, you go down and see to the evac."

"Roger that," Kim said. She looked over her shoulder at Nance. "Better alert the commandos, and get us in touch with the Confederates on the ground."

Nance nodded.

"And we might as well let Ben know," Kim said.

She didn't mind flying, but she always felt better knowing Ben was behind her, calling the shots and making sure things were taken care of. She might have to do some fancy flying, and if so, she wanted her full attention on piloting the ship.

Chapter 42

"They've sent two small raids against us," Captain Lawrence said. "We pushed them back, but the problem isn't firepower."

Ben was listening to the report Captain Lawrence was giving Holt. Ben still didn't know what Holt's position in the Confederacy was, but they all seemed to give him deference.

"What is?" Holt grumbled.

"Passing fifteen thousand feet," Nance said.

Ben keyed his mic. "Landing team, let's hold here for now."

There were four quick replies, including Duke Simeon. The adventurous royal claimed his ship could set down on the roof of the palace to evacuate the staff and crew of the *Plato* who had taken that building as their refuge.

"The problem is the darkness," Captain Lawrence said. "We don't see them until they're less than a hundred yards out. If they get that close en force, we might not be able to hold them."

"We can't land if the street is compromised," Ben said. "Captain Lawrence, how's the tunnel to the staff village?"

"We've cleared the tunnel, but if I send men through there, the rest of us might be overrun. I propose that we combine our efforts and destroy the alien army before evacuating."

"Negative," Holt said. "We're working within a pretty tight window. We need everyone on board one of the ships within the hour if we're going to make our escape window."

"Fine, I've just sent Lieutenant Gabianelli to prepare our withdraw. But you'll have to hold off the devils. Have you seen them, Holt? They're savages."

"Yeah, I'm aware," Holt said. "We're going to hit them pretty hard up here. When you hear the shootin', get to scootin'."

"Roger that. Lawrence, out."

Ben had already checked the thermal display. There was a group of aliens amassing on the banks of the lake just east of the city. Fortunately, the staff village was to the west. It looked to Ben as if the aliens were waiting on the stragglers before attacking with their full army.

"Pounds, Schumacher, head to the village," Ben said. "Use your thermal imaging to check for the enemy. There may be a few out that way."

"Copy, heading out," James Schumacher said.

Ben saw the two ships leave on their plot.

"Kim, take us to a hover about fifty feet off the ground on the west side of town," Ben said. "Magnum, give her laser control."

"Here we go," Kim said with enthusiasm. "Time to bake a few bad guys."

"Just remember, we've got enough battery power for two full cycles on the lasers," Ben said. "I'd like to keep the second auxiliary battery bank as a backup just in case we run into trouble."

"Yeah, yeah. Don't go spend the power all in one barrage. I get it," Kim said. "Don't spoil the fun."

Ben glanced over at Lieutenant Mark Baker, who was sitting at the communications console. It had been Professor

Jones's spot on the bridge, and Ben felt a pang of anguish not seeing the older man. Corporal Dial and Amadi were standing just behind him, watching the rescue and battle on the big bridge screens.

Kim brought the ship down into a smooth hover at the end of the street. They were close to the royal palace, and the well-lit hotel tower loomed in the distance. The Confederates with Holt were lining up for their attack run.

"Okay, gang, here we go," Holt said. "Starting our assault."

They were far enough away that Ben couldn't see the ships, but they started in with missiles of some type that impacted with bright explosions. It looked to Ben like lightning in the distance. Then, after a few seconds, came the rumble of thunder.

"Ben, now seems like a good time to pick up passengers," Duke Simeon declared.

"You sure about that rooftop?" Ben asked.

"Absolutely. I've spent half my life in that palace. It'll hold."

"Fine," Ben said. "You're a go. Nance, let's go back to normal on the camera feed."

A second later, the greens and yellows of the thermal imaging switched to normal, and the long cobblestone street that ran the length of the tiny resort town came into view. It was lit with antique lamp posts and bright floodlights mounted on the buildings. The effect was to bathe the street in light while the green space beyond was shrouded in darkness.

The *Hyperion* descended slowly. Ben was watching it and almost didn't see the attack coming from out of the darkness.

Magnum, Dial, and Amadi called out simultaneously, "Incoming!"

"I've got this," Kim said.

Ben hit the transmit button and spoke into his mic, "Attack from the green space! I repeat, the aliens are attacking Royal City from the green space."

There were hundreds of aliens running with strangely shaped axes, dashing through the well-trimmed grass and leaping onto the cobblestones. Kim fired two quick shots with the lasers mounted on the wing engines of the ship. They flashed out, one after the other, streaking along the road and vaporizing the aliens unlucky enough to have been in their path. The bright flashes shocked the aliens, many of which faltered in their charge. But some were already past and rushing up the steps to the palace or smashing through the glass on the buildings down the row.

Kim fired again, killing several of the aliens, but on the whole, it wasn't enough.

"We can help," Corporal Dial shouted.

"Open the back hatch, Ben!" Magnum added.

Ben touched a few controls on his console as the *Hyperion* slowly settled onto the roof of the palace. The royal residence was probably the most exquisitely designed building Ben had ever seen, but it was also sturdy. The aliens threw themselves against the glass windows and chopped at the handsome wooden doors, but unlike the other structures, the palace was built with materials designed to withstand such an attack. Ben was confident that the refugees in the palace would escape, but he wasn't as certain about the Confederates in the other buildings.

Ben's com-link beeped, and Magnum's voice was heard through the tiny speaker. "Take us slowly down the street," he urged.

Ben glanced at the camera feed showing the cargo hold. The rear hatch gaped open and the commandos were leaning out, firing their rifles in quick bursts.

"Kim," Ben said.

"I heard him," Kim snapped.

She rotated the ship around so that the rear of the vessel was pointed down the street, making it easier for the soldiers to fire their weapons. Magnum was blasting away his Lancet assault rifle, but from the buildings themselves, there was nothing. Ben realized that Captain Lawrence must have called a full-scale retreat.

A soft bang was heard, then another.

"The aliens are throwing their axes at us," Nance said, bringing up a video feed from one of the posterior cameras.

Ben saw several more of the aliens directly below them throw their axes up. The weapons came spinning toward the camera.

"Take us up," Ben said. "Twenty more feet, maybe."

"It's good for us they don't have rifles," Lieutenant Baker said.

"I've got everyone from the palace," Duke Simeon said, his voice laced with static over the radio. "Lifting off."

Ben saw another aircraft come charging toward them out of the darkness. It swiveled in midair, then opened fired on the hotel tower. Ben saw that it was Holt's ship. He wasn't flying it, but it was the largest of the Confederate vessels and he had set himself up as squadron commander inside it.

Explosions rocked the ground hard enough to make some of the aliens topple over. Smoke and fire billowed out of the hotel's opulent lobby. Ben couldn't help but despair at the richly appointed hotel being destroyed.

"Timber!" Holt shouted over the radio.

His ship raced away just before the tower fell. It came down like a tree, falling over the street and into the green space. Ben had no doubt that Holt relished destroying a building owned by the Royal Imperium as much as, or even more than, stopping the aliens. The ship came back out of the darkness, moving toward the royal palace.

"Don't do it, Holt," Ben said into the mic at his console. "Save your ammunition for the escape."

"I don't take orders from you," Holt snarled.

Missiles shot out from the ship and exploded against the palace.

"Why's he doing that?" Lieutenant Baker cried. "Doesn't he realize the tunnel his people are escaping through leads right beneath the palace?"

"Holt, stop," Ben urged. "The escape tunnel is right beneath the palace."

Reason might have sunk in, but the palace was barely damaged by the missile attack. Fires burned on the steps and walls from the detonations, but the weapons didn't penetrate the building or even shatter the windows.

"The *Ulysses* is loaded and heading out," James Schumacher declared. "But we can't get all the soldiers. We need another ship."

"Holt," Ben said. "Go to the village and get the last of the soldiers."

"You'd love that, wouldn't you?" the Confederate leader snarled.

"We should do it," Nance said. "The commandos can cover the retreating soldiers."

"Kim?" Ben said.

"I'm already going," she said.

"We'll pick them up," Ben said over the radio.

The ship flew quickly across the forest that separated the staff village from Royal City. Ben felt a tightness in his chest. Max Pounder's ship, a fat-looking freight hauler, was just taking off when they arrived. There were soldiers milling at the fringe of a clearing. The *Echo* had just enough room to land.

The soldiers didn't need any encouragement. They came racing on board. Then came civilians, more than Ben expected, racing out of a building where he guessed the tunnel from Royal City connected. Some were covered in dust and dirt. Ben saw Captain Lawrence limping for the back of the ship. There were children too, every one of them looking terrified.

A glance at the cargo hold showed nearly fifty refugees. Most were lined up in the aisles between pallets of food, and some even crawled up on top of the carefully packed pallets.

"That's the last of them," Corporal Dial said over the com-link. "Get us out of here."

The ship rose straight up into the air, and the planet was lost in the darkness beneath them. Ben heard voices over the radio calling for all the ships to retreat. The battle was over, and Ben had no idea of the toll. It seemed like they had rescued the Confederates and civilians, but Royal City was lost. He knew it shouldn't matter. If the professor's device worked, the entire planet would be boiled away to nothing but subatomic particles, yet it felt wrong to know that the aliens had taken the only human settlements on the planet.

Chapter 43

Eight alien ships lay in ruins. General Pershing had hoped for more. But what really bothered her was the fact that the *Eclipse* had let her gun crews slack. They came out of hyperspace unprepared, and when the aliens followed seconds later, they were hit with a barrage of space debris the alien ships had picked up in the Celeste system.

"The aliens are adapting," Captain Davis said.

General Pershing ignored her. Stating the obvious was of no concern. It was time to make the jump back to the Celeste system. But without the *Eclipse*, it wouldn't be very helpful to the ships trying to escape Gershwin. The Confederates were expendable, but the crown prince was not. The *Modulus Echo* had to escape and fire off the singularity weapon Professor Jones had built or the entire operation was for nothing.

They had destroyed perhaps thirty of the enemy ships, but that wasn't even a tenth of what the aliens had in their fleet and they still controlled the wormhole and could bring more vessels from their own galaxy to reinforce their numbers.

"The last rescue craft is returning," the communications officer proclaimed.

"It's about time," Pershing said.

The *Eclipse* had lost power and succumbed to several hull breaches. A maintenance crew could set her right again, but there was no telling how long it would take the fractured Royal Imperium to send one out. And with the ship's power offline, the life-support systems wouldn't last long. All of which forced Pershing's hand, and a rescue was ordered.

Fortunately, no more alien ships followed them through hyperspace. If they had come under attack while trying to ferry the survivors from the *Eclipse* to the *Tradewind*, things could have gone south. Nothing was certain during war, and Pershing knew how best-laid plans often went awry, but she laid the blame for the loss of the *Eclipse* squarely on the shoulders of her captain. Pershing would deal with the disgraced officer later. As soon as the transport was docked, they would make the jump to hyperspace and return to the Celeste system.

"Navigation, set the jump straight to the Celeste system," Pershing ordered. "Somewhere above Gershwin."

"Aye," the navigation officer said in a loud voice. "Recalculating jump to the Celeste system."

"Weapons are ready," the tactical officer said.

"Very good," Pershing said. "Helm, be prepared for evasive maneuvers."

"What should we do with the crew from the *Eclipse*?" Captain Davis asked.

"Send the officers to the wardroom," Pershing said. "The rest of the crew should stand in reserve in case they're needed to help man the weapons."

"Jump point is set," the navigation officer announced.

"Helm, take us out," Pershing ordered.

"Aye, preparing to jump to hyperspace," the helmsman said. "In three, two, one."

The ship was operating flawlessly, and General Pershing noted the time. The jump back to the Celeste system would take eighteen minutes. Just enough time that she could relieve herself, get a little caffeine in her system, and return to the bridge.

"Captain, you have the con," Pershing said.

"Aye, General, I have the con."

Fifteen minutes later, Pershing was back, and the crew was ready for round three. So far, they had been victorious, but it would only take one mistake to lose the *Tradewind* and every soul on board. Pershing watched the seconds counting down and wondered what the *Echo* was doing.

"Sixty seconds until we transition from hyperspace," the helmsman called out.

Pershing didn't respond. She was ready and there were no more orders to give. The crew was primed and knew what was at stake. Captain Davis ran a tight ship and Pershing could appreciate that. If it were in her power, she would promote Davis to admiral and give her a battle cruiser, but Pershing wouldn't be on the command staff when the Royal Imperium was finally pieced back together. Squabbling over what the fleet should be doing or how concerned they should be about a band of rebels was beneath her. The hero of the Krah conflict, as she liked to think of it, would retire to bask in the glow of her military fame. Even if the crown prince offered her admiral general, she would pass. Administrative work simply wouldn't do after having fought the biggest threat humanity had ever faced.

The helmsman was counting down to transition, and Pershing shook the fantasies from her mind. There was a moment—less than a second, really—that felt like the ship was in slow motion. Then everything snapped into place. Unlike before, the Krah fleet was in motion. Every ship was moving, spreading out.

"Fire, fire, fire!" Pershing said.

Once more, laser bolts flew. Six different Krah ships were hit. The *Tradewind* was above the planet's orbital plane, and almost all the Krah vessels were below them. It took her missiles and torpedoes several long seconds before they caught their targets. The laser cannons fired three volleys before the first explosions lit space.

"Helm, take us forward, thrusters at full," Pershing said.

"Aye, thrusters at full," the officer repeated.

It was only seconds before the larger chunks of ruined starships were snatched up by the long, waving arms of their sister vessels and hurled toward the *Tradewind*.

"Their aim is off," the tactical officer said.

"They have no experience tracking moving targets," Pershing said. "Keep firing! We have to hold their attention for as long as possible. Captain Davis, scan for our rescue ships."

"Aye, General. Scanning for rescue ships."

"I want to know as soon as the *Modulus Echo* reaches orbit."

"The *Modulus Echo*?" Captain Davis said.

"That's right. She's a Kestrel class ship. You can't miss her."

"Aye, Kestrel class, General."

Pershing took a deep breath and hoped that the crazy plan she had cooked up would actually work.

Chapter 44

The *Modulus Echo* led the way into orbit. The other ships were fast, some bristling with weapons, but Kim could tell that their pilots and crews were still getting used to the converted commercial vessels. The moment they broke atmosphere, it was clear that getting out of the system wouldn't be easy. Every ship in the alien fleet was underway, not just drifting in orbit but preparing for something.

"There's the *Tradewind*," Nance said, bringing one of the ship's cameras up on the main bridge display.

Kim didn't have time to look. She was surrounded by smaller displays that showed every side of the ship. It was like looking through windows and gave her a sense of the entire vessel, even though their artificial gravity made it seem like they weren't moving at all.

"They've stirred up the hornet's nest," Ben said.

"Can we even make it out of the system like this?" Lieutenant Baker asked.

"What, this?" Kim said. "Piece of cake."

"Head toward the system star, Kim," Ben told her. "I'll contact the Confederate vessels."

She heard him on the comms, calmly encouraging the other ships to spread out and make the jump to hyperspace as soon as possible. Kim felt sorry for the other pilots. There were no clear lanes of escape. Perhaps that was why the alien fleet was maneuvering, although Kim found the idea of that much coordinated movement to be mind boggling. Still, it also limited the alien ships. She could maneuver between them, and they wouldn't be able to pursue her without running the risk of colliding. It would only take one or two collisions to put the entire fleet at risk.

"She's giving them all she's got," Magnum said, referring to the general.

"It's just one ship," Nance said.

"They must have lost the other," Ben replied. "Kim, any chance you can get us out of here?"

"You know it," Kim said, ignoring the lump that had formed in the pit of her stomach.

She pressed the throttle forward and tipped the toes on her right foot down while lifting her left foot. The result was a spectacular spin that sent them racing through space and straight between two large alien ships. She saw their gangly, grappling arms reaching out for her, but they were too slow. The *Echo* was almost at full speed, her main drive roaring. Kim could feel the slight vibration in the ship's hull made by the engines. It was a comforting sensation, as the images on the displays spun and shifted.

There were more ships behind them than in front. Most of the alien fleet was between the planet and the wormhole, but there were easily eighty or ninety ships between the planet and the system star. And Kim knew the farther she got from the crowded center of the fleet, the more maneuvering room the aliens would have.

She put the ship into a dive to avoid a behemoth of a ship that was directly between them and the star. The cameras hit by the direct sunlight were washed out, and Kim realized that she needed a different way to keep track of the aliens. Visuals weren't reliable.

"Nance, I can't see," Kim said. "The sunlight is flooding the cameras."

"We can use the radar and project a simulation of surrounding space," Nance said. "I'll send it to your screens now."

"How accurate is it?" Kim said.

"Completely," Nance said in her usual calm, as if the idea of the projection being inaccurate was ridiculous.

"Real time?" Kim asked again.

"Absolutely," Nance said.

Kim felt herself relax a little, but she couldn't afford a little. The alien ships were aware of her and moving to intercept. They were still too close together to alter their course too much, but every ship was extending their grappling arms. Kim slipped wide around another of the ships.

"Magnum, give them something else to think about," Kim said.

"Firing missiles one and two," the big man said.

Two missiles shot out, flying close together and then suddenly splitting apart. They both struck one alien vessel, blasting away dozens of the grappling arms. Kim flew past the ship that could no longer reach her and chuckled.

"That's what I'm talking about," Kim crowed.

"Speaking of missiles, Mark and I will head down and get the device ready," Ben said.

"No problem," Kim said. "Nance can you set a jump point out there beyond the alien ships?"

"I'll start the calculations," Nance said.

Kim turned all her attention back to flying. They only had four more missiles, which were small-yield weapons that were only really capable of taking out the grappling arms. They had no chance of destroying the alien ships, but fortunately for them, the aliens didn't know it. Kim slipped around one of the vessels, slipping just outside the range of its grappling arms, and noticed that two of the ships ahead of them were moving to block her escape. They even had their grappling arms at only half their true range, trying to lure her between them.

"Not today," Kim said.

She flew straight toward the two ships, as if she were falling for their trap, then pulled up at the last moment, changing directions. She was losing ground but heading for wider space lanes between the alien ships.

"The *Savanna* is gone," Nance said.

"It made the jump?" Magnum asked.

"No," Nance said. "Destroyed."

Kim felt the lump in her stomach as if it suddenly weighed twice as much. Sometimes flying felt like a game, but she knew that she held the lives of every person on board the ship in her hands. It was daunting, especially with the cargo bay full of refugees.

"Has anyone made the jump?" Kim asked.

"The *Tradewind*," Nance said. "They just jumped."

Kim wanted to know more about the other Confederate ships, but she was afraid to ask. Another alien ship was coming for her. The *Echo* and the alien ship were on a collision course. Kim heard the warning alarm but ignored it. She started to dive beneath the large alien ship but realized too late that another vessel was in the way. She reversed her course, but it was too late. Her breath caught in her throat as the grappling arms reached out for her. Kim knew their momentum had carried the

Echo too close to the alien vessel. They were in range of those arms that would tear them to pieces.

Suddenly, flashes of light shot past the *Echo* and vaporized the grappling arms.

"What the hell?" Kim shouted.

"Thought you might need a hand, *Modulus Echo*!"

Kim recognized the voice but couldn't believe what she was hearing. Duke Simeon on the *Hyperion* had come out of nowhere and saved them at the last second.

"Thanks," Kim said, keying her mic with a tap of a button, "Your Grace."

"Well, maybe I should let you get destroyed, seeing as how you have my cousin on board and all, but why throw the baby out with the bathwater?"

"You should get clear and make the jump, *Hyperion*," Kim said.

"Just as soon as you do, *Echo*."

"I can't promise that we can both find a way out of this mess," Kim said.

"None needed," the duke declared. "We're all members of the Royal Imperium on board this ship. Getting you clear is more important than all our lives."

"The *Star Runner* is gone," Nance said.

"This is getting dicey," Kim said. "Ben, how's it coming with that package?"

Chapter 45

Ben had to push his way through the crowd of people in the cargo area. He was thankful that no one had moved into the engineering bay. The device was sitting on his workbench. They had already slung cargo straps underneath it to make moving the heavy device more manageable. There were two missiles attached to either side of the boxy contraption.

"We'll need a couple more hands to carry it," Ben said to Mark. "See if you can get a couple of the Confederate soldiers to give us a hand."

The lieutenant in the Royal Imperium Fleet nodded. He didn't seem to mind taking orders from a civilian, or giving them to who just weeks before had been his enemy. Two frightened-looking men followed Mark back into the engineering bay. They each took a strap and Ben gave a nod. They lifted the device and shuffled their way out of Engineering and through the cargo hold to the air lock door.

Ben's com-link beeped, and Kim's voice was heard.

"Ben, how's it coming with that package?" she asked.

"Almost there," Ben replied.

He hit the control switch that opened the inner air lock door, then shuffled inside with the heavy load, trying not to think about the fact that the only thing separating him from the hard vacuum of space was the small air lock door.

"Okay, that's good," Ben said.

He and Mark had to climb back out of the air lock, and then Ben sealed the door. The two men hurried back up to the main deck. Captain Lawrence followed them, along with Corporals Dial and Amadi.

"What was that thing?" Captain Lawrence asked.

"Just a surprise for our friends," Ben said. "An experimental device. It might not do anything at all. We'll have to wait and see."

He dropped back into his seat and pressed the buttons to cycle the air lock. Eighty percent of the air was pumped out, but Ben left just enough to create a strong suction when the outer air lock door was opened.

"How close are we?" Ben asked.

"Close enough to launch," Kim said. "Not close enough to make the jump to hyperspace."

Ben could see that one of the alien ships was racing alongside them, slowly angling to try and reach the *Echo*. He wanted to warn Kim, but he thought it best to let her do the flying. She didn't need him pointing out what he was sure she already knew.

Laser blasts raked down the side of the approaching alien ship from behind the *Echo*. Dozens of grappling arms were destroyed in a blink of an eye.

"What was that?" Ben said.

"Duke Simeon in the *Hyperion*," Nance said.

"I think he likes me," Kim said with a giggle.

Ben had no idea how she could stay so calm during such stressful times, but he didn't question it. It was one of her strengths and something he found incredibly appealing about her.

"What's the duke doing out here?" Ben said.

"Trying to be the hero," Kim said. "And so far, he's succeeding."

"The *Ophar* and the *Salient Dream* are gone," Nance said. "The *Pilgrim* too, but I couldn't tell whether it was destroyed or made the jump to hyperspace."

"The *Pilgrim* was Holt's ship," Ben said. "Has any of the other ships survived?"

"Three," Nance said. "But it doesn't look good for the rest."

"Those with passengers?" Captain Lawrence asked.

"They made it," Nance said. "The other Confederate ships made sure of it."

"Alright then," Ben said. "Time to deliver the package. Magnum, fire away."

"Firing missiles three through six," Magnum replied.

"Opening the air lock," Ben said.

He pressed the controls and the outer door slid open in one quick movement. The device was sucked out, just as planned, and went tumbling through space. Ben tracked it on the screen of his console. Using the controls at his station, he activated the flux shield and waited while it spun up.

"Well?" Kim asked.

"It's powering up," Ben said.

"No rush," she said, her voice dripping with sarcasm. "We've got all day."

Ben ignored her. The boxy device was spinning toward an alien ship, but the vessel moved, trying to get ahead of the *Echo.*

Suddenly, there was a flash of light. Not like the passing of a laser bolt, but a brighter, more sustained flash. Ben looked up, his mouth suddenly dry.

"What was that?" he managed to ask.

Nance looked at him and slowly nodded. "The *Hyperion*," she said in a quiet voice.

Ben felt like he was going to be sick again.

"Damn it!" Kim snarled. "I told him to get clear."

Tears blurred Ben's vision when he looked back at his screens. He wiped them away, feeling a void opening inside him as another person he considered a friend vanished from the galaxy forever. He didn't know what happened when a person died, but it seemed wrong somehow to think that Duke Simeon and the passengers on his ship were all just suddenly gone, as if they had never existed in the first place. He clenched his teeth so hard it felt like they might shatter, then hit the button that brought the flux shield online.

There was no sign that the gravity shield was working. Ben had to just trust his work. He pressed another button and the missiles activated, flaring to life, shooting toward the sun. A timer popped up on his console. Eighty-six seconds and it would reach the coordinates marked for it.

Ben looked up. There were only a few alien ships near them, but they were faster than the *Echo*. Kim was doing all she could to keep them safe, but it was going to be close.

"Can we make the jump now?" Kim asked. "I've got a lane."

"No," Ben said. "We have to stay in the system to activate the device."

"I thought it was on a timer," Kim snapped.

"It is. We'll have ten seconds when I activate it."

"Ten seconds?" Kim said. "That's cutting it kind of close, don't you think?"

"I thought you would appreciate the difficulty. That's how you like things."

"We're the only vessel left in the system," Nance said.

"We won't be for long," Kim said.

Ben glanced at his screen. Fifty-eight seconds was left.

"I just need a minute," Ben said.

"I can maybe last half a minute," Kim said.

"Just don't jump without telling me."

"Just tell me as soon as I can jump."

Thirty-six seconds remained. Kim took the ship into a spinning dive. The aliens were closing in. The tension on the bridge was palpable. Sweat was running down Ben's forehead, but he needed a few more seconds.

"Ben!" Kim said. "I can't shake them any longer."

There was eighteen seconds left on the timer, but Ben knew they had run out of time. He pressed the activation button.

"Make the jump!" Ben shouted.

Time suddenly slowed. On the bridge displays, Ben saw alien grappling arms reaching for them from two different directions. And then, suddenly, the image on the screens changed to the swirl of hyperspace. It lasted less than a second, and then the strange slowing returned.

It was as if someone had snapped their fingers and the ship popped back into regular space, but they weren't in the clear. The rendezvous point was beyond the heliosphere of the Celeste system. Had Ben looked, he would have seen a star only slightly larger than the multitude of stars all around them. But there was no time to look. Dozens of alien ships surrounded them. Kim had to swerve to avoid an alien ship's spindly arms that were reaching for them. She dove and was almost smashed to smithereens by a huge chunk of metal that was being flung toward the *Tradewind*. There were flashes of laser light and missile explosions.

"Jump to the secondary escape point," Ben said.

"The nav computer is still generating the flight path," Nance said.

"This is worse than the Celeste system," Kim said.

"It's up," Nance said. "You can jump."

"Thank you, Nancy! Here we go."

The chaos of war disappeared, and a second later, they came out into empty space.

"Where are we?" Ben asked.

"Close to the secondary rendezvous point," Nance said. "I moved us about a hundred miles out, just in case."

"Smart thinking," Kim said.

"Looks like we're safe," Mark proclaimed. "I have to admit, I've never been that scared in my life."

"Give me long odds on the ground any day," Captain Lawrence said.

In the distance, the *Tradewind* popped into sight, followed by three Confederate vessels. Ben was just breathing a sigh of relief when two alien ships suddenly appeared. Fortunately, the *Tradewind* was ready for them. Multiple laser strikes made quick work of the alien vessels, but more were coming out of hyperspace before the first two blew apart.

"Did it work?" Kim asked.

Ben looked at his console. They were far out of range to see anything happening in the system. "I don't know," he said. "We'll just have to wait and see."

"I just got new rendezvous coordinates," Nance said. "Calculating jump point."

"I feel like we should help somehow," Kim said.

On the big bridge screens, Ben saw the alien ships gathering the shattered sections of their own ships to use as ammunition against the *Tradewind*. The lasers were redirected to shoot down the hunks of debris. The tension began to ratchet up again, and Ben was frustrated that they couldn't do more.

"Jump point is set," Nance said.

"Alright, let's go," Ben said.

They made another microjump, only this time they were alone.

"Where are the other ships?" Ben asked.

"The *Tradewind* sent us all to different locations," Nance announced. "I'm calculating the next jump in case we're followed."

They waited for several minutes, feeling strangely alone. Ben couldn't relax, even though he tried. It felt as if the entire galaxy was suddenly deserted and they were all alone.

Chapter 46

The Krah fleet was still in motion, spreading out, searching for more enemies. The humans were much more destructive than any race the Krah had encountered. Yet they were also so incredibly wealthy. Decisions had been made and passed down from the alphas and priests to move the entire empire to the new galaxy. Holding the portal and the system it was found in was paramount, and fortunately the verdant world was ideal for raising up a new army of Krah warriors.

The fleet was assembling and would eventually go out in large armadas to take what was needed from the other nearby star systems. But until the chaser ships sent after the human vessels returned, the fleet would stay close to the planet. No one among the alien fleet noticed the bulky device racing toward the system star. There was debris from dozens of ships that had been blown apart by the humans and their cowardly weapons. When they did finally notice, it was too late.

There was a surge of strange energy. Not like a weapon, but more like a gravitational anomaly. Sensors beeped and flashed, but the readings were abnormal. The only thing that was certain was that the energy reading was emanating from somewhere close to the star. Too close, it seemed, to those studying the data. Nothing could survive that close to the immeasurable heat of a star. And then the light wavered, almost like a light fixture flickering from a power surge.

Celeste went supernova, sending a wave of energy so powerful it turned the first planet in the system to atoms, and the second blew apart like a snowball impacting a wall. When it reached the first Krah ship, the vessel exploded in a ball of sparks. The other ships fell like dominos. No amount of armor or shielding could resist the heat and power of the blast. Some crumpled; others were completely vaporized in a blink of an eye.

On the planet, a bright light was the only warning that something was amiss. Then the heat turned everything on the surface of the planet to ash in less time than it took for a human heart to beat. Royal City was lost. The glass melted, the metal ionized, even the cobblestones of the street were blown to dust. The shock wave sent Gershwin, burned to a scorched rock, hurtling through space.

The only thing that remained was the wormhole. The glowing ring of fire was unfazed by the star's explosion. The star itself grew dark red and seemed to expand behind the shock wave. But as suddenly as the explosion had destroyed the system, the star began to collapse back on itself. Minutes later, there was more light, a powerful swirl of gravity waves. The wormhole had survived the supernova, but nothing could survive the black hole. The incredible power of gravity twisted the tunnel in space, stretching it flat and crushing anything inside, including a huge chain ship controlled by an alpha of the Krah Empire. The tunnel between the galaxies was closed forever, leaving only the opening on one side. Any ship that tried to pass through the portal would be destroyed at the other end.

On the *Modulus Echo*, there was a flare of light so bright it caught them all by surprise. For a second, Ben thought that he had died and that the bright light was the other side, beckoning to him. But then the light faded a little, and on the bridge display screens, they could see Celeste. It was larger than before, the size of a marble.

"What just happened?" Captain Lawrence said.

"The star, Celeste," Lieutenant Mark Baker said. "It just went supernova."

"Good God in heaven," Captain Lawrence said.

Ben knew that God wasn't to blame. He was. He had built the device, at least most of it. He had set it in motion and activated it. The destruction of the Celeste system was on his head. He sat back, feeling strangely numb all over.

"It worked," Kim said.

The star, a bright, red marble on their screen, began to shrink. Ben knew it was collapsing on itself, creating a black hole that would seal the Celeste system forever. His mouth tasted sour, and a gloom settled over him.

"Kim, make the jump," Ben said. "Let's see who's left."

"You don't have to sound so sad," Kim said. "We're finally free."

"Once we drop off the crown prince and the other passengers," Ben said.

"Sure, but we can do that anywhere, can't we?"

"I suppose," Ben said.

"Nance, set a course for the Yelsin system. We'll take the commandos home," Kim said, taking charge.

Ben wasn't sure, but he thought that perhaps she was stepping up so that he didn't have to. It was a relief. He didn't want to be in charge anymore. He didn't want to be responsible for anyone but himself. And he needed to sleep.

"How long will it take?" Ben asked Nance.

"Five hours or so," Nance replied.

"Good. Let's do it. Great idea, Kim."

"Sure," Kim said. "We'll make the jump and get some food for the passengers. Why don't you get some rest?"

Ben looked at her. There was a strange look in her eyes. He thought perhaps it was compassion, but he couldn't be certain.

"You sure?" Ben asked.

"Absolutely," she said. "We got this."

"Okay," Ben said, suddenly so tired that just walking to his cabin was difficult. "Thanks."

He went inside the small room. It was his home. He shut the door and collapsed onto the bunk. He wished Kim were with him, but he was fading fast and knew she was busy. The darkness seemed frightening as he flicked off the lights to his quarters. The things he'd done threatened to haunt his dreams, but he pushed them away. He would deal with his guilt another time. For now, he just wanted to sleep. And it took him away from everything, for a blissful few hours of sweet oblivion.

Epilogue

The mood on Yelsin Prime was subdued. The Special Forces wing of the Royal Imperium military was waiting for the dust to settle. Queen Ultane had been removed from the Mersa system, and no one knew where she was or if she was even alive. Duke Simeon was dead, a tragic casualty in the fight with the Krah. Crown Prince Godfred was alive, but clearly insane. And no one had heard from the *Tradewind*. There was still time for General Pershing to discover what the *Echo* had done and show up with orders to arrest Ben and his friends, but it had yet to happen.

"We made it, eh?" Staff Sergeant Visher asked as he was being moved off the *Modulus Echo*.

"Yes," Ben said. "Thanks in no small part to your Corporal Dial. He took charge of your platoon and was of great service to us all."

"Yeah, I'm not surprised. Don't tell him that, though. He'll be a pain in my backside once they make him a sergeant," Visher said. He was still weak, but he extended a hand. "It was an honor to fight with you, Ben. Good luck."

"Thank you," Ben said.

Kim ambled over. The cargo area was still packed with supplies, but the passengers had all disembarked save for a last few who were still saying their goodbyes. She leaned down and kissed the crusty staff sergeant on the forehead.

"Goodbye, Visher," she said.

"So long and good luck," he told her just before the doctor ordered him to be moved into the base hospital.

"I suppose this is goodbye, then," Lieutenant Baker said. "You could stick around, you know. There might even be a parade for saving the galaxy."

"Somehow I doubt that," Ben said, extending a hand. "We couldn't have done it without your help, though."

They shook hands, then the lieutenant disembarked, obviously glad to be off the *Echo* and back where he felt safe again. Ben's com-linked beeped and Nance gave him an update.

"There's a new ship in the system," she said.

"The *Tradewind*?" Ben asked with a sense of dread building inside him.

"No, it's the *Pilgrim*," Nance said. "They're hailing us."

"Put it through," Ben said as he and Kim headed back up to the main deck.

A video appeared on the large bridge display screens. Holt looked cross, but then he always did.

"You made it," Ben said. "Congratulations."

"Save it," Holt said. "The general survived too, and she's vowing to have your heads for decorations on her ship."

Ben's hopes dropped, and he felt a sense of panic rising inside.

"She'll have to catch us first," Kim said.

"Then don't wait around too long," Holt said. "If I can find you, so can she."

"Why is she angry?" Ben said. "Everything worked the way we planned."

"Except that you took off with the crown prince. Apparently, that was a deal breaker in her opinion."

"We can lift off now if you're ready," Nance said.

"What about the Confederates?" Ben asked. "Captain Lawrence and his companions are still on the base."

"I'll get them," Holt said. "You better get going while you can. If you run out of Zexum, look me up. I'm sure we could find something for you to do."

"Yeah, well, don't hold your breath," Ben said. "And thanks for the warning."

The screen went blank, and Ben felt a sudden sense of pressure again. They needed to leave soon. Major Le Croix was coming down from the upper deck with Corporal Dial. Le Croix's robotic legs clanked on the metal stairs, and he looked miserable.

Ben walked over and shook Dial's hand. "Looks like we're taking off."

"Where are you headed?" Dial asked.

"Away from the fighting, someplace quiet for a while. We've earned a vacation."

"I'll say," Dial said. "It's too bad, though. You make a great captain. Damn fine ship too."

"Thank you," Ben said. "What's going to happen to the major?"

"Oh, you know," Le Croix said, putting on a brave face. "I'll be a cripple again in no time."

"They'll have to debrief him," Dial said. "There's no telling how long that will take, or what it will entail. Of course, there are only a few of us who know he was on our ship, and not the duke's. If he were to stay on board, no one would be the wiser."

Ben looked over at the rest of the crew. They were all at their stations, and he could see they were eager to leave. But no one shook their heads or acted as if letting Major Le Croix stay with them was a bad idea.

"We're game if you are, Major," Ben said.

"You mean it?" Le Croix asked.

"Sure," Kim said from the bridge. "I'll do some medical work on those fancy legs of yours. How hard could it be?"

"Alright, then," Le Croix said. "It beats being treated like a prisoner."

"Welcome to the *Modulus Echo*," Ben said.

"Good luck to you all," Corporal Dial said. "I hope our paths meet again."

"Under friendly circumstances," Ben said.

They shook hands, and Dial headed off the ship. Ben and Le Croix joined the others. Ben sat at the engineering console, and Le Croix sat carefully at the communications station.

"We're ready," Ben said as he hit the buttons to close the rear hatch.

"I've alerted the base," Nance said. "We're cleared for takeoff."

"Good, let's get out of here."

The *Modulus Echo* lifted off, rising straight up into the air. It took them half an hour to reach orbit. They were moving steadily away from Yelsin Prime, and it would be another fifteen before they would be able to jump into hyperspace.

"Where are we headed?" Le Croix asked.

"Somewhere far away," Ben said.

"Good," Kim said. "A long hyperspace jump is just what we need. I could use some sleep."

"Will we be fugitives again?" Nance asked.

"Maybe," Ben said. "But I'm sure General Pershing has plenty to do to keep her busy. In the meantime, we'll make ourselves scarce."

Ben's messaging service pinged, and he checked the incoming messages. Only one was of any importance. It was from the Brimex Corporation. He scanned it quickly.

"Well, what do you know," he said.

"I know that tone of voice," Kim said guardedly. "What is it?"

"The flux shields are going into production, and there are already enough orders to keep them busy for six months," Ben said. "We're going to be rich when the payment starts rolling in."

"And when will that be?" Nance asked.

"Not before we run out of food or fuel," Ben said.

"Hey, good news for a change. That's refreshing!" Kim said.

She hit the controls and time seemed to stretch for a long second, then they disappeared into hyperspace.

Ten minutes later, Ben was the only crewman left on the bridge. Everyone else had gone off to get some much-needed rest, and Ben was alone with his ship. He loved her, almost as much as he loved Kim. Getting the *Modulus Echo* off Torrent Four had been difficult, and the journey had left some scars. Not just on him and the crew, but on the entire galaxy. Still, they had fuel and food, and money coming in before long. They weren't exactly wanted fugitives, and for once the future looked bright. There were still a lot of questions to answer, but for the moment they were safe and that was all Ben wanted. No more surprises, no more obligations.

"Ben," Kim said softly.

He jumped.

"You scared me. Don't go sneaking up on a person like that," Ben said. He couldn't help but notice the strange look on Kim's face. "What's wrong?"

"I need to show you something?"

She took his hand and led him away from the bridge. She was going to her quarters, and while he knew that leaving the ship unmanned wasn't the wisest thing they could do, the systems were all green and they were safe enough in hyperspace. He decided not to resist this time.

"What d'you have in mind?" Ben asked, playful.

"Not this," Kim said, pressing the button that opened the door to her quarters.

Ben's jaw dropped. On the brightly colored bedspread, sitting up with a grin on her face, was a little girl.

"Who's she?" Ben asked.

"One of the refugees?" Kim said, shrugging her shoulders.

"I want to be a pilot!" the little girl declared. "I'm going to fly ships and have adventures."

"Where are your parents?" Ben asked.

"My mom didn't make it," the girl said, "when the monsters came to the village. I guess I'm on my own now, but that's okay." She was proudly defiant. "I can take care of myself."

"Remind you of anyone?" Kim said with a smirk.

"I'm not sure this ship can handle more than one of you," Ben said.

Kim wrapped her arms around him and pulled him close. "Who knows, maybe it'll be nice having a sweet little girl on board."

"Eww!" the girl declared.

She hurried over and shut the door to the cabin. It swooshed shut, leaving Ben and Kim alone in the atrium.

"Or not," Ben said.

"But we can keep her, right? She's got nowhere to go."

"We'll figure it out," Ben said, giving her a soft kiss on the forehead. "We always do."

Author's Note

Thank you so much for joining me on this journey. I wrote Kestrel Class for me and I'm so honored that thousands of readers joined me on such a grand adventure.

I've been busy since completing the manuscript for *Planet Fall* writing a new adventure. It's a coming of age story about a young man in a galaxy divided by rival mega-corporations, companies that have grown bigger than governments and control entire planets.

Some book ideas begin with a character, or the world the story is set in. But this book started with the opening scene, an attack on an isolated colony and one young man's response. Sometimes you have to take the opportunities that come your way and ride them for all they're worth. That's exactly what happens to Alex Chester Evans.

It's a fast paced book that combines elements of space opera, military, and thriller. I'll be publishing *War INC* in early May,

*9 7 8 1 9 5 2 2 6 0 0 5 6 *